PRAISE FOR C

Wife by Wednesday

"A fun and sizzling romance, great characters that trade verbal spars like fist punches, and the dream of your own royal wedding!"

—Sizzling Hot Book Reviews, 5 Star

"A good holiday, fireside, or bedtime story."

—Manic Reviews, 4 1/2 Stars

"A great story that I hope is the start of a new series."

—The Romance Studio, 4 1/2 Hearts

Married by Monday

"If I hadn't already added Ms. Catherine Bybee to my list of favorite authors, after reading this book I would have been compelled to. This is a book *nobody* should miss, because the magic it contains is awesome."

—Booked Up Reviews, 5 Stars

"Ms. Bybee writes authentic situations and expresses the good and the bad in such an equal way . . . Keep[s] the reader on the edge of her seat . . ."

—Reading Between the Wines, 5 Stars

"*Married by Monday* was a refreshing read and one I couldn't possibly put down . . ."

—The Romance Studio, 4 1/2 Hearts

Fiancé by Friday

"Bybee knows exactly how to keep readers happy . . . A thrilling pursuit and enough passion to stuff in your back pocket to last for the next few lifetimes . . . The hero and heroine come to life with each flip of the page and will linger long after readers cross the finish line."

—*RT Book Reviews*, 4 1/2 Stars, Top Pick (Hot)

"A tale full of danger and sexual tension . . . the intriguing characters add emotional depth, ensuring readers will race to the perfectly fitting finish."

—*Publishers Weekly*

"Suspense, survival, and chemistry mix in this scintillating read."

—*Booklist*

"Hot romance, a mystery assassin, British royalty, and an alpha Marine . . . this story has it all!"

—Harlequin Junkie

Single by Saturday

"Captures readers' hearts and keeps them glued to the pages until the fascinating finish . . . romance lovers will feel the sparks fly . . . almost instantaneously."

—*RT Book Reviews*, 4 1/2 Stars, Top Pick

"[A] wonderfully exciting plot, lots of desire, and some sassy attitude thrown in for good measure!"

—Harlequin Junkie

Taken by Tuesday

"[Bybee] knows exactly how to get bookworms sucked into the perfect storyline; then she casts her spell upon them so they don't escape until they reach the 'Holy Cow!' ending."

—*RT Book Reviews*, 4 1/2 Stars, Top Pick

Seduced by Sunday

"You simply can't miss [this novel]. It contains everything a romance reader loves—clever dialogue, three-dimensional characters, and just the right amount of steam to go with that heartwarming love story."

—Brenda Novak, *New York Times* bestselling author

"Bybee hits the mark . . . providing readers with a smart, sophisticated romance between a spirited heroine and a prim hero . . . Passionate and intelligent characters [are] at the heart of this entertaining read."

—*Publishers Weekly*

Treasured by Thursday

"The Weekday Brides never disappoint and this final installment is by far Bybee's best work to date."

—*RT Book Reviews*, 4 1/2 Stars, Top Pick

"An exquisitely written and complex story brimming with pride, passion, and pulse-pounding danger . . . Readers will gladly make time to savor this winning finale to a wonderful series."

—*Publishers Weekly*, Starred Review

"Bybee concludes her popular Weekday Brides series in a gratifying way with a passionate, troubled couple who may find a happy future if they can just survive and then learn to trust each other. A compelling and entertaining mix of sexy, complicated romance and menacing suspense."

—*Kirkus Reviews*

Not Quite Dating

"It's refreshing to read about a man who isn't afraid to fall in love . . . [Jack and Jessie] fit together as a couple and as a family."

—*RT Book Reviews*, 3 Stars (Hot)

"*Not Quite Dating* offers a sweet and satisfying Cinderella fantasy that will keep you smiling long after you've finished reading . . ."

—Kathy Altman, *USA Today*, Happy Ever After

"The perfect rags to riches romance . . . The dialogue is inventive and witty, the characters are well drawn out. The storyline is superb and really shines . . . I highly recommend this standout romance! Catherine Bybee is an automatic buy for me."

—Harlequin Junkie, 4 1/2 Hearts

Not Quite Enough

"Bybee's gift for creating unforgettable romances cannot be ignored. The third book in the Not Quite series will sweep readers away to a paradise, and they will be intrigued by the thrilling story that accompanies their literary vacation."

—*RT Book Reviews*, 4 1/2 Stars, Top Pick

Not Quite Forever

"Full of classic Bybee humor, steamy romance, and enough plot twists and turns to keep readers entertained all the way to the very last page."

—Tracy Brogan, bestselling author of the Bell Harbor series

"Magnetic . . . The love scenes are sizzling and the multi-dimensional characters make this a page-turner. Readers will look for earlier installments and eagerly anticipate new ones."

—*Publishers Weekly*

Doing It Over

"The romance between fiercely independent Melanie and charming Wyatt heats up even as outsiders threaten to derail their newfound happiness. This novel will hook readers with its warm, inviting characters and the promise for similar future installments."

—*Publishers Weekly*

Not Quite Perfect

Also by Catherine Bybee

Contemporary Romance

Weekday Brides Series

Wife by Wednesday

Married by Monday

Fiancé by Friday

Single by Saturday

Taken by Tuesday

Seduced by Sunday

Treasured by Thursday

Not Quite Series

Not Quite Dating

Not Quite Mine

Not Quite Enough

Not Quite Forever

Most Likely To Series

Doing It Over

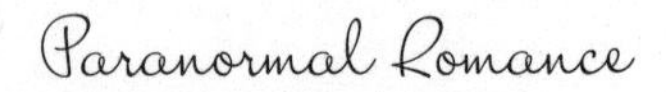

MacCoinnich Time Travels

Binding Vows

Silent Vows

Redeeming Vows

Highland Shifter

Highland Protector

The Ritter Werewolves Series

Before the Moon Rises

Embracing the Wolf

Novellas

Soul Mate

Possessive

Erotica

Kilt Worthy

Kilt-A-Licious

CATHERINE BYBEE

This is a work of fiction. Names, characters, organizations, places, events, and incidents are either products of the author's imagination or are used fictitiously.

Published by Montlake Romance, Seattle

www.apub.com

ISBN-13: 9781503937291
ISBN-10: 1503937291

Cover design by Shasti O'Leary Soudant

Printed in the United States of America

This one is for Marina Adair
Our friendship means the world to me

Chapter One

The problem with plumbers was every single stereotype in print, film, and gossip was true. Mary folded her arms across her chest and attempted to keep her eyes from the disturbing crack of ass peeking above the overzealous waistband of Leroy's Dockers pants.

He pointed at the small screen showing the image of the pipe from her toilet to parts unknown. "This is where the real problem is," he said with a grin that yelled dollar signs.

All she saw was sludge. "What is it?"

"Roots."

"Roots? What kind of roots?"

"Probably from that pepper tree in your front yard. Nasty buggers. With the drought being as it is . . . we're finding this all too often. Poor trees need water and your pepper has found a mainline IV of the stuff."

"In my toilet?"

"In the drainage *from* your toilet."

The postage stamp front yard of her condominium had a space of grass the size of her thumbnail and one tree. The grass was all but dead with the water police happily fining anyone found watering their yards outside the mandated times.

Leroy tugged on his camera and unearthed a smell that had her shoving a finger under her nose in an attempt to block it.

It didn't work.

"What are you doing?"

"I'll remove the roots and see how bad the damage is to the pipe."

The putrid smell intensified and had Mary placing her full hand over her mouth.

Leroy simply smiled as if he were a flippin' doe frolicking in a meadow.

"How long will this take?" she asked.

"Depends on how long these roots have been here and how far down they go."

One more tug and Mary did what she had to do. "I'm going across the street to my friend's. I'll check back in about an hour."

Leroy released a toothy smile and waved a gloved hand in the air as she turned and nearly ran out the door.

Once the door closed behind her, she shivered and sucked in a breath of fresh air. It helped that the morning had left a blanket of fog that reached to her portion of Orange County. If only that moisture had resulted in actual raindrops, problems with tree roots clogging up her pipes might not have happened.

She jogged across the street even though there wasn't any traffic to speak of. Most of those who worked normal hours had left before the sun rose to rush to the freeway and crawl their way to the sources of their employment.

With Walt's car missing from the driveway, Mary felt comfortable opening the door of Dakota's condo without knocking.

Noise from the floor above told Mary that her BFF was up and walking around. "Hey, Baby Mama."

"Up here," Dakota's singsong voice called from upstairs.

Mary climbed the stairs of what she considered her second home.

Dakota was in the nursery Mary and Walt had personally painted while Dakota watched a couple of months prior.

Dakota stood over the chest of drawers, folding baby clothes she'd unwrapped during the baby shower, which had happened the previous weekend. Even with a belly the size of a small city, Mary's friend was stunning. With dark hair and skin that easily accepted the sun, she had the most expressive eyes and an attitude to match whatever life tossed her way. She'd still be wearing four-inch heels if not for her doctor husband, who threatened to throw her expensive collection in the trash if she didn't give them up willingly. Truth was, Walt had asked Mary to hide them until after the baby was born if Dakota's stubborn streak didn't wane.

Thankfully, Dakota Laurens, romance author, had relented to Dakota Eddy, soon-to-be mom.

"I feel like a house," Dakota complained as she closed the drawer of the dresser.

"If it helps . . . you only look like a cottage."

Dakota's wicked gaze snapped into a smile. "I love you."

"I know." Mary pulled the bulk of her long, curly blonde hair behind her back and stepped close to take the laundry basket from Dakota's hands.

"I got it."

"Humor me. Watching you move makes me hurt."

Dakota didn't argue as she let her belly lead the way out of the nursery. She did a little hop in the threshold. "I keep jumping in hopes Junior will get the eviction notice."

Dakota sat at 39½ weeks and grumbled every day since her OB told her she could safely deliver at any time. In Dakota's head that meant labor day was every day.

Junior had other ideas.

They'd all grown accustomed to calling the baby Junior, though Dakota and Walt had no intentions of giving the baby that title. The nursery they were walking away from was a plethora of yellow and green with a sprinkling of pink and blue. Everyone left tags and gift receipts for gender specific stuff. The one thing about baby gifts was the practicality of those giving. It was amazing how many people added a massive box of diapers as a joke. Dakota had added cloth diapers into the mix, organic girl that she was . . . but Mary didn't give that much time before her friend caved to the tossable variety.

Dakota hesitated on the stairwell and held her belly.

Mary watched with a hawk's eye.

Dakota shrugged and continued. "Not that I don't like the company . . . but why are you here so early?"

They moved into the kitchen, where Mary insisted Dakota sit while she helped herself to the coffee that must have been made by Walt before he left for his twelve-hour ER shift. The man was pulling all kinds of overtime so he could stay home once the baby arrived.

"Want some tea?" Mary asked, knowing Dakota's preference.

She released a moan. "God no. Can't stand it this month."

Mary laughed and thumbed the pink box of doughnuts on the counter. "Refined sugar?"

Dakota offered an enthusiastic nod.

Laughing, Mary placed a maple glazed on a napkin and brought it to her friend, who sat on a cushioned kitchen chair. "I'm going to love rubbing this in six months from now when you're past all this stuff."

Dakota bit into her doughnut with her eyes rolling into the back of her head. She chased a bit of sugar with her tongue before offering a comment. "Junior is bound to be a sugar-holic."

"That's crazy talk."

"Has to be some kind of explanation."

Dakota didn't eat refined sugar, or a ton of processed food, before she was knocked up. The switch had tossed Mary for a loop when she realized she could explore the world of fast food with her friend for the first time.

Dakota bit into her doughnut again and shifted in the chair with a hand to her belly. "This has been great and all . . . but I'm about done having my ribs kicked."

"Junior will come when they're done."

She looked down and scolded her unborn child. "You're done! Let's get on with it . . . shall we? Team. Team effort."

Mary loved the misplaced logic.

Dakota laughed at herself and glanced up. "Why are you here again?"

Mary explained about her plumbing issue before launching into the story of the proverbial plumbing crack that wouldn't stop winking at her while she was standing by.

"Roots?"

"That's what he told me."

"Sounds expensive."

"I just want my toilet to flush . . . call me crazy."

"You have a second bathroom," Dakota reminded her.

"Yeah, but it's slowing down, too. If I don't fix it, I might be walking over here all the time when I need to go."

"You're here all the time anyway."

A tiny, transient sense of insecurity nibbled at Mary's psyche. She purposely, forcefully, pushed it away. "Is Walt working?" The question was rhetorical.

Dakota answered with a nod. "He wanted to cut his shift today."

Mary glanced up from her task. "Why?"

"Says the baby dropped."

From where Mary stood, the baby hadn't done anything but push Dakota's belly further into next week. "Dropped?"

"Yeah . . . I don't get it either. Junior is still baking. I think I'd know if they were going to make an appearance before Walt does."

Mary stopped staring at her best friend's stomach and noticed the ripples on the surface of the coffee in her cup.

"I'm only twenty minutes away at any given time if Walt's at the hospital."

Dakota shifted positions again. "I know, hon . . . I appreciate it."

Dakota was the closest thing Mary had to a sister, and they'd only known each other for just over a half a dozen years. They'd connected because they were neighbors and cemented their friendship when they realized how alike they were. Dakota was completely OCD when it came to prepping for the apocalypse, or the more likely event of a nasty earthquake . . . and Mary was obsessive about analyzing every person who crossed her path. It helped that Dakota was a writer and tended to study people without realizing it. She'd often turn to Mary when they were in a restaurant and point out a habit the waiter displayed . . . or a customer with an unusual tic. People watching was a shared pastime between a psychologist and a romance novelist.

"What's on your agenda today?" Dakota asked, her mouth twisting as she attempted to get comfortable and obviously failed.

"I have a client at one and another at three." Mary felt her face contorting to mimic her friend's. "You look miserable."

Dakota huffed out a breath and pushed off the stool. "I am. And I need to pee. Again!"

Mary chucked as Dakota heaved her pregnant belly, along with the rest of her, off the stool and rounded the corner. The sound of her friend walking up the stairs had Mary shouting, "You have a bathroom downstairs."

"This is the only exercise I'm getting these days."

Mary opened her mouth to argue and snapped it closed.

With the squeak of the floor above her for company, Mary moved around the kitchen island to look out at the backyard. It looked a lot like hers, only with more flowers. It was a postage stamp, like most of those in Orange County. Add the fact that they were in a townhouse condominium development, and that yard became even smaller, bumped up to the attached condo on one side. Mary knew it was only a matter of time before Dakota and Walt . . . along with Junior, moved to a bigger place.

Just the thought of her best friend moving away left her empty inside.

She allowed herself a half second of self-pity before shaking away the cloud that had started to form over her head.

Hearing the sound of a toilet flushing, Mary forced herself to smile. If Dakota saw her staring out the back window with *poor me* written all over her face, she'd put her friend in an awkward place. The last thing Mary wanted was to dampen Dakota's joy at being a new wife and soon-to-be mom.

"You know, Mary . . ." Dakota called from the stairs.

Mary started to move around the dividing wall from the kitchen to the living room when Dakota yelled.

"Son of a—"

A horrendous thud followed Dakota cussing and had Mary running toward her friend.

Dakota sat crumpled at the bottom of the stairs, one hand on her belly, the other on her leg.

"What the heck?"

"Oh, damn. Oh . . ." Dakota started to rock back and forth, her eyes closed and her face squished in pain.

Mary managed to put her cup on the floor as she knelt down beside her. "What hurts? Did you fall?" Stupid question, but Dakota didn't call her on it.

"Slipped," she said, gritting her teeth.

Mary glanced at the stairs, noticed liquid on the surface of the polished wood.

"Did you spill something?"

Dakota finally opened her eyes and pulled up the edge of her pants on her right leg. It was already turning red.

"Damn . . . just, son of a bitch!"

"Are you okay?"

"No. I think I broke it."

Mary's heart leapt in her chest. "Really?" She peered closer.

"Oh, damn."

Mary swept back her hair and tried to catch Dakota's eyes. "Should I call an ambulance?"

Dakota shook her head.

"I'll call Walt."

"No . . ."

"What?"

"Yes. Oh, God it hurts!"

"Your leg?" Mary glanced down again.

"No."

"Your leg doesn't hurt?"

"It. All. Hurts!"

Mary stood quick enough to feel a little dizzy. "I'm calling an ambulance."

"No, Mary . . . Walt will freak."

Mary didn't listen and found the cordless receiver sitting on the counter in the kitchen. She dialed 911 and hurried back to her friend.

"Mary, I'm okaaay." Dakota winced as she said it and closed her eyes.

"Nine one one, what's your emergency?" The operator sounded bored.

"Yeah, my friend fell down the stairs."

"Is your friend awake?"

Dakota started to pound her fist on the floor beside her. At first Mary thought maybe it was a tactic to end the phone call, then she noticed the grimace on her face.

"She's awake."

"Any visible injuries?"

"Her leg. But she says everything hurts."

It took Dakota moving her hand from her leg to her belly for Mary to report the obvious. "She's pregnant. Nine months pregnant."

"Is she in labor?"

"No . . . uhm." Once again the liquid on the stairs had her pause. "Dakota?"

"What?" Her friend bit the question out.

"Did your water break?"

"No my water didn't—" Dakota didn't finish her sentence. They both looked down at the same time.

"Oh, shit." This time it was Mary cussing. And Mary didn't cuss out loud.

"Ma'am?"

"Uh, yeah. Her water . . . yeah, she's in labor."

"How far apart are her contractions?" The monotone questions coming from the operator sounded as if they came from a computer and not a person.

"How far apart are your contractions?" Mary repeated the question.

"How the hell should I know?" Dakota barked.

Mary tilted the receiver to her mouth. "She doesn't know. It all just happened. Is an ambulance coming?"

The operator confirmed the address and told her the paramedics would be there within four minutes. When Mary tried to end the call, the operator continued to ask questions. *Are the contractions coming fast? Was the baby crowning?* Mary's eyes moved to the wet spot on Dakota's pregnancy pants.

"What are you staring at?"

"They want to know if the baby is coming out."

Dakota shook her head as the sound of an ambulance rang closer.

"Thank God," Mary muttered as she left Dakota's side and moved to the front door. As soon as she saw the lights, she thanked the operator and hung up.

The small fire medic truck pulled into the drive just as the full-size truck rounded the corner onto their street.

The medic stepped from the truck without rushing.

"She's inside." Mary forced her breathing to slow.

The fortysomething man offered a nod and followed her in while the second medic went to the back of the truck to grab some kind of box.

Another siren filtered into the mix while neighbors started to emerge from their houses.

Within the course of ten minutes the medics had cut Dakota's pants away, splinted what did appear to be a broken leg, gotten up close and personal enough to know the baby wasn't flashing the color of its hair, and had loaded her friend onto a gurney.

After a brief argument as to which hospital the medics were going to take her to, Dakota finally met Mary's gaze.

"Call Walt."

The medics extended the gurney and started to roll her out of the house.

"And grab my purse. My overnight bag is by Walt's side of the bed," she yelled.

"I got it."

"And lock the door."

Mary smiled. "I'm right behind you."

"Call my mom . . . but don't tell her about the fall."

She's going to find out eventually. "Okay."

"Mary?"

"Yeah?"

"Hurry."

"Right behind you!"

Dakota let out a long string of expletives as the medics bumped the gurney over the threshold of the home.

"It's going to be a long day!" Mary whispered to herself.

Chapter Two

Thank goodness someone had the sense to invent the hands-free car phone. By the time Mary had packed up all of Dakota's things, she was a good ten minutes behind the ambulance. It didn't help that Mary had to run across the street and tell Leroy the plumber to lock up when he left.

Instead of calling the ER directly to catch Walt, she went for his personal cell phone. He answered on the fifth ring. "Dr. Eddy."

She'd been practicing this call for a good five minutes in her head. "Who is going to be a daddy today?"

Silence met her ear.

"Walt?"

"Mary?"

"Well, now that we have the names straight, I thought you might like to know that Dakota's in labor."

She heard him suck in a breath before blowing it out.

"Labor?"

Mary felt a smile teasing her lips. "First there is sex, then there is conception . . . nine months of baking . . . then labor. Didn't they teach you this in medical school?"

"Okay . . . yeah . . . all right. Labor. Okay. I've gotta . . . damn it . . . is she there? Let me talk to her."

"Nope, she's in the ambulance. I'm behind her by ten minutes."

"Ambulance? Why? Was she delivering?" Poor Walt was working himself up.

"No." Mary looked over her shoulder and attempted to merge into traffic. "She couldn't walk."

"What? Why?"

The BMW behind her wasn't letting her in without a little persuasion. She nudged the nose of her Honda into the other lane in hopes the other driver would show a little compassion. "She fell down the stairs."

The Beemer ignored her like she wasn't there. "Thanks, dude."

"Fell down the stairs?" Walt's voice elevated.

Looked like the Subaru was going to cut her a break. "Yeah, broken leg. I'm sure she's fine. Broken, but fine."

"What the hell! Back up, Mary. What are you talking about?"

Now that she was in the correct lane to merge onto the freeway, which would bring her to the hospital faster, Mary focused on the conversation. "Dakota's water broke, she slipped, fell . . . she thinks she broke her leg."

"You're serious."

"Yep."

Walt offered a few expletives before asking which hospital the medics were taking his wife to.

"I'll call your parents and Dakota's. Just get to the hospital."

It sounded as if Walt was rushing around the ER, barking orders while carrying the phone pressed to his ear. "And call Monica. Let her know what happened, that she and Trent need to take the conference call without me."

Monica was a new friend to her and Dakota, and a nurse practitioner who worked alongside Walt with his Borderless Doctors and Borderless Nurses organization. Trent was Monica's husband and one of the Fairchild brothers who owned Fairchild Charters, a private jet and helicopter company that had recently started working with Borderless Doctors for humanitarian relief.

"I'm on it, Walt. Just stay calm and drive safe."

He paused on the line. "I'm going to be a dad."

Mary grinned as she exited the freeway. "Get a hustle, Daddy."

"Right, right . . . I'm on my wa—" He didn't finish his sentence before the line went dead.

—

Dr. and Mrs. Eddy were quick to answer the phone and tell her they would be booking flights and awaiting word.

Dakota's parents weren't as easy . . . well, not Elaine in any event. "She isn't due for two more weeks."

"Tell that to the baby." Mary was attempting to find a parking spot in the elevated structure.

"Well, that is very inconvenient."

There were some times Mary realized not having any parents could be a blessing. "I'm not sure what to tell you, Mrs. Laurens, your daughter went into labor, and I think she could use your help after the baby arrives." And if Dakota had in fact broken a leg . . . then she'd take all the help she could get. Including her uptight mother.

"Well, bless her heart. Who goes into labor early on their first baby?"

Mary rolled her eyes.

Once again, Mary gave Elaine the hospital information and asked that she inform Dakota's sister.

"We'll do our best to get a flight in the next day or so."

"That would be great."

"Leave it to Dakota . . ." Elaine's voice trailed off as she hung up the phone.

Mary squeezed her car between a long-bed dually truck and a minivan. There wasn't much space between the cars. The truck looked relatively new, giving her the sense that maybe the owner would be extra careful not to ding a door when sliding inside. The minivan, on the other hand, was oxidized and a couple of decades old. Mary went ahead and backed out of the space and pulled back in a little closer to the truck.

She left the engine running while she fumbled through her contacts in her phone in search of Monica's number. On her third time through her list, it dawned on her that she hadn't replaced all the numbers when she'd upgraded her cell earlier in the year.

She considered calling Walt back, then decided against it. The man would be stressed enough. If he didn't know Monica's number from memory, he'd be fumbling with a cell phone while on the highway.

Mary tapped her fingers along her phone as she debated. There was one person she could call who would have Monica's number, one someone whose number she'd memorized months ago.

A chill went over her body when she considered her options.

Before she could talk herself out of it, she dialed.

In a completely childish act, she chanted in her head that the call go to voice mail. On the fourth ring she held her breath.

"Hello?"

One simple greeting and her insides did the wobble. "Hi, Glen."

"I saw your name pop up on my screen and thought, no way. After all this time she finally calls."

His words made her pause. "Y-you were supposed to call me."

"I was?"

She squeezed the bridge of her nose and closed her eyes. "Yes, you . . . never mind. That isn't why I'm calling."

"Of course not. Because if you were calling for *that* reason, you would have done so before now."

She remembered the words he'd said to her the last time they'd had a private conversation. *The invitation is always open.*

"So there is a statute of limitations on your invitation," she said, her voice clipped. "Good to know." Not that she'd planned on taking him up on said invite.

"I didn't say that."

"Whatever! I'm calling to get Monica's number. Do you have it?"

"I do have it."

She waited.

"Well?"

"Well what?" He was playing coy.

"Monica's number. What is it?"

"Don't you have it?"

She wanted to bang her head on the steering wheel. "I do, at home. I have a new phone. I didn't transfer her number into it."

"Oh." He had a lift to his voice. "But you transferred mine?"

"No!" The man was exasperating. "I knew your number."

"You *memorized* it?"

"Yes. No . . . darn it." She hadn't meant to tell him that. "Can I have her number, please?"

His soft laugh had her gripping the steering wheel.

"Glen!"

"Am I the only one who finds it interesting that you memorized a number you had no intention of using?"

"Am I the only one who recognizes how huge your ego is?"

He laughed. "I think there are a lot of people who know that about me."

"How proud you are." The reason it would never have worked between them.

"Life is short, Counselor. Insecurity doesn't move one forward in life. You should know that."

"Of course I know that." *I don't always practice it, but I know it.* "Now are you going to give me Monica's number or not?"

"Someone is upset."

"Someone is infuriating."

He laughed again. "Do you have a pen?"

She opened the glove compartment in her car and pulled out a notepad and pen. "I'm ready."

She jotted down the number Glen finally surrendered.

"What's the big hurry?" he asked.

"Dakota's in labor. Walt asked me to call your brother and Monica so they could take a conference call or something."

"So Junior is finally here."

"Soon, in any event."

"Give my best to Mom and Dad." He sounded sincere.

"I will."

She paused, waiting for him to say something . . . good-bye, great talking to ya . . . something.

Silence.

"Glen?"

"Yeah?"

The man made her crazy. "I've gotta go."

"Okay, go then."

"I will . . . I'm going."

He didn't hang up.

"Glen?"

"Yeah?"

"You make me crazy!" she all but yelled. "I'm deleting your number from my brain."

He laughed. "No, you're not."

"I am."

"Good luck with that."

"I'm hanging up now . . ."

No click on his end.

Mary's thumb hovered over the cancel button on the steering wheel of her car.

When it became obvious he wasn't going to say anything, she let out a frustrated sigh. "I'm . . . oh, forget it." She hung up to his laughter.

—

Glen leaned back in his office chair, his feet resting on the edge of his desk, and stared at the cell phone in his hand.

She'd called.

Took the woman damn near a year, but she'd called.

Sure, the excuse about needing Monica's number was handy, and maybe she actually did need Monica's number . . . or maybe Mary wanted to open a conversation between them and wasn't sure how to do it and save face.

He thumbed through his contacts and dialed his brother.

"Hey, Glen."

Gotta love cell phones. Everyone knows who's on the line before they answer.

"Trent, you sound good."

The youngest Fairchild was the most allergic to the office. He only came in on Tuesdays and Thursdays, and avoided that whenever he could. Didn't mean the man didn't work, he simply didn't do it at a desk.

"I was just there yesterday."

"But it feels like forever."

"Bite me."

Glen laughed. "Listen, I just got a call from Mary, she's trying to get ahold of Monica."

"Monica's on the phone with her right now."

So that part wasn't a lie. A twinge of disappointment fluttered in his head. "Good, good." Glen searched for an excuse to stay on the line. Maybe get a tidbit about Mary he didn't already know.

"Is that all?" Trent asked.

"Uhm . . . yeah."

From Trent's end he heard Monica talking. "You're kidding."

"Is everything okay?"

"Hold up," Trent said before the sound from the other end became muffled.

"She what?"

"What is it?" Glen asked again.

All Glen caught was the word *broken*.

"That's crazy."

"Trent?" Glen attempted to catch his brother's attention. "What's broken?"

"Mary . . . hold on."

Mary was broken? She didn't sound busted when he spoke with her.

He repeated his brother's name a few times before Trent responded.

"According to Mary, Dakota fell and broke a leg."

"I thought she was in labor."

"That, too."

Glen didn't know a lot about having babies, but he didn't think a broken anything would aid in the delivery.

"I'll call you back." Trent moved on in a hurry.

"If you need me for anything."

"Okay . . . yeah." The line went dead.

Glen was leaning over his desk, sliding his fingers over his cell phone. So Mary did need Monica's number. But she'd memorized his.

That was a juicy piece of information that had him smiling.

Now how was he going to wiggle his ass all the way to California without being obvious?

As it turned out . . . he didn't need to wiggle at all.

His phone rang.

"Forget something?"

Trent didn't bother with hello. "I need you to fly Monica to California. I'd do it myself but I have that meeting tomorrow with the transplant coordinator and the Red Cross."

"Anything I can do to help."

A few minutes later Glen pushed away from his desk in search of one of his top brokers. He needed to find out what planes were available and round up a copilot.

There was something to be said for being the CFO of Fairchild Charters.

Chapter Three

There was no reason to hurry. As it turned out, eight hours after the rush of phone calls and breaking the speed limit, Dakota was holding on to Junior a little longer.

Walt stuck his head out into the lobby on occasion and informed Mary of the progress. "She's at seven now."

It had taken her two hours to go from six centimeters to seven.

"How is she?"

Walt ran a hand through his hair. "Better. The epidural . . ." He paused. "Thank God for the epidural."

Mary grinned.

"Does she need anything?"

He shook his head. "I have it covered."

Mary knew that was coming. It didn't hurt to ask. "What about you? Do you need anything?"

Walt glanced over his shoulder. "I'd kill for chocolate."

"I doubt it has to come to that." She pushed herself off the waiting room sofa and tucked the book she'd been reading into her purse. "Any particular kind?"

"Any . . . all."

"Sounds like Dakota's sugar cravings have been passed on to you."

Walt grinned. "Thanks, Mary."

It felt good to get off the labor and delivery floor. Mary already knew that the vending machines closest to the emergency room had the best selection for after-hours pickings. But since the gift shop and the cafeteria were still open, she went ahead and started her search there.

One look at the line out the cafeteria door and she turned to find the overpriced gift store. The store window held the usual suspects. Pink and blue teddy bears, get well balloons, and several sprays of flowers and live plants. Inside, an elderly woman in a blue volunteer uniform greeted her with a smile. She considered a gender specific stuffed toy but decided to wait until Junior was born. Unlike everyone else in the free world, Dakota wanted to be surprised when the baby was born, so Mary had no idea what color to pick. Next to the tiny teddy bears was a gangly legged stuffed monkey holding crutches.

Oh, what were the chances of that?

Mary reached out a hand just as someone behind her did the same.

"Excuse me," she said without looking up.

"I touched it first."

That voice.

She closed her eyes, rested her hand on the monkey, and turned. "What are you doing here?"

Tilting her neck to look at his face was an effort. It wasn't that Mary was terribly short, but Glen was a full head taller than she was. And those eyes. Piercing, brown with just a hint of gold. Strong jaw in need of a shave.

Her heart fluttered and parts of her she'd rather not mention started to melt. One side of his mouth lifted in a half smile as he dipped just enough for her to notice the pilot's hat sitting on top of his full head of dark brown hair.

The man needed a warning label.

"I had to give a friend a ride."

Only a pilot would call a cross-country flight a ride.

"A ride," she repeated for good measure.

He shrugged. "Damn, you're beautiful."

She hated the fact that her cheeks warmed immediately.

I'm not going to smile. I'm not going to smile.

"Always the player."

His eyes swept her face. "Because I speak the obvious?"

Her psychology hat popped onto her head as quick as Mary Poppins could snap open her umbrella. "Because you say things like that to disarm your opponent and put yourself in a dominant position."

Glen blinked several times, his eyes never changing focus. "I-I do what?"

"Oh, forget it." She attempted to grasp the monkey from his hand, but he kept hold. "Glen, please."

"I like when a woman begs."

She let loose the monkey. "You're impossible."

He snatched it into his hands. "Maybe, but I get what I want."

Mary started to leave the gift shop before remembering why she was there.

Doing her best to ignore Glen as he stepped up to the register to purchase the lame stuffed toy, Mary randomly grabbed a half a dozen candy bars and waited for her turn.

The seventy-plus-year-old woman behind the counter offered a full smile as she rang up Glen's purchase. "Are you a pilot?"

Mary had a strong urge to roll her eyes.

"Yes, ma'am."

"It's always so nice to see those clean white uniforms. So few young men pay attention to their whites."

"It's hard to attract the attention of beautiful women wearing dingy yellow," he told her.

She blushed at Glen's words as she handed him his change. "I'm sure you have no trouble there."

He had the nerve to glance over his shoulder at Mary.

Instead of pretending she wasn't listening, Mary met his eyes.

"You'd be surprised," Glen told the clerk.

He took the bagged-up monkey and took two steps back and waited.

Mary dumped the candy on the counter while Glen stared.

"What?" she asked him.

"Well, that explains why you're so uptight."

She narrowed her eyes and looked down.

"Excuse me?"

"Women need chocolate on occasion."

Her breath caught in her throat. "It's not . . ."

"It's okay, Mary. Everything makes sense."

"It isn't . . . it's for Walt."

Glen looked beyond her at the volunteer behind the register and winked. "I'm sure it is."

"It is." The fact that he was insinuating she was on her cycle had her wanting to toss the candy at him. The last thing she wanted to discuss was something as personal as her period.

"Whatever you say, sweetheart."

The man made her want to scream.

She snatched dollar bills from her purse, tossed them on the counter, then took Walt's bag of chocolate before storming out of the gift shop without taking her change.

As she expected, Glen followed behind.

She hit the button to the elevator twice. "You were going to give that poor woman in the gift shop a heart attack."

"Is that right."

A woman and a toddler moved to stand beside them.

Once the elevator arrived and six people filed out, they pushed in and stood in silence until the mom and son left on the third floor.

"Do you flirt with everyone who wears a bra?"

Glen glanced at the ceiling. "Was she wearing a bra?"

Mary felt a smile tugging at the corner of her lips and fought it back. “Seriously, Glen. You must know how out of line it is to flirt with a woman her age.”

“Seriously, Mary.” He used her words against her. “Why are you so worried about my reputation?”

“I’m not worried about your reputation.” *Am I worried about his reputation?*

The doors opened on the sixth floor and she stepped out.

They rounded past the glass partition to the room holding all the infants born that day. Inside were four cherub faces, one wrapped in blue, the other three in pink.

Glen’s step faltered. “Are any of these . . .”

Mary kept walking. “No, she hasn’t delivered yet.”

Glen rubbernecked at the nursery as he walked beside her.

For a moment, the smirk he wore on his face waned.

The next corner brought them to the open waiting room.

Monica jumped up when she saw them.

Mary greeted her with a hug. “You didn’t have to rush.”

“If I broke my leg on the way to the hospital to deliver a baby, someone better rush for me.”

Mary loved friends like Monica.

“Did you tell the nurses you’re here?”

Monica nodded.

Mary sat, setting her purse and the bag of candy on the floor beside her.

Monica immediately picked up Mary’s stuff and set it in the chair. “Hospital floors,” she said as if Mary understood her point without question.

“It’s going to be a while. Walt said Dakota was only at seven centimeters,” Mary told her.

“Could take hours then.”

“Seven centimeters?” Glen asked.

Both women turned his way.

"The cervix has to dilate to ten before she can push."

Glen stopped smiling. "Ten centimeters?" He rounded the fingers on his right hand with his left. "That has to hurt."

"That's why they call it labor," Monica said with a laugh.

Mary noticed Glen swallowing as he separated his hands and rested them on the arms of the chair.

"Hard to picture, isn't it?" she asked him.

"Thinking about it makes me glad I'm a man."

"I bet."

Once again, Walt popped his head from the locked delivery wing. "Monica!"

The two embraced as old friends did.

"How is she doing?" Monica wasted no time in asking.

"Good. Baby is fine. No decels. Looks good for a normal delivery."

Glen leaned close and whispered in Mary's ear. "What's a decel?"

Mary shrugged. "Must be doctor-nurse talk."

"How is Dakota's blood pressure?"

"Within her normal limits." Walt placed a hand on Monica's arm. "We're watching it closely."

Dakota had had early pregnancy blood pressure problems that caused some worry in her first trimester. Mary knew that there was always a possibility of her having more issues during delivery. While the risk sat in the back of her head, Mary hadn't really thought much about it until Monica brought it up.

Walt glanced over and noticed Glen.

Glen stood and they did the man handshake thing. "How does it feel?" he asked.

Walt shook his head. "I've delivered dozens of babies, but it's a hell of a lot harder watching your wife laboring with your own."

Monica patted him on the back. "You'll be fine."

"I should get back," he told them.

It was Mary's turn to make her way to his side. "Here." She thrust the brown paper bag full of candy in his hands.

He glanced inside, grinned, and kissed her cheek. "You're a godsend."

She smiled, glanced at Glen with a smirk, then returned her attention to Walt. "If you need more, just ask."

He waved the bag in the air and disappeared behind the door.

Chapter Four

Walt's parents arrived just after nine, and Dakota's parents weren't going to leave the East Coast until the morning.

The only other person Mary had been instructed to call once Junior was born was Dakota's agent. Only Desi didn't want a late night wake-up call unless something went wrong. "No one calls at two a.m. with good news. Call me in the morning," she'd told Mary.

A few other families had filtered into the waiting room and out again once their new member of the family had been born.

Monica had curled up in one of the chairs and fallen fast asleep.

Mary made small talk with Walt's parents for a couple of hours, but the day started to wear on her. She leaned the back of her head on the wall and closed her eyes.

Glen sat beside her quietly thumbing through a magazine. He had to be exhausted. His internal clock was three hours ahead of hers, and she was shot.

Instead of asking, she allowed her mind to drift.

He smelled good. Like he'd just splashed aftershave over his skin. And not the perfumey sweet smelling stuff, but the musky, sexy smelling stuff.

She pictured his cocky grin and striking eyes and smiled as she lost her fight with sleep.

"Mary." His voice was a soft whisper in her dreams. Even though her back hurt from the stiff bed she must be lying on, his breath on her ear made it all right as he whispered her name. "Mary?"

She snuggled closer, not wanting to break from the dream she knew she must be having. "I'm sleeping," she heard herself mutter.

She heard his quiet laughter. "But you need to wake up, sweetheart."

She shook her head.

"Mary?"

Other voices mixed with Glen's and had her opening her eyes.

It all came back.

Dakota.

Maternity waiting room.

Babies.

Someone was pushed up against her cheek.

No, scratch that, she was all but collapsed on someone's shoulder.

Crisp white shirt, stripes on the sleeves.

Glen.

"Are you awake now?"

"Oh, God."

She felt moisture out of the corner of her mouth. Mortified, she glanced down and noticed a wet spot on his shirt.

"Well?"

Her horror at finding herself leaning on Glen quickly faded when she noticed Walt standing in the doorway, his eyes bright and shiny, his face illuminated despite the late hour.

"We have a son."

Mary felt the tired snap away with his words.

Questions ran through the room. How was Dakota? When could they see her and the baby? How was the delivery?

Mary just stood beside them lost in thought.

A nephew . . . well, as close to a nephew as she'd ever have.

Walt led them back to the suite where he'd spent his entire day.

Lying in a bed, her long dark hair pulled back, her swollen cheeks flushed from what had to be a grueling experience, Dakota smiled as they all filed inside the room.

In her arms was a quiet little bundle wrapped in a tiny blanket with a blue little cap on his head.

Mary felt her eyes swell with unshed tears. It took a lot for Mary to cry. In fact, she never cried.

There were oohs, and plenty of aahs. And though Walt's father was a cardiologist, he asked about Dakota's splinted leg poking out from under the sheets.

"Well, that just adds to the stories you can tell over cocktails later in life," Dr. Eddy said as he pointed to her leg.

The older Dr. Eddy leaned over and kissed Dakota's cheek before smiling down at his grandson.

"Have you picked out a name?" Monica asked.

"We have. And no, it's not Walter the Fourth."

Mary had already heard that Junior and Walter were off the potential list. There were three generations of doctors with Walter Eddy's name, and forcing the newest Eddy to carry the burden of being a doctor, or carry the burden of breaking the trend, wasn't something Dakota and Walt wanted to do.

"Well, don't keep us waiting," JoAnne implored.

"Leo Michael Eddy."

Mary caught Dakota's gaze and smiled. "A strong, heroic name."

Dakota winked and the memory of so many brainstorming sessions over names surfaced. Not for naming the baby, but for naming the heroes in Dakota's books. At one point they'd brought up the name Leo, but Dakota hadn't used it until now.

"We don't have one Leo in the family." JoAnne sounded unconvinced.

"Precisely," Walt said to his mother.

One of the nurses stepped into the room, bringing another chair. "I'll be taking baby Leo for his first bath in about half an hour," she told them. "I know you've been waiting all day, but I'm going to have to boot you all to the door when I do."

"We're all shot anyway," Monica told her.

"Not as shot as me." They all chuckled at Dakota's comment.

Walt lifted Leo from Dakota's arms and walked to his mother.

While JoAnne and Dakota had had a rocky start, the two managed to bond during the holidays.

JoAnne pushed back in the chair and held out her arms. The second Leo was in them, JoAnne grew misty-eyed. "Aren't you just the most beautiful boy."

Mary took that moment to move beside Dakota.

"How are you feeling?"

"Exhausted."

The gaggle of people centered around the baby, giving them a chance for a few quietly spoken words.

"How's the leg?"

Dakota narrowed her gaze. "Freakin' broken. How the hell am I going to manage a baby with a broken leg?" she whispered.

Mary looked around the room. "With lots of hands. Your mother will be here tomorrow."

"I'm not sure that will be of any help."

Mary held in a laugh. "I'm right across the street."

Dakota placed her hand on hers. "I know. Thank you. I don't know what I would have done if I'd fallen and you weren't there."

"You'd have crawled to the phone and dialed 911. It's not like you're ninety and had a stroke."

"Still."

Words between best friends weren't needed, but always nice to hear.

"Have we figured out where everyone is staying tonight?" Walt asked when Leo had been passed to his father.

"I suppose we can get a hotel."

"It's a little late for that. I have a pullout in my living room." Mary's two-bedroom condo had her office space and her bedroom. She didn't often have overnight guests, so the pullout was perfect. Dakota and Walt's place was larger, but the nursery took up the guest bedroom.

"I'm staying here a little longer. Mom, Dad . . . you guys can take our room. I'll crash on the couch when I get home."

Mary glanced at Glen.

Glen in her space . . . how was that for irony? "Monica can bunk with me . . . you can take the pullout."

"How can a man pass up an offer like that?"

"Perfect," Monica said with a yawn. "The thought of dealing with a hotel this late sounds painful. I'll call Jessie in the morning and book rooms at The Morrison for everyone."

Once the sleeping arrangements were made, Mary switched car keys with Walt since he had the SUV he'd purchased just a month before in anticipation of Junior . . . ah, Leo. It was going to take some time to get used to calling Leo something other than Junior. Her compact car would be fine for Walt solo.

When the nurse made her second appearance, no one made her crack the visitor whip.

"You didn't get to hold him," Dakota noticed.

"I'm sure I'll get my chance," Mary said.

Walt returned Leo to Dakota's arms and several cell phones came out to take pictures of the three of them.

"How do I look?" Dakota asked when Mary checked the picture.

"Like crap. But I'll clean it up before I post it to your fans." Yet one more thing Mary loved doing for Dakota and her famous author self.

"I love you."

"I know." Mary tucked her phone away and turned toward the door.

Glen had said very little while in the room and now stood by the door, waiting to leave.

He visibly shivered while they waited for the others to join them. "What's the matter, Glen? Allergic to babies?"

"Maybe I'm cold."

"You're a terrible liar."

And he was. She'd yet to meet a player, especially one who had the gold card for the club, who didn't run from single women with biological ticking clocks. Or a delivery room with a bitty bundle wrapped in a blanket.

"Not allergic," he conceded. "Just not ready."

She paused, met his gaze. "I think that's the first honest thing I've heard pass your lips."

For a brief moment he actually looked offended.

And for a brief moment, she felt bad for saying her thoughts aloud. "Something I should probably work on."

—

Mary didn't own a cat.

It took every ounce of propriety to *not* point that out when he stepped into her home.

"The plumber was here working on the downstairs bathroom when I left with Dakota. I'm not sure it's working."

Mary pushed past him, turning on lights.

"We'll make do," Monica said as she set her small overnight case at the base of the stairs.

"There is another one upstairs." Mary no sooner let them into the condominium before she was walking back out the door. "I'm just going to make sure Walt's parents are settled."

And then she was gone.

"How is it she has so much energy?" Monica asked once Mary flew out the front door.

"Beats me."

Monica walked into Mary's small kitchen and opened the refrigerator. She found a bottle of water and waved it in the air. "You might wanna see if her bathroom works down here before we dominate the one upstairs."

If there was something Glen was not used to doing, it was exploring a woman's home without her in it. He glanced around the space and moved to a closed door. One look at the toilet lying on its side told him all he needed to know.

"Bummer," Monica said over his shoulder.

Glen lifted his overnight case and started toward the stairs. "I won't be long."

Monica leaned against the counter and tilted her water bottle back.

The doors upstairs were open. He glanced in to see a perfectly made bed, simple white linen and only a couple of pillows. Nothing overly feminine but not a room a man would claim unless he was married.

He didn't step inside, instead he found a door to the room he needed in the hall. Here, too, everything was perfectly set. Not the messy feminine space he usually identified with the opposite sex. The bathroom had a Jack and Jill setup with one door leading to the master bedroom and the other to the hall. He took another quick look into Mary's room before closing both doors.

He wanted to linger . . . open doors and search for something, anything that may give him a few more clues to the most evasive woman he'd ever met.

The most intriguing woman, if he was honest with himself. Maybe it was the fact that she didn't fall over herself to grab his attention that fascinated him.

If he searched her space, would he find something telling? A box of condoms? A prescription of some sort?

God, he was an asshole.

He shook the desire to invade her privacy away and got to the business at hand.

He worked quickly, mainly to get the hell out of there. Or he'd give in to his internal devilish side and poke around. Because the place was so tidy, he found himself making sure there wasn't one drop on the counter after he brushed his teeth.

When he turned off the light, he heard voices drifting from the bottom floor.

"He'll be fine," Monica said.

"I didn't realize this sofa bed was so short."

Glen found the two of them moving furniture around in the living room and staring down at the bed he'd call his for the night.

"Looks good to me." He caught Mary's eyes.

"You'll have to sleep sideways."

He was about to suggest that Monica take the downstairs accommodations and he'd take the space next to Mary, but didn't think his comment would be well received. "I'll be fine," he said instead.

Monica patted Mary on the back. "You play hostess, I'm going to take a quick shower."

"Okay."

"Good night, Glen," Monica said before leaving them alone.

"I'll get a blanket and pillow."

Once again, Mary buzzed out of the room, returning less than a minute later with her hands full. "Sorry about the downstairs bathroom," she apologized. "I thought he'd have it fixed."

"It's not like you expected guests."

"I almost never have guests," she told him while spreading a sheet over the tiny mattress.

He leaned down to help her. "We appreciate you offering."

Together they pulled the blanket onto the bed. Glen tested the sofa bed with his weight. The springs offered a little protest but didn't feel that bad. "Perfect."

"Probably not. But it will have to do."

"I'll be fine, Mary."

She turned away, then back again. "Help yourself to the kitchen. I'll leave the hall door open to the bathroom upstairs."

"Got it."

She tilted her head and regarded him. "Good night."

He smiled, purposely waiting for her to look directly into his eyes. "Good night, Mary."

Her cheeks flushed and he had to hold back a wicked grin.

Thirty minutes later, when the noise of the two women upstairs stopped and all Glen could hear was the hum of the refrigerator, he stared at the ceiling and wondered what Mary wore to bed.

As soon as he grew comfortable with the ill-placed spring in the pullout bed, he closed his eyes and fell fast asleep.

The sound of a phone ringing had him springing awake.

Chapter Five

Mary jumped out of bed at the first ring. Her hand reached for the handset by her bedside to find the space where the phone usually lay empty.

In a fog, she scrambled for where the thing could be and all but fell out of her bed.

On the second ring, Monica stirred beside her.

The phone sounded distant. Outside her bedroom door, it grew louder.

Her home phone nearly never rang unless there was an emergency, which gave her feet wings as she flew down the stairs toward the ringing phone. In the reaches of her mind, she noticed dawn breaking through the closed curtains of her living room.

On the fourth ring, she saw the phone on the other side of the sofa bed and went for it. She vaguely realized she'd done a tiny hop, skip, sputter over Glen's legs before landing on the other side with the phone in her hand. "Mary Kildare," she answered as if she'd been up for hours.

"Mary, thank God. I'm so sorry to call you on this number."

The voice was male, not one she recognized at first syllable. "It's okay . . ."

"It's Jacob. Jacob Golf."

The flood of information that followed the man's name made her sigh. A client, one struggling to keep his marriage together, he was someone who never called unless it was to make or break an appointment. "Hello, Jacob."

"Nina's gone. She didn't come home last night. I called her cell, she didn't pick up. I texted her, nothing. Her sister doesn't know where she is."

He was borderline manic. Though she wasn't at liberty to diagnosis her clients like a psychiatrist, she knew someone was manic when she saw it. Or in this case, heard it.

"Jacob, calm down. Take a deep breath."

"Calm down? My wife is gone, Mary."

"Jacob, listen to me. You've called me instead of the police, so you must think she's not a missing person."

Her mind was focused on her job, but the man in the bed beside her leaned close when he heard the word *police.*

"Who's Jacob?"

"Quiet." Mary waved Glen's question off and turned to stare at the wall.

"Why should you care? You get your check every week. And who are you with? I thought you were single?" Jacob started to shout.

That had escalated quickly. "What happened before Nina left?"

"We fought. She'd been out with her friends . . ." He paused. "Drinking. She looked guilty . . . I don't know what to think."

Mary knew from her private counseling sessions with Nina that the woman was less than faithful and had encouraged her to come clean with her husband more than once.

That hadn't happened.

"Did she take any of her things with her?"

"No."

Mary rubbed her eyes with her back of her hand. It was too early for this. "Then she'll be back. Unless you think she's away against her will . . ."

She waited for Jacob to voice what they both knew.

There was a moment of silence too long. "You knew this was going to happen."

Yes, she did, but she wasn't about to say that aloud. "Nina didn't confide in me on this subject."

"You should have told me." His voice grew short.

"Jacob—"

"You women stick together. I knew better than to trust in a chick to listen to our problems and make them better."

This was always hard to hear, even if she knew all of it was misplaced anger and a slightly unstable mind. Sadly, there was more instability out there than not these days. At least with those she worked with.

"I think we should talk when you're not upset."

"You probably know where she is."

Nina had told her Jacob could get unreasonably angry. He'd controlled it during their counseling sessions but seemed to be having a hard time now. "I assure you, I don't."

Beside Mary, Glen had swung his legs over the bed and sat listening to her side of the conversation.

"Such a bitch." His voice was loud enough for Mary to pull the phone away from her ear. "Fucking—"

The word exploded and Glen grabbed the phone.

Before Mary could grab it back, he was yelling into it.

"Listen, asshole, that's no way to talk to a lady."

Mary reached for the phone only to have Glen turn away, his bare back to her. "Glen, stop. I have it." She did not need this intervention.

"I don't care who you are. Have some respect."

Mary heard Jacob yelling on the line but couldn't make out the words. "Glen!"

One more final outburst from the phone and Glen dropped it from his ear. "He hung up."

She dropped her hands in her lap and glared. "Why did you do that?"

"The guy's a psycho."

No use denying that. "And?"

"What, and?"

"I'm a therapist. Dealing with people who aren't always of a completely sound mind isn't uncommon."

Glen ran a hand through his hair and stared at her as if she'd grown horns. "Men calling you, cussing and screaming, is a normal thing?"

"No." She glanced around the room, ran a hand over her face. "Not at home." Which gave her pause. How had Jacob gotten her home phone number? She only gave her clients her cell to use in an emergency, a number that offered an automatic reply after business hours to call 911 if there was anything life threatening in progress.

A wife leaving a husband didn't fall into that category.

"How did Crazy Guy get your home number?"

That she didn't know.

She shook her head and felt a tiny shiver of worry run down her spine, and dropped her eyes. That's when she realized that Glen wore tight underwear. Underwear that didn't leave a lot to the imagination.

Mary diverted her eyes to her own attire.

Tiny shirt and an even smaller pair of sleeping shorts.

Leaving the room without a bathrobe while having guests over was an unexpected event.

"That man sounded unstable to me."

"You're the pilot. I'm the therapist."

Glen sat tall, tossed the phone on the bed between them. "I'm a man unwilling to listen to a woman accept abuse from another man."

She forced her eyes to his. "So it's a sexist thing?"

"It's how I was raised," was all he offered.

It could be worse, she supposed. "This is my job. People call me when they're upset and need guidance."

"At home, in the middle of the night, to blame you for their problems?"

She couldn't deny that had happened. "Sometimes."

"I think I'll stick to flying planes."

Mary took the phone and stood. "You do that."

Unlike her initial sail over the bed, this time she walked around it, doing her best to ignore his eyes as they followed her around the room.

"Mary?" He stopped her.

"Yeah?"

"Do you think that guy is really crazy?"

She turned to see him looking directly at her. "His wife just left him. My guess is that would make anyone a little off balance."

Glen sat taller. "Do you have a gun?"

She narrowed her eyes. "A what?"

"A gun." He made a motion of pulling a trigger with his fingers. "You know."

Mary shook her head in despair. "No. I do not own a gun." To own a gun would mean she could use one. And she didn't think she could.

"I'd feel better if you had a gun."

She regarded him for a moment. "It's a good thing my welfare is none of your concern then."

His stare went directly through her, his lips lost all expression.

"That was uncalled for. I'm sorry."

He broke eye contact, leaned over the bed, and grabbed the jeans he'd been wearing the night before.

"I'm . . . really sorry."

"Let it go," he told her as he jerked his pants on.

A voice told her to drop it, but her heart sang a different tune. She approached him and placed a hand on his arm. "I could tell you I'm not awake, that I'm upset about that call. But the truth is I'm not used to hearing that someone cares about my well-being. I wasn't sure how to respond and I did so poorly."

He stopped short of zipping up his pants and let his arms drop to his sides. "I think that might be the first honest thing I've heard come from your lips."

She thought of her own observation she'd made about him the previous day and let a slow smile simmer over her lips. "Touché."

They arrived back at the hospital just before noon.

The place had exploded with people and flowers. While Glen had no real need to return to baby central, he kept his return flight on standby, using the excuse that he needed to await his brother's arrival before justifying his trip home.

"You really don't have to babysit me," Monica told him as they took one more trip down to the lobby of the hospital.

"I'm not babysitting you."

His sister-in-law regarded him out of the corner of her eye. "Is this about Mary?"

He shrugged. "That guy who called this morning was a complete freak."

"A freak she calls a client."

He couldn't shake the edge of the man's voice from his system. Nor the way Mary's face had looked when Glen had asked her how the guy managed to find her personal phone number.

Oh, she might try and act as if all was running normal in her world, but he somehow knew this wasn't standard operating procedure.

Then there was the part about her not having someone in her life to care. He knew Mary and Dakota were tight, but he'd also heard just enough about her history to know he and Mary were both orphans. Although Mary's biological parents had never been a part of her life,

Glen's had passed away when he was an adult. He'd always had his brothers and the company his father had founded to keep him occupied.

What did Mary have?

No siblings, one good friend, and a handful of freakish clients.

No wonder women like her owned a gaggle of cats. He hated that he stereotyped her, but couldn't seem to prevent his head from going there.

They stepped outside the sliding doors of the main lobby while they waited for Trent's arrival.

"You know, Glen . . . you should just ask her out."

Hadn't he already done that? Twice?

Not that Mary had shot him down. More like ignored his request. Twisted the invitation and made him question whether he'd actually uttered the words *Let's go out.*

"She has my number," he said as he placed his sunglasses over his eyes to avoid looking at his sister-in-law.

Monica released half a snort, half a laugh. "Testosterone truly rots the male brain," she said.

"Is that your medical diagnosis?"

"That's my *female* diagnosis. Mary is not the kind of woman to make the first move. I'm sure you can see that. Waiting for her to ask you out is an exercise in stupidity."

He paused. "I think you just called me stupid."

Monica nodded and pointed two fingers in the air toward him. "Brighter than you appear, flyboy."

"She's not interested."

Monica did that snort thing again.

"She'd be smart not to be interested, but she is."

"Wait, what? She'd be smart not—"

Monica rested one hand on her hip. "You're a player, Glen. Admit it."

"I am not." He was so a player. Denying it was a knee-jerk reaction.

"When was the last long-term relationship you had?"

He thought about that for a good ten seconds. "Define long-term."

"Exactly. I'm not sure if it's by design, intention, or simple bad luck. But you haven't been terribly unhappy since I've met you. Which means you're either happy being a bachelor and a player or you're happily holding out for the right girl." She took a deep breath and continued, "I think you like playing the field."

"What's wrong with that?"

"Nothing. I enjoyed the field at one time. I don't think Mary knows there is a field out there. Yet she can spot someone on it a mile away. Hence her being smart to avoid seeing someone playing it."

Glen tilted his sunglasses and made sure Monica looked directly at him. "So why are you suggesting I ask her out if you're so sure I'm wrong for her?"

Monica had this snarky smile that snuck up on you when you weren't watching. One that told him she knew a hell of a lot more than she let on.

"Because I like Mary. I think she'd find more joy in life if she were less guarded. Dating you could break open that free spirit and help her grasp life a little more than she's allowing herself. If there is something I've learned about you in the past couple years, it's that you enjoy living."

Damn, Monica had nailed Mary in a couple of sentences.

"I can see what Mary would get out of our dating . . . what do you think I'll gain?"

That snarky smile appeared in spades. "So much more."

What the hell did that mean?

He was about to ask when a car pulled into the turnaround and out stepped his younger brother.

Sister-in-law bonding time was over.

Chapter Six

He'd left.

Mary had known he would. He lived on the East Coast for crying out loud . . . but he'd left without so much as a smile. Well, there was a cordial *Thanks for putting me up* comment, and a group of *See you laters* to those sharing in the joy of baby Leo, but nothing more than a nod in her direction.

Then he left.

She hated the disappointment inside her. Mary had always been one to guard herself against caring too deeply about a man. As Dakota was fond of saying, it was a wonder she'd ever slept with anyone. As she'd gotten older, she'd avoiding putting herself out there because staying emotionally detached was getting tougher to do.

Here she was, an hour after Glen had left the hospital, still picturing him walking away. And she hadn't even dated the man.

They'd met at a Florida writer's conference Mary had attended with Dakota. Glen was there with his brother Trent for an emergency medical response convention taking place in the same hotel. And since Fairchild Charters was pioneering personal aircraft to come to the aid of people affected by natural disasters, as CFO of Fairchild Charters, he needed to be present.

They'd had some serious eye chemistry from word one. But in less than twenty-four hours Glen had flown back to Connecticut and she was on her way home to California. They'd exchanged phone numbers . . . but her phone never rang.

Because of Dakota's connection to the Fairchilds through Walt and Monica's friendship, Mary had found herself face-to-face with Glen a half a dozen times over the last year. Each one her heart kicked a little harder, each time she was reminded that he wasn't interested enough to initiate a real date, each encounter left her a little heartbroken.

She understood. He was as commitment-phobic as any wealthy bachelor should be. Mary remembered saying nearly those exact words to him within hours of meeting the man. Probably not one of her best decisions. Analyzing people and recognizing what motivated them to do the things they did—or in this case, not do the things they should—was her job. Keeping her analysis to herself was close to impossible.

Dakota had warned her for years to keep her mouth shut unless she was kissing someone.

Mary didn't listen.

Her stomach started to rumble when the smell of food blew in from the hall. She'd been at the hospital for two solid days and needed a little solitude. Having been on her own most of her life, she could only take a large family for so long before she needed to be alone. It was something she and Dakota had in common.

Walt's parents were talking about leaving and checking into a hotel so Walt could have some privacy at home, but Dakota's parents had been at the hospital a few hours and showed no signs of leaving anytime soon.

"I have a block of rooms waiting at The Morrison," Monica announced.

"Oh, that's perfect," Dr. Eddy said. "Then we can all ride in together tomorrow."

"How about giving me a call in the morning before rushing over. The orthopedic said he'd be by first thing in the morning to cast Dakota's leg. I'm going to push to have her discharged," Walt said.

"Why the hurry?" Elaine asked.

"She'll heal faster at home."

"Hospitals are full of germs," Monica added.

Mary listened to the exchange at a distance. "I have clients in the morning," she said as she stood, grabbing her purse. "If you need anything, I'm a phone call away."

Dakota offered a tired smile.

"Does anyone need a ride?" Mary asked in slight encouragement for the others in the room to leave.

"We're okay," Walt's parents chimed in together.

"All right then. Everyone has my number." She leaned over and kissed Dakota's cheek. "I'll see you at home."

"Thanks, Mary."

She drove with the windows down to push the hospital smell from her head. Instead of driving straight to her empty house, broken toilet, and a microwave dinner . . . she decided to make a detour to the beach. It was after six and most of the beach crowd had left hours before. Spring in Southern California offered beach weather on most days, but the time shift and the cooler nights kept people from lingering too long.

Mary kept a beach blanket and a simple chair in her trunk on standby for nights like this. Nights where she felt the melancholy setting in and when she analyzed her life way too closely. Watching the sun set and the tide pull in reminded her of how lucky she was. How rich she was for the friendships she had and the blessings she'd been given. She didn't think she used the beach for meditation, but in a way she did.

She snuggled into a thick sweater, slung her purse over her shoulder, and stepped onto the warm sand. Once she was close enough to hear the waves but not right on top of the water, Mary spread out her blanket and set up her chair.

There wasn't a cloud in the sky, but with the sun low on the horizon the air had a perfect crispness to it. She closed her eyes and faced the breeze. The salt air cleansed the taste of the hospital from her palate.

Dakota had looked exhausted. Her normally snarky comments were mild at best as the day had trailed on.

Even Walt appeared worn out.

The grandparents, both sets, were on fire, competing to hold baby Leo and preach which family member he took after. Then there was Monica . . . the woman was a true friend. She spoke with the nurses on staff, talked with a supervisor about having a physical therapist make a half dozen home visits once Dakota was discharged. Her mind turned to Glen and she purposely shook her head and stared at the setting sun. The vibrant purple and pink that skirted along the blue sea helped her mind clear.

In her purse, her phone buzzed.

She dug it free without losing sight of the last moments of the sun. "Mary Kildare."

"Most people just say hello."

Mary let her eyes close and fought the smile that attempted to cross her lips.

"Most people don't start a conversation with an insult."

Glen, with a husky sound she'd become a little too fond of, chuckled.

"Hello, Mary."

She followed his lead. "Hello, Glen."

There was a slight delay in the line, which made their conversation stutter. "Where are you?" she asked.

"Somewhere over Texas."

So he was on a plane. She assumed as much. Instead of asking why he was calling, she waited for him to speak.

He hesitated . . . or maybe it was the delay. "Do you have plans this Saturday?"

She gripped the phone a little too tight. "Why are you asking?"

"We both know why I'm asking."

Mary paused and held her breath. "I don't have any plans."

"Great. I'll pick you up at four."

The sun was already gone. "I don't believe I said yes."

He laughed. "I don't believe you said no."

Any other man, any other time, she'd tell him to ask . . . make him work a little harder to secure a date. "Fly safe."

"See you Saturday."

He was about to hang up.

"Wait . . . what should I wear?"

"I'd like to say those tiny shorts you wear to bed, but I think a simple dress will do."

Mary covered her face in her hand. Her boy shorts . . . he'd seen her butt hanging out of her pajamas.

He hung up laughing. No good-bye, not a see you later . . . simply disconnected the call.

And Mary smiled.

The morning provided her with a wake-up call from Nina. Apparently the Golfs were going to do their best to ensure her sleep deprivation for the week. At least Nina called her cell phone.

"He is crazy."

He being Jacob, and on that they could both agree. Though Mary wasn't about to say it.

It took ten minutes to talk Nina down and another ten to set an appointment for later in the week. According to Nina, she'd left the house after Jacob had accused her of lying about where she'd been the other night. And according to Nina, she went to a girlfriend's house who Jacob didn't know well and stayed with her. Not that any of this

Instead of it upsetting her, she looked a little closer and saw the lift in his eyes. The one that said he liked what he saw.

How had that happened? She hadn't been so much as glanced toward in months, now she had a date with Glen before the week ran out and Mr. Duvall was giving her the eye.

Carla arrived with two Reubens, giving them both something to do other than talk.

"That is one thick sandwich."

It took both hands to pick it up, and still pickled cabbage managed to drip onto her plate. "Enjoy."

It was salty, fatty, and sinful, but oh so good. Mary enjoyed her first bite and watched Kent as he took his. He smiled as the flavors hit his tongue.

"That's amazing," he said once he swallowed.

Mary acknowledged with a hum and went in for bite number two.

Kent quizzed her on other places close by to catch lunch and asked where happy hour took place when the mood struck.

She offered lunch suggestions but explained that she didn't do happy hour close by and he'd have to ask his office staff for that connection.

By the time she'd made it through half of her sandwich, Carla had already dropped off a small box for the other half along with the bill. As often as she tried, getting through the whole meal proved impossible. Besides, lunch the next day or dinner that night was instant.

Her phone buzzed in her purse as she finished boxing her lunch.

It was Dakota with a text. `I'm leaving the hospital by three.`

`Do you need anything?`

`Xanax for my mother. She's already driving me crazy.`

Mary grinned. `You'll have to ask your husband for that prescription.`

was news . . . or that believable, from what Nina had told Mary in the past. But perhaps the woman was justifying her possible split of the relationship. Much as Mary attempted to help couples in turmoil work things out, sometimes some relationships were destined to fail. Unfortunately, her ratio of marriages that held out with counseling was about fifty percent. That only counted the splits she'd been told about. No telling if a couple called it quits years later once their counseling sessions had ended.

Truth was, by the time couples stepped into her office, a lot of damage and miscommunication had already taken place. Years of problems that took a lot of dusting under carpets weren't easy. It was in part why Mary was so brutally honest with her dates. She couldn't see sugarcoating anything from day one.

She didn't always work with couples. In fact, only half of her clients were attempting to keep their relationships with their significant others intact. She had clients who struggled with depression and phobias. Those with abusive pasts, both as victims and perpetrators. But in truth, she didn't often take on clients on the latter end of that scale. She was a counselor, not a doctor, and although she'd been trained to speak with just about anyone about anything . . . people with a past of hurting others fell into a criminal category and needed more help than she could offer. She cut them out as quickly as she could and offered a multitude of psychiatrists they could seek out to meet their needs.

Mary made it to her office, which was a rented space in a professional building that held a single sitting area, a comfortable chair for her, and a desk against a wall surrounded by glass.

Thirty minutes after she arrived to her office, her first client showed up. Four hours after that, she was locking the door.

A deli around the corner from her office was her go-to choice for a late lunch. They had a counter that wrapped around the kitchen and offered her a view of the cooks as they moved like squirrels scrambling to store food away for the winter.

She greeted the hostess by name and moved past the line of people waiting for booths. She set her notebook on the counter and tucked her purse under her feet. “Hey, Carla.” The waitress smiled as she passed.

“Hi, Mary. The usual?”

“Creature of habit.”

Carla waved and kept walking.

Mary opened her notebook and scribbled a few things about her first client. She wrote down her observations and her predictions. So far, the single mother of two was making classic post-divorce decisions that were less than healthy for her fragile state of mind. The woman was a man pleaser, a typical middle child who felt the need to make everything great for everyone, often neglecting her own needs in the process. Now, two years after her divorce, she was entering into a relationship identical to the one she'd just left. As much as Mary could see that each week when they spoke, telling the client that her new guy was just like the old one wasn't seeping in. Mary spun things around this week, asking about her client's past more than her current life and comparing the two. Her client left the office in a state of confusion.

The woman was thinking . . . and that was what Mary wanted.

“Is anyone sitting here?” a male voice asked to her right.

Mary glanced up with a smile and nudged her notebook away from the other dining space. “Looks like you are.”

The man wore a suit. Probably walked from one of the many professional buildings in the area. He lifted a menu and blew out a breath. “That's a lot of choices,” he said.

He was obviously speaking to her.

She took him in from the corner of her eye. Handsome enough . . . a little younger than she preferred, but a nice smile and kind eyes. “I haven't had a sandwich here I didn't like.”

Carla set an iced tea by her place mat and joined the conversation. “You've only eaten one sandwich on the whole menu.”

Mary felt her cheeks warm. “And I liked it.”

The stranger next to her laughed. “And which sandwich is tha

“The Reuben,” both Mary and Carla said at the same time.

He placed the menu down and offered a nod. “Then that's w
I'll have.”

Carla waved her pen in the air.

Mary placed her focus back on her notes to find herself being pu
out of them once again.

“Is it always this busy in here?”

“Weekdays. The breakfast crowd on Saturday and Sunday keep
open on the weekends.”

“It sounds like you come here a lot.”

The stranger had settled into his seat, twisting his body just enou
for her to know that he wasn't going to let her ignore him. So inste
of being rude, she went ahead and put her pen down and closed h
notebook.

“At least once a week. Are you new to the area?”

“I started my new job at Owen, Peters, and Masons last week.”

She recognized the name of the firm. Their offices sat behind th
building she was in. “So you're an attorney?”

He shook his head. “An accountant.”

She pushed her unruly hair over her shoulder.

“I know, boring, huh?”

“Numbers are important,” she told him.

“They do a lot of forensic accounting over there. Something I spe
cialize in.”

“Congratulations on your new position then.”

He lifted up his glass of water and she followed his lead. “And to
new friends.”

Mary went ahead and lowered her glass and extended her hand. “Mary Kildare.”

“Kent Duvall.” He held her hand a fraction too long.

The symbol of a heart and the letter *U* appeared, which Mary sent back before tossing her phone back in her purse. She set the money on the counter for her lunch, the same amount she always did, and twisted out of her chair.

Kent seemed disappointed she was leaving. "It was a pleasure to meet you," she told him.

He wiped his face. "Maybe I'll see you here again?"

She felt the need to move quickly . . . like if she didn't, this stranger, who wasn't hard to look at and hadn't given her one red flag during their brief conversation, was going to ask for her number . . . or something . . . if she didn't run away. On any other day, or week, she might linger and see where things went, but since Glen had just asked her out, her insides twisted with the thought of juggling two men.

"I am a regular," she reminded him.

His eyes did that connecting thing again. "I'll look forward to it."

She was blushing. Felt the heat in her cheeks and tried her best to stop it. "Have a nice day."

"Good-bye, Mary."

She shuffled a little too quickly and felt his eyes follow her as she walked out of the deli.

Chapter Seven

Glen sat in a meeting with all the senior brokers for Fairchild Charters. Because he'd called a meeting, the men wore suits and ties, where on most days they'd feel free working in more casual attire.

"As you all know, our bookings are down from last year."

"Damn recession." Chris was his number two when it came to sales. The man had been with the company for close to fifteen years and had lost most of the hair on his head to prove it. He'd been on the team longer than Glen had held the position of CFO.

"Even our regulars are holding back on their flights this year," Scott said.

Glen leaned forward on his elbows. "Last year we offered the two-thousand-dollar recession coupon and our flights increased by eight percent over the holidays."

"Are you suggesting another coupon?"

Glen shook his head. "I think we need new promotions."

The half a dozen men sitting at the table stared at each other.

"Nothing?"

"We've been here before, Glen. Discounts, empty leg incentives, it's all we have outside of giving away free flights." Scott probably had the most lucrative broker clientele. He pulled in over seven figures annually even with the recession.

"There has to be more ways to pull in new clients."

Jay, a thirty-five-year-old previous Wall Street stockbroker, was the newest addition to their senior team. "If you don't mind me saying, Glen . . . I think you're asking the wrong group of brokers."

All eyes turned to the newbie. A few men instantly protested.

Glen stopped them. "Who should I ask?"

"The guys on the floor . . . those putting out cold calls in an effort to find the next rock star, the next basketball player who signed a big contract and doesn't want to fly commercially anymore. The new guys are listening to the excuses as to why someone with the means says no. All of us are in the black. We don't hustle like we once did."

"Speak for yourself, Jay," Chris scolded.

"Do you even know where to find the cold call list?" Jay asked.

Glen knew cold calls were taken off of the Contact Us page on their website. But even he had no idea how to access it.

Chris started to argue. "I'm beyond cold calls."

"Exactly my point."

"I do my job."

"Damn, Chris . . . let it go. Jay has a point." This came from Gerald, another onetime stockbroker who made the switch to selling private charters after the market crash. And like Jay, he'd made a name for himself in a short amount of time. That seemed to be the case with Fairchild Charters. Their brokers circulated quickly because of the stress of the job. It was all high sales, not something Glen could remove. The incentive his brokers had to fill more flights was what kept his birds in the air.

Glen stopped the arguing with his words. "Here's what I want from you. I need a list of names from the floor. Guys who have been with us long enough to taste what they want, know the system, but haven't hit the point where their client list pays them enough to work less than five days a week."

"I don't know that many of the newbies," Scott confessed.

Glen leaned back and crossed his arms over his chest. "Maybe we need to start up a mentorship incentive."

There was one thing Glen had learned about the brokers. They were a competitive lot who didn't take a ton of shit from their coworkers.

Glen pushed back from the table. "I want a list of three names minimum from each of you by Monday."

He left the men muttering to themselves with thirty minutes to spare before meeting with his brother for lunch.

He waltzed past the secretary of his chief operating officer with a simple point of his finger. "Is he with anyone?"

"Nope."

Glen smiled and noticed the flush on the secretary's cheeks. Cute, but he didn't mix work with pleasure.

The door was open to the corner office that had been held by Chuck Nielson almost since the inception of Fairchild Charters. The older man had been one of Glen's father's best friends in addition to one of his most valued employees. "Gotta minute?" Glen asked as he let himself in.

"Always." The man never turned him away. Sure, he was technically Glen's employee, but he'd been a mentor of immeasurable importance after Glen's parents had died in an unexpected plane crash and was always treated like an extension of the family.

"I just got out of a broker meeting." Glen closed the door behind him.

"Learn anything invaluable?"

"Disturbing, actually."

Chuck regarded him with a crick of his head. "Oh?"

"Our team didn't have any ideas, general or specific, to increase sales."

"That's not unusual," Chuck told him. "They're not the hungry ones."

Glen pointed two fingers in Chuck's direction. "Exactly. So I asked them to give me names of newer brokers who we can tap into for ideas."

"Excellent idea. So what was disturbing?"

Instead of answering the question, Glen said, "We need different levels of broker meetings."

"I'm listening."

Glen paced the office instead of sitting. He liked working on his feet whenever he could. Sadly, a lot of his job was behind a desk.

"How many employees do we have on our sales team?"

"Just here? Or in our other locations?"

"Here." They had brokers in their satellite locations, but the majority of their calls were funneled through the main office.

"Fifty to seventy. Depends on the turnover."

"That isn't including the exec team?"

"No."

"Damn."

"Mind sharing, Glen?"

He met Chuck's gaze. "I'm slacking. I know a few of the guys on the floor based on the payroll that comes across my desk, but I couldn't match a face to the name."

"Your job isn't in personnel."

"No. But that doesn't mean I shouldn't know a little more about the team bringing in business." The memory of his father talking about an employee, a broker . . . a secretary, even someone in the mail room came to mind. He'd always taken the time to meet the employees, even if only once. It's part of why Fairchild Charters had done so well. It wasn't a family business in the full sense. They had hundreds of employees from all walks of life. They commissioned planes all over the globe for their clients. They did have a small fleet of their own aircraft and several pilots on call to fly within a couple of hours when need be. It would be impossible to know everyone.

But Glen could certainly take the time to meet his brokers.

"You know, son, it's not disturbing to stumble across an idea that stares you in the face. It's disturbing if you don't."

Chuck was right. He felt better listening to the man's wisdom.

Glen moved to leave the office.

"Glen, Mimi and I haven't had you over for dinner for months. This weekend good for you?" Mimi was Chuck's wife of over thirty years.

"I have plans." A mass of blonde curly hair filed his head and made all the disturbing thoughts blow away.

Chuck offered a smile. "Good ones, I hope."

"I'm not sure yet."

Save me!

The text from Dakota followed Mary's last client of the day. It was after five, later than she normally worked, but she'd had to squeeze her clients in from the two days she spent at the hospital with her BFF.

That bad? Mary texted en route to her car.

They're fighting over who needs to stay here and who can come next week.

The image of Dakota's small-town Southern mother fighting with Walt's metropolitan mother made her chuckle. I'm on my way.

Hurry. My mother is in my kitchen rearranging everything.

Mary placed her phone in her purse and nearly ran straight into a chest.

She snapped her eyes up and stepped back. "I'm sorry . . . I wasn't—" Her words fell away. "Jacob?"

Jacob Golfs was standing beside the driver's side door of her car, his expression stoic, his clothes slightly disheveled. "Hello, Mary."

She'd always given her clients permission to use her first name. But standing this close to one who had recently started to act out of character made her wonder if that was a good decision.

"What can I do for you?" She tried to keep her stance at ease even when the hair on her neck was standing up.

"You spoke with Nina."

"Briefly, this morning."

"What did she say?"

"You know I can't talk about that. If you'd like to discuss something we all spoke about together . . ." She left her words open-ended, knowing he understood the rules.

He blinked a few times. "She won't talk to me."

Nina had told her that Jacob was calling obsessively, even when she told him she needed time to think, time away from him.

"Sometimes a little distance helps us see things clearly," Mary told him.

"Did she say that?"

Mary knew how to use his words to help her cause. "Does that sound like something she'd say?"

He shook his head. "She said to stay away so she could think."

"And are you giving her space?"

He was rubbing his thumb to his forefinger on both hands. "If I can't talk to her, I can't make it right."

The man was codependent with his wife and would probably never admit it.

"Perhaps if you gave her a couple days to cool off she'd talk to you."

Jacob kept shaking his head no. "This is making me nuts."

Obviously.

"One of Nina's concerns in counseling is that you don't communicate effectively,"

"I can't *communicate* at all if she won't pick up the phone or tell me where she is." He spat out the word *communicate* as if it left a sour taste in his mouth.

"She told you her needs, Jacob. Time to think. If you are listening to her and trying to meet her needs, which you tell me you want to do, then you'll give her some space."

He ran his fingers through his hair. "Space. Fine."

"Good."

Jacob turned a full circle before twisting toward his car on the other side of the lot.

Mary scrambled a little quickly inside hers and locked the door. She knew a conversation about her personal boundaries was in order, but she didn't dare have it while standing alone in a parking lot.

The drive home helped clear her thoughts. It would have been nice to drive by her favorite beach spot, but the text from Dakota had pushed her to get home before the in-laws made a frazzled time even worse.

Mary made quick work of dropping off her car, her notebook, her briefcase holding her laptop, and the leftovers from lunch at her place before heading across the street.

After a single knock, Mary let herself in as she had for years.

Something savory cooked in the oven, filling the house with a scent Mary had never experienced in Dakota's place.

"Biscuits are about the easiest thing to cook, JoAnne," Elaine was scolding the other grandmother.

"Mine come from a box."

"That's a shame."

Mary poked her head into the kitchen. "Hello."

"Hi, Mary. I didn't hear you knock." JoAnne was one for propriety.

"She doesn't have to knock." Dakota sat perched on the couch, her cast leg elevated on several pillows on the coffee table.

Mary did a quick head count. She saw the men outside in the backyard. A tiny bassinet sat beside the sofa. Inside, a sleeping Leo puffed with pink lips. She moved beside Dakota and sat next to her. "So how is *Grace* doing today?" She stared at the cast as she spoke.

"It feels better now that I can't move it."

"Blue suits you." The baby blue cast looked like Leo's blankets.

"I thought it worked."

Mary ran her thumb under Dakota's left eye. "You're exhausted."

"He's up every two hours needing a boob."

"Then you should try sleeping now."

Dakota glanced toward the kitchen. Both Elaine and JoAnne were huddled around the stove, their backs to them. "Need I say more?"

"What is Walt saying?" she whispered.

"That it will only be a couple of days. But they keep talking like they will be here for weeks."

Yeah, but Dakota needed her rest now. "Where is Monica?"

"She and Trent went to visit Monica's mother today. She's going to stop by tomorrow before flying home."

"This should be ready in fifteen minutes," JoAnne said.

Dakota's strangled smile told Mary she was more tired than hungry.

"When will Leo wake up?"

"I don't know. Seems like he was just feeding."

Mary stood and pulled the blanket up around Dakota's legs. "I'll be back." She didn't offer an explanation and walked out the back door to the men.

They stopped talking and greeted her in unison.

She did the rounds and got straight to the point. "Walt, Dr. Eddy . . . Mr. Laurens. I have a favor to ask."

They waited.

"I need one or two of you to help get Dakota up to her bed so she can sleep."

Walt looked over his shoulder inside the house and stood. "I knew she was pushing herself."

Mary stopped him from opening the door. "Dinner is almost done, but my guess is Dakota would covet an hour of sleep and she can eat later. Which means you men need to help your wives understand it isn't personal."

Dr. Eddy followed his son's lead and stood. "C'mon, Dennis, it's time to remind our wives what it was like those first weeks after our kids were born."

They filed into the room together.

Walt beelined to his wife and whispered in her ear before removing the blanket from her lap.

She offered a tired nod and buried her head in his shoulder.

"Dinner's not quite ready," Elaine told them.

Everyone spoke in softer tones than normal and occasionally glanced over at Leo to see if they woke him.

Walt lifted Dakota off the couch and carried her.

"Don't drop me," Dakota teased.

"Have some faith."

Walt was walking Dakota up the stairs before the conversation in the kitchen began. "She's exhausting herself, JoAnne. Keep a plate for when Leo wakes up."

JoAnne had an expression of shock before pulling it in. "Bless her heart, she should have told me. I could have waited to put the roast in."

"Sleep when the baby sleeps, remember?" Elaine said, wiping her hands free of the biscuit mixture.

"I understand there is some debate on who is staying around to help." Mary glanced at both women.

"Well, I should," Elaine said first. She left the notion that Dakota was *her* daughter unsaid.

"And you drive her a little crazy, Elaine," Mary said flat out.

Elaine sucked in a deep breath, and for a moment Mary thought she'd deny the truth.

"She's right, hon," Dennis calmed his wife before she could respond.

Mary leaned against the counter and offered her advice. "You know what I think will be the most helpful thing right now?"

The collective silence in the room kept her talking.

"Spend the next two days cooking meals for Walt and Dakota so all they have to do is pop stuff in the microwave or oven. Walt isn't going back to the ER for at least a month. He even took himself off the call list for Borderless Doctors. I'm across the street for emergencies, and I'll come by every day to do laundry or shop, or whatever they need."

"But—"

"Just listen, Elaine."

"Give them a couple of weeks to figure this parent thing out. Dakota has enough hospitality genes in her to not want to offend you by saying she's too tired to eat. Imagine keeping that pace for the next few weeks. I promise to call you back if they're struggling or need another set of hands."

Elaine and JoAnne exchanged glances. "Two more days with the baby."

JoAnne painted on a properly insincere smile. "Why do our children live so far away?"

Mary mentally patted herself on the back.

An hour and a half later she received a text from Dakota.

`I managed an hour-long nap. Thank you. I don't know what you said, but I owe you.`

`You'd do the same for me.` Only they both knew that Mary wouldn't have family clamoring around to help if she had a baby.

`I would!`

Mary considered letting the conversation fade there . . .

`BTW...I have a date with Glen this Saturday.`

Giddy excitement bubbled up inside her as she watched the instant dot, dot, dot on her tiny phone message screen.

`OMFingG! About damn time! I'm in a room full of in-laws or I'd call you over to squeal about it.`

`You're a little busy right now. We'll chat later when you're awake.`

`Bet your ass we'll talk later. I'm gonna want details.`

Mary looked forward to a little normalcy so she could provide them. But to dominate any of Dakota's time right now would be selfish, all things considered.

Chapter Eight

Monica called Mary the next morning, asked if they could have lunch before she flew home the next day.

"I love pizza." Monica removed a slice and let the cheese drip down the sides.

"Me too. Glad you suggested it. I feel guilty ordering a whole one on my own."

Monica closed her eyes as she bit in. "Not as good as New York, but . . ."

"Mmm, Chicago is still my favorite."

Monica added an enthusiastic nod.

"Dakota and I were there for one of her conferences. We ordered a large, which on the right day we can put down. The waiter looked at us like we were crazy."

Monica stopped chewing so she could laugh.

"I know. The pizza arrived and I looked at the guy . . . 'dude, we ordered pizza.'"

"How much did you get through?"

"One slice. And that took serious effort." The memory of the loaded Chicago style pizza with its one-inch thickness and sauce on top made her mouth water.

"So . . ."

Every conversation that started with the word *so*, in Mary's experience, was the reason for the invite for lunch, cocktails . . . or dinner.

"So?"

"I understand Glen asked you out."

She wiped her mouth and set the slice aside. "Dakota told you."

Monica was quick to shake her head.

"Glen?"

She shook it again. "Trent. Who heard from his brother Jason. Who found out because Glen set aside a plane to fly back."

"Sounds like a long list."

"Not that long. They're a tight-knit group. I don't think either of them would have mentioned Glen dating anyone if they weren't . . . I don't know . . . excited to see where it goes."

Mary tried not to read into that. "I have to be honest," she said. "Your brother-in-law drives me a little crazy."

"The Fairchild charm. I know. They all will, trust me."

"No, I mean . . ." What did she mean? "He challenges everything I say. Even that silly stuffed monkey he gave Dakota in the hospital. I saw it first, but he swiped it right from under me to give it to her."

Monica chuckled. "Sounds like Glen."

"And he's a player. I know he's a player."

"But you said yes to a date anyway."

Mary paused. "He is cute."

Monica lifted a brow.

"Sexy. Okay . . . cute is for boys. Hot. And all those cocky parts are a bit of a turn-on if I were being honest."

"The Fairchild charm," she said for the second time.

"I don't normally go for that kind of charm. I'm more reserved." More like the girl who said yes to Mr. Accountant from the deli. "I'm probably going to regret it."

Monica picked up her pizza and waved it in the air. "Don't regret it."

"What?"

"Take the experience for what it's worth but don't regret trying something new. Yeah, it's not your norm . . . but Glen isn't a creepy-scary dude."

No, he wasn't.

"Whatever happens, don't regret." Monica set her pizza back down without taking a bite. "Here is the thing. We all know you. It's not like he can casually date you, treat you like crap, and none of us hear the details. I mean . . . I like to think we're friends."

"We are."

"And I'm super close to Walt and now Dakota. And you and Dakota are tight. So the grapevine is woven in ways none of us want to change."

Mary really hadn't thought of it that way. "And if things aren't cool between Glen and me, or get ugly . . ." She hated personal conflict. She could handle it in her professional life. But she had enough as a child and avoided it as an adult whenever possible. "Maybe I should cancel before anything gets—"

"No! That's not . . . no. Listen, I'm not going to deny that Glen has been a player. But I haven't heard of him being a jerk to the women in his life. And every player eventually calms down."

"Some pretend to calm down but still play."

Monica acknowledged her with a nod. "I'm not convinced that's Glen. From what I've been told about his mom and dad . . . they instilled integrity in their marriage."

"I'm going on a first date, Monica. No one is talking about that kind of thing."

"So date. And unless there is a conversation about monogamy . . ." Monica's words trailed off.

"Then assume it's not monogamous."

Her lunch date didn't confirm or deny.

Could she do that? Assume Glen was seeing other women while seeing her? She knew it happened all the time, but . . .

Monica pushed her plate aside, giving up on the pizza. "And another thing."

"More words of advice?"

"More statement of fact. Whatever goes down between you and Glen. We're still friends. He's family . . . but you and I are friends, and I don't want anything to wiggle between that."

"Deal."

Dakota's in-laws and parents all shuffled off to the airport Friday afternoon. By two, Mary was finished with her clients and heading home. Leroy met her at two thirty with a crew of men.

"See here." The same camera was snaked down her plumbing that she'd seen the first day he showed up to her house. "The pipe is crushed at this point."

Mary glanced at the screen, saw the pipe in question.

"Okay . . . what does that mean?"

"Means we need to replace the pipe or you'll be calling us back out here in no time with the same problem."

"Roots in the plumbing."

"Yeah. As long as the roots find their way into the pipe, and they find water . . . you're going to have this issue."

Mary glanced beyond her bathroom. "So where is the pipe?"

Leroy walked outside of the bathroom and into her living space. He stopped about six feet in front of her front door and pointed down. "Here. Under the slab."

Mary glanced at the tile entry and the carpet that filled her living room. "How do you get to the pipe?" She hated to sound blonde, but she knew she did anyway.

"We have to dig it out. My guys have saws to remove the slab. Once we unearth the pipe we'll cut apart the bad section, replace it with new . . . then fill in the slab with new concrete."

Mary's jaw dropped. "So you have to rip up my floors?"

Leroy removed his baseball cap and scratched what was left of his hair. "The tile has to be knocked out. We can try and pull the carpet up at the seam, but there is a chance it will be damaged and need replacing."

Mary shook her head at the magnitude of a simple clogged-up toilet.

"So you rip it up and put new tile down?"

Leroy shook his head. "We take care of the pipe, ma'am. We don't lay tile."

Oh, great. "And how long will this take?"

"We can pull out the tile and rip back the carpet today . . . mark where we need to cut. Might even get some of that cutting down before five. Then we can be back on Monday to pull the rest out. Once I get in there, fixing the pipe is quick. But then we need to fill it all back in. So I should be done by Wednesday unless I find a bigger issue."

"Bigger issue?"

"Yeah . . . there is a junction here that comes from your kitchen. I'll wanna pull the camera up that way, make sure there isn't any issues."

She did not want to think about pulling up her kitchen floor.

"Got it . . . okay. How much is this going to cost me?"

He started to talk about the steps, the things he'd already done. "Cut to the chase, Leroy."

"About five."

Mary blinked . . . "Five?"

"Thousand."

She choked.

"You might try and check your homeowners policy, see if this is covered."

"And that doesn't cover fixing the floor once it's all torn up."

Leroy shook his head. "You might have an insurance claim."

"Do I have to get their approval if I have a claim?"

"Nope . . . it's not like medical insurance. If you're covered, you present them with a copy of the bill and they reimburse you."

That was marginally better.

"So are we good to go?"

"I guess."

After three hours on the phone with various people at the insurance company, Mary determined that the destruction of the floor was covered, where the pipe and every one of those five thousand dollars to fix it was not. She had an emergency savings for things like this, but five grand was going to seriously cut into that account.

She was clicking out of her online bank account when her phone rang.

"So are you coming over now that the masses have left?"

Dakota always made her smile.

"You sound awake."

"Leo slept for four hours last night, and I had a solid two hours this afternoon. Who knew sleep would be my crack?"

"All right. Give me five minutes."

"I have wine."

"Okay, two."

Dakota laughed and hung up.

The plumbers had taped up the area they were going to work from floor to ceiling. A plastic zipper was a walk-through barrier from the front door to the rest of the condo. After making sure the front door was locked, Mary went ahead and used the garage as her entry.

There was music drifting from Dakota and Walt's place, and laughter when she let herself in after one knock.

"We're back here."

Dakota sat at the kitchen counter, her foot elevated on a stool beside her . . . Walt moved around the kitchen assembling food.

"I hope you're hungry," Dakota said. "My mother cooks for a village."

"I could eat." Mary glanced around the room to see Leo sleeping in the same place he was the last time she was there. "Does he ever wake up?"

Both Dakota and Walt laughed. "All night long," Walt said.

She detoured to Leo and watched him sleep for a minute. "He is beautiful."

"He is, right? Not just . . . you have to say it because you're my best friend."

"No." His cherub face and tiny pink lips with a tuft of dark hair. And so itty-bitty it was hard not to get caught up in him. "He's lovely."

"How about some wine?" Walt asked.

"I'd love some." Mary placed the keys and the remote to her garage on the coffee table and turned to the kitchen. "Can I help with anything?"

Walt motioned to the stack of raw salad greens on the counter. "Knock yourself out."

Mary moved to the sink and turned to Dakota.

Then her eyes dropped. "Holy cow! When did that happen?"

Dakota glanced down at her chest and giggled. "My milk came in."

Boy did it. Mary had always been a tad envious of her friend's boobs, but now . . . wow!

"Do they hurt?"

"Like you wouldn't believe."

Walt laughed from the stove. "I like 'em."

"Such a man."

They talked about boobs while Mary prepared a salad.

"Enough about my rack," Dakota cut the conversation off. "I wanna hear about Glen."

Walt turned off the flame on the stovetop and asked, "What's up with Glen?"

Mary glanced at her friend. "You didn't tell him?"

"Wasn't my place."

"Well?" Walt asked again.

A measure of surprise that Dakota hadn't spoken with Walt about the date actually made Mary happy. They could still keep secrets . . . though this one wasn't meant to be one . . . even though her BFF was married to the love of her life.

"I have a date with Glen tomorrow night."

Walt nodded at the information. "I guess that's a long time coming."

"Where's he taking you?" Dakota asked.

"I have no idea. I didn't ask."

"Hmm, well . . . the fact he's flying in from the East Coast to see you means he'll figure out someplace nice."

"When you say it like that it seems so stupid."

"Say it like what?"

"He's flying in . . . I said yes to a date with someone who lives in a time zone three hours from my own. That's crazy."

"It's romantic. I would never have thought of a plot like that."

Mary watched as Dakota glanced at the ceiling and smiled. "Oh, no. I know that look."

"Brilliant idea. You've heard of the May-December romance . . . how about the East-West romance?"

"I thought you were taking the year off," Walt chided.

"I can't keep down a stellar idea for a novel, Walt. It's not how it works."

He removed a pan of something casserole-ish from the oven as he spoke. "Then jot it down and return to it later."

Dakota glanced around, found a pen, and waved it toward the coffee table.

Mary saw the notepad in question and brought it over. "So what are you going to wear?" Dakota asked.

"On my date?"

Dakota rolled her eyes as she kept writing. "No, to bed. Yes on your date!"

"He suggested a dress."

"Nothing floral." Dakota waved the end of her pen in Mary's direction. "I know you have two perfect little black dresses."

Power dresses, as Dakota had called them when they'd gone shopping the last time they were in New York.

"Not that I don't love women's fashion and hate to change the subject . . . but why are the plumbers always at your house?" Walt asked.

While they ate dinner, Mary explained her plumbing dilemma and the money it would cost to fix it. "I guess it's time for me to put in those wood floors I've been threatening to do since I moved in."

"Yeah, if the insurance company is going to help with the cost, you might as well get something shiny for all your trouble."

Dakota glanced around her kitchen and into the living space. Her place had come with hardwood floors, only the honey oak color wasn't something any of them were excited about. "I'd switch these out if it would make a difference on resale."

Mary felt a chill of shock run through her. "Are you thinking of moving?"

Dakota exchanged glances with Walt. "We're keeping our options open. This place is going to get smaller as Leo gets bigger."

"And the market is turning around," Walt added.

She hated the thought of her friend moving away but smiled and agreed anyway. "Any idea where you guys will move?"

"We haven't really thought about location . . . just that here isn't going to work long-term."

Mary painted on a fake smile and pushed her plate away. "You know how much I love shopping with other people's money."

"I won't be up for house shopping until this thing comes off." Dakota patted the blue cast on her leg and groaned. "I still can't believe I broke my damn leg."

The conversation drifted to the cast, baby Leo, and the excitement over midday napping while Mary helped Walt with the dishes.

As Leo started to stir Mary started to make her excuses.

"I want to hear all about tomorrow's date," Dakota said.

"I don't." Walt laughed.

"I'll come over Sunday." Mary let herself out and turned to look back. She hated the *poor me* thoughts coursing through her veins. Despised the feeling of loneliness when she walked past her car in the garage and into her place.

It was quiet.

Too quiet.

No wonder women pushing thirty owned cats.

Mary shook her head and muttered to the wall, "I hate cats."

Chapter Nine

Dakota had the best shoes, and Mary felt no shame in borrowing a pricey pair for her date.

"You're like a sister I never had," Mary called out as she ran back home with a pair of Pradas dangling from her fingertips.

"I want details."

Dakota stood in the doorway with crutches. She'd managed to get dressed in something other than sweatpants and was starting to lose the dark circles from under her eyes.

Something told Mary that Dakota would be sitting at her living room window peeking out when Glen was due to pick her up. The thought delighted her.

She hadn't been much of a girlie girl before she'd met Dakota. But her friend had taught her the finer things about being a woman. From the dresses she wore that were snug on her hips and made her sensible "girls" have a little more pow, to the extra eye liner and red on her lips. This was the *let's go out and have fun* Mary . . . the Mary that didn't present herself to her clients, and didn't appear too often.

She slid her hands down her hips and turned to the side. The newest of her black power dresses hugged her waist and stopped short of her knees. The cap sleeves offered style to the neckline that dipped low enough to be enticing but high enough to avoid advertising her cup size. Not bad.

Her mass of curly blonde hair had a mind of its own. She messed with a few bits in the front, put way too much hair spray over them to tame them down, and left it alone. She'd considered putting it up, but Dakota usually helped her with that style and Mary wasn't about to ask.

She was sliding her feet into her borrowed strappy Pradas when the doorbell rang.

One look out the front window showed her a black sedan, the kind that had a hired driver, sat at the curb.

She unzipped the plastic divider and stepped over the broken out tile.

There were butterflies in her belly. The giddy girlie kind that were a little out of place considering she'd seen Glen on so many occasions the newness should have worn off.

She opened the door and sighed. He wore a jacket, minus the tie . . . and dark slacks. Even from where she stood she could smell he'd just taken a shower. And he held flowers in his hand.

While she was looking at him, his ever-ready cocky smile slowly dropped as his eyes swept over her twice. "I'm sorry, I'm looking for Miss Kildare." He looked beyond her at the tarp and tapped the concrete floor with the toe of his dress shoe. "I'm not sure I have the right house."

"My plumbing problem turned into a nightmare."

His gaze returned to hers. "You're, uhm . . . wow!"

Glen speechless was a rarity.

She liked it.

"Are those for me?"

He lifted the bouquet. "First date flowers. It's in the rule book."

She took them, smelled one of the half dozen roses in the mix, and smiled. "Not everyone read that book."

"Makes those of us who did look even better."

She nodded toward the inside. "Let me put these in water and grab my purse."

Glen followed her through the tarp and into her kitchen.

The four-inch heels made it easier for her to reach the shelf where she stored her vase, but as she reached for it, Glen stood beside her and helped.

God he smelled good.

"Thanks."

He simply hummed as he handed it to her.

She tried to ignore the heat in his eyes as he stared.

"I'd say you didn't have to."

"But that wouldn't be sincere."

"You can't go wrong with flowers. Candy is hit and miss."

She removed the wrap and fanned the arrangement in the vase as it filled with water. When she was done she set it in the window and turned to find Glen still staring.

"Ready?"

He didn't move. "Have you ever had dessert before dinner?"

She shook her head. "Are you trying to tell me we're having cheesecake for dinner?"

He smiled, took a step closer. "When we were kids, every once in a while my mom would have some kind of bridge night, or girls' night . . . I don't know what it was. But we loved it, Trent, Jason, and I. Our dad always brought out the pie, cake, even ice cream sundaes before we'd have dinner."

"Did you finish your dinner?"

"Not always. But we enjoyed it more because we'd done it backwards."

"That's sweet. If we're not having cake first . . . then what made you think of that story?"

Glen took another step closer and reached over to push one of the curls from her shoulder. Heat rose in his eyes, and the response of her body was chemical. "Because of this."

His hand slid behind her neck and encouraged her into his arms as he lowered his lips to hers.

She was stunned. From head to toe her body short-circuited. He was warm and smelled delicious . . . and utterly confident as he pressed her body next to his. The span of his hand wrapped around her waist but didn't move beyond that spot. She slowly woke up, closed her eyes, and kissed him back. It felt good to be kissed. She barely tasted his tongue before he backed away.

With her eyes closed she felt his stare.

"I wanted to do that for a very long time," he confessed.

She slowly opened her eyes and kept looking at his chest. "You caught me off guard."

He placed his finger under her chin and forced her to look at him. "We're even then. Now we can have a nice evening without either of us wondering what that was going to taste like."

"You had your dessert first."

Glen shrugged. "What can I say? I have a sweet tooth."

She grabbed her clutch on the counter. "Shall we?"

He placed his hand on the small of her back and led her outside.

Glen had been told by one of his very first girlfriends that women obsess over the good night kiss on the first date. Through all the years of dating, all the women he'd played tonsil hockey with while in college, he'd never kissed one when she opened the door.

Damn, he was happy he'd done it with Mary. She tasted like cinnamon, which was probably gum, or maybe toothpaste, but she smelled like an ocean breeze. He glanced over at her, sitting in the seat beside him in the back of the Lincoln Town Car. She had long legs and wore sexy heels that should be impossible to walk in. Damn, the dress. He envied the fabric that hugged her skin. Mary was a beautiful woman, a fact he'd known since they met . . . but tonight she was sexy. Something in the way she smiled . . . or maybe it was the lack of challenging him with every word? He didn't want to question it.

"So where are you taking me?"

This was where Glen had all his cards. "Have you ever had a progressive dinner?"

"Like hopping from one place to another?"

"Yeah, I have a great place for drinks before dinner. The view is spectacular. A short ride from there we have dinner reservations."

He liked when she smiled at him. "And dessert?"

"You want more dessert?" he asked.

Her eyes narrowed.

"You mean something with sugar?"

She lost her frown and giggled.

"You need to do that more," he said.

"Do what?"

"Laugh."

"I laugh all the time."

"Not around me."

She sighed. "When you're not infuriating me, you're quite witty."

"I'm witty *when* I'm infuriating you."

She giggled again.

The driver pulled through the gates and onto the tarmac.

"I should have guessed," she said under her breath.

"Yes, you should have."

A Hawker 800 stood ready. Mary presented her ID to airport security as a precaution, and he helped her up the small staircase and into the plane. It wasn't a huge aircraft, but it wasn't without its bragging points either. "Sit wherever you like," Glen encouraged her as he took the three-step detour to the cockpit. "Ready when you are, gentlemen."

The copilot followed him back and secured the door. "If there is anything you need, Mr. Fairchild, let us know."

"We will."

The plane started moving nearly as quickly as the copilot closed the cockpit door.

"I thought you'd be the one flying."

He took the seat across from her and fastened his belt. "I like being in control, but I don't always have to be the pilot. Besides, I'd need a bigger plane for there to be enough room for you to join me up there."

She smiled again.

He was on a roll.

"Do you take all your first dates on planes?"

"You might assume that, but no. Never."

"Really? Why?"

So many reasons, he thought but didn't say. "I guess it comes down to expectations."

"Expectation of taking a private flight for a date every time?"

"There is that."

"There is more you're not saying."

Glen took in her expression. She had this shine behind her eyes when she was reading you. Something that made you hope the closet you wanted closed was firmly shut because if it wasn't, she was going to bust that shit open and find all the laundry you shoved in the corner. He wasn't ready to reveal all his reasons, but he had a few he could disclose. "I'm a pilot, and one of three brothers who own and operate one of the largest personal jet charter companies out there. I know my mode of transportation is set aside for a very few of us in the world. I'm also aware that plenty of people would use any one of us to tap into that ride. When you take that away from the start when you're dating, it lets you know if you're being used."

Mary started to chew on that.

"No one likes being used."

The pilot took that moment to call into the cabin, "We're next for takeoff, Mr. Fairchild."

Glen reached over and pressed an intercom button to reach the pilot. "We're ready."

Even though he trusted the pilots, Glen still felt a tiny bit of tension in his spine until they leveled off in the air.

"So why did you break your rules with me?" Mary asked.

He unbuckled his seat belt and tapped her knee before he stood. "Because you're not a user. Now, what can I get you to drink?"

"I *could* be a user."

Glen did a little eye roll. "No, you can't. It's not in your DNA." He opened the compact icebox that held all the liquor and removed what he'd seen Mary drink in the past. "Red or white?"

"White. How can you be so certain about my character when we've only seen each other, what . . . half a dozen times?"

He considered pointing out that on three of those occasions Mary went out of her way to attempt to pay her share. If she was shot down, she made sure to send a thoughtful gift pack, or wine basket . . . or some such thing to let her host know she appreciated the invitation. "Give me one example of when you used someone for something."

She opened her mouth, closed it, then looked at her shoes. "Does borrowing shoes count?"

That brought his eye to the sexy shoes on those sexy legs. "If you broke them and didn't replace them, then yes."

"That would be rude."

He made quick use of the wine opener and poured them both a glass. "A user wouldn't care about appearing rude."

"I suppose." She took the glass with a thank-you and leaned back in the plush leather seat. "I'm not going to pretend that sitting in a private jet isn't amazing."

He glanced around the cabin and wondered how she saw it. "It's a luxury that's easy to get used to."

"That's the truth. When Dakota and I traveled to her conferences before her books hit, we always flew coach." She cringed. "The first time Dakota sat in first class we argued for a week about me letting her help with my ticket so we could fly together."

"See, not a user."

Mary sipped her wine and continued, "On the way home she used her miles and upgraded me. Now I save a little bit every month to sit in the front. It's worth it."

"I've never flown coach," he said matter-of-factly.

"Really?"

"Never. I learned to fly before I could drive a car. We all did. Our father was adamant about it. Some people switch drivers while on their family vacations, we switched pilots." He remembered the first time he'd joined his father in the cockpit with his entire family in the back. *You have their lives in your hands, Glen. Always fly like your family is riding with you.*

"You miss him." Mary was doing that staring thing again.

"I do. Both of them." Glen knew Mary had been told he'd lost his parents in a plane crash years ago. Just as he'd been told that Mary grew up without parents. "Did you ever know yours?"

She shook her head. "I was left at a church when I was close to a year old. No note . . . no witnesses to see who left me there. Sister Mary Frances found me. I don't know if my parents were kids or unable to take care of me, or maybe they're dead and Grandma didn't wanna do it all again. I try not to think about it."

"A lot of people would take a beginning like that and never turn it around." Glen couldn't picture anyone giving away a child.

"I was a troublemaker as a kid."

That was news. "Really? What kind of trouble?"

She took another sip of her wine; the glow on her cheeks became more evident. "Most of my formative years were spent in and out of a school for children . . . which was a fancy way of saying orphanage that Mary Frances volunteered for. Since Sister Mary Frances was the one who ultimately named me, she was the one who did a lot of my molding. She's very pragmatic. Calls people on their bull straight up. And she was a nun . . . who argues with a nun?"

"I don't know."

"No one! I followed her lead. If I saw a disservice or an inaccuracy, I called it out. Didn't matter if I was in the middle of my math class or church. Mary Frances and I have had a lot of conversations about faith. She also encouraged me to keep thinking and never take words at face value."

"And that landed you in trouble?"

"Yeah . . . I didn't last with a foster family for long, and a lot of the reason why was my mouth. I would question everything to the point of driving my foster parents crazy."

"All kids ask why the sky is blue." He could understand it being annoying, but not to the point of walking away.

"No, I would ask why Mr. Van Goosen was watching naked people exercising on his computer."

Glen felt laughter deep in the pit of his stomach. "Oops."

"Yeah, and when Mrs. Van Goosen delivered a *because he likes it* answer, I went to school and asked all of my classmates if their fathers watched naked people lying on top each other. And when their answers didn't work for me, I'd ask my teacher . . . who knew the Van Goosens because Mr. Van Goosen was a deacon in the church."

Glen had to stop drinking his wine or risk spitting it out. "Whoa!"

"The scandal rippled and I was back with Sister Mary. I bounced two more times. When I was a senior in high school I filed the necessary paperwork for emancipation, which the state was eager to approve when they saw I held a job, was finishing school with already a full year of college under my belt and a five-year plan."

"Who did you stay with?"

"Sister Mary."

"With the nuns?"

"No. Sister Mary had left the church by then. Remember all those scandals with sexual abuse that came out a while back?"

He nodded.

"She couldn't take the hypocrisy. That *don't take orders, make up your own mind* she'd instilled in me was deep in her. She's still a devout Catholic, don't get me wrong . . . she just doesn't say she's married to God anymore."

"Where is Sister Mary now?"

"In Phoenix. The dry heat helps with her arthritis. *All those years of prayer*, she'd tell me."

"How often do you see her?"

"Not often enough."

"What keeps you from visiting?"

She glanced out the window. "Life. My clients keep me busy. I don't care for driving through the desert by myself, and hundred-dollar flights to Phoenix never seem to apply when I have the time to go. I get there in spring and again in the winter . . . usually around Christmas."

Glen felt the plane starting her descent and heard the chime into the cabin from the captain. He stood and took the nearly empty wineglass from Mary's hand.

"We're here?" she asked, looking out the window.

"Feels like it."

"Where are we, anyway?"

He winked. "You'll see."

She didn't quiz him, which caught him by surprise. "That's it? No questions?" He snapped his seat belt in place, glanced at hers, which she'd never taken off.

"I actually kinda like surprises. I'm the kid that didn't have Santa Claus, remember?"

Her words were said with such casualness it took a moment for them to sucker punch him in the gut.

His parents had been ripped out of his life long after Santa was dead . . . but to never have had that thrill, that fantasy . . .

It wasn't until he felt the earth under the wheels of the plane that he snapped out of his thoughts.

"Well, Mary Kildare, I'm not Santa, but I do have a few things in my bag of misfit toys."

The plane came to a stop and Glen opened the hatch.

Chapter Ten

In Mary's life, she could count on one hand how many times she'd been truly spoiled. Most of them had been in the past year since she and Dakota had met the Fairchilds. The previous Thanksgiving, she, Dakota, and Walt found themselves on a private plane en route to the East Coast, where they enjoyed a full weekend of food, friends, and then a ride into New York City, via helicopter, to shop. Then there was the unexpected charter when Dakota had gone missing in Denver with her mother-in-law. Mary was told a plane was waiting for her and to get in. She did! Then there was the last book release Dakota had . . . private planes, penthouse suites, even a full day at the spa and five-star meals the entire week. She'd tried to pay for some of it . . . any of it. It would put her behind in her savings plan for the future, but she was willing. The occasion was that important. But no one would take her money. Monica's connections to The Morrison Hotel chain and the Fairchilds' unlimited ability to use the air as their private freeway was equivalent to her suggesting she pay for gas when it was under three dollars a gallon . . . *No, hon, we've got it this time.*

Now . . . here she was moving from a private plane to a waiting town car for a date that was apparently going to take place in San Francisco.

Who did that? Who took their dates to San Francisco from LA?

Glen, apparently.

The town car didn't take them far. In fact . . . it didn't take them anywhere at all. She'd no sooner reclined in her seat than the car stopped and someone opened her door.

"What is this?"

Glen shrugged. "A helicopter. The drive in would take an hour at this time of day."

Mary simply shook her head and popped this into her memory book.

The helicopter required her to put on a big set of earphones to talk. "I'm officially using you now," she told him.

He shook his head with an unconvinced smile. "It's not using if you're going along for the unexpected ride."

She didn't agree.

Flying never bothered her. In fact, the thrill of the takeoff and landing on a normal plane always made her smile. She didn't worry about crashing. She was pragmatic enough to know that more people died on the freeway en route to the airport each year than those who died in the air. The helicopter was an extension of a roller coaster at a theme park. The vertical, the horizontal, the tiny dip to the side. Her cheeks hurt from smiling so much. She didn't even care that the silly earphones were probably messing up her hair.

"If you took all your dates out like this, you'd be married by now." The noise inside the earphones was tinny and full of the sound of wind.

"Getting married requires more than a helicopter ride."

"Women can be crafty. You should watch out."

"For other women?"

She nodded and glanced at the city fast approaching.

"I'm on a date with you and you're talking about other women."

She glanced over her shoulder and caught his shocked eyes. "Oh, don't give me that look. We will get along a whole lot better if you don't pretend you don't date often."

Shock gave way to acceptance.

Mary turned back to her window. "Lying is a deal breaker, Glen. I think you should know that."

"Then I won't lie."

She took in his chiseled jaw once again. "What about you? Any deal breakers?"

He opened his mouth—

"No, let me guess."

He closed it.

"Users."

He pointed one finger in the air and smiled.

The Top of the Mark sat on Nob Hill in the Mark Hopkins Hotel. The view of the city was remarkable. Other than a helicopter hovering over, this was the best view money could buy.

The lounge had a fair number of guests with an accomplished pianist entertaining the room.

The first course of their evening would take place here.

Glen requested a view of the Golden Gate Bridge and smiled as he sat across from Mary to enjoy it.

"Wow."

"My favorite West Coast city," Glen confessed.

"I can see why."

"Don't tell me this is your first time."

Mary quickly shook her head. "No. There was a conference of therapists that brought me here a few years ago. I didn't get out of the hotel much to explore the city, I'm afraid."

He couldn't help but wonder if the conference was held with a bunch of red sofas in the meeting halls instead of tables and chairs. Why he assumed every therapist had a red couch, he couldn't say.

"That's too bad. There are a lot of things to do here."

They ordered more wine and a couple of appetizers.

"What do you do when you're here?" she asked.

"Depends on the occasion and who I'm with."

She questioned him with her eyes.

"My brother Jason and I are here a few times a year to check on our satellite office. There are usually dinners involved, sometimes a little elbow rubbing with certain business owners."

"Define elbow rubbing," she said while sipping her wine.

"Like the building we landed on in the business district. There is a bit of a war going on here when it comes to helicopter traffic. We try and have access to as many helipads as we can, which requires us to hold relationships with the owners of the buildings, sometimes the prominent tenants of those buildings. While Jason and I don't actively look for people to use our service, it never hurts to have some of the top companies know what we can provide."

"Putting a face to a name."

"Exactly. Elbow rubbing can mean dinner, drinks, or rounds of golf."

"Do you golf?"

"If you're asking if I can hold a club and hit the ball, yes . . . if you are asking if that ball ever goes in a hole, then no."

Mary's chuckle started slow and built. "Let me guess, you're good at basketball."

"Now that ball I can dunk." He joined her laughter. "Football on occasion."

She shook her head. "I remember Thanksgiving. Halftime game in the yard and you all came in holding a body part and grabbing beer."

"It *is* a contact sport. What about you . . . any sports?"

"My constant movement as a kid kept me away from anything formal in school. I always wanted to ice-skate, but there wasn't a rink close by . . . and lessons were never going to happen."

"What about as an adult, find anything you enjoy doing now?"

"I love the ocean, but I've never surfed. Swimming always energizes me. I don't know . . . there are a lot of things out there I haven't tried. Haven't thought much about it."

Glen wondered if there was anything out there he hadn't tried. He suddenly felt very privileged.

"Do you like museums?"

Her eyes lit up. "Love them, you?"

"Nope . . . well, does the Hard Rock museum count?"

Her shoulders deflated a tad. "What about walking tours of a new city?"

"I don't think I've done that."

"New Orleans is on my bucket list. They have graveyard tours, ghost tours, Garden District tours."

"Sounds like you've been there."

"Nope. Bucket list. Dakota and I travel really well together. I usually scope out where her conferences are and plan a few things for us to do outside of her classes and signings."

Glen didn't see that staying the same now that Dakota had Walt and the two of them were recent parents.

"Do you both have a trip planned?"

Mary shook her head. "The spring conference happened last week. She obviously couldn't go."

"Let me guess, it was scheduled in New Orleans."

A flash of disappointment crossed her eyes. "It will come around again. And if not, we can go another time, or I'll find a way to go myself."

He opened his mouth to offer to help and she put her index finger in the air. "No. Thanks, but no."

"I didn't say anything."

"You were about to. And I would never take you up on it."

We'll see about that.

—

Glen went from supersnazzy, over-the-top fancy to Fisherman's Wharf, where the two of them were entirely overdressed. But Mary loved it.

He pulled her into what looked like a fish and chips shack and said they were having another course there. "Best clam chowder in the city."

And it was.

They walked through the crowd toward the bay. The wrap she'd brought for her dress wasn't doing the job and the first gust of wind had Glen placing his jacket over her shoulders.

When he directed her into a swanky restaurant with an up-close view of the bay, she took a minute and excused herself to the ladies' room.

Her hair was a mess . . . well, it was always unruly, but the moist air and wind had done a proper job of making it crazy. She tamed it the best she could, reapplied a little lip gloss, and stood back. She was smiling. Her cheeks were rosy, from the wind or the company, she couldn't really say. Both, she guessed.

Before leaving the ladies' room she sent a quick text to Dakota.

`I'm in San Francisco having the best time.`

She didn't wait for a reply and put her phone back in her purse.

Once again, Glen had procured a table with the perfect view. More wine appeared, as did the waiter with the menus.

She glanced at the selections. "I honestly don't know how much more I can eat."

"I won't be offended if you don't finish."

She put her menu down. "Then how about you order, and I'll have a bite of yours."

"Oh, no. I've played that game."

"I'm serious. You've been feeding me since we got here."

"Uh-huh." He didn't look at her, just kept reading the menu.

"Really, Glen. I'm fine with the wine."

"Uh-huh!"

The waiter reappeared.

Glen gave her one look, turned to the waiter, and ordered two filets mignons. "Medium rare?" he asked her.

He did not play fair. "Medium," she corrected him.

He gave her an *I won* smile before completing their order.

"I told you I wasn't hungry."

"I ordered a salad to share."

And they did. Halfway through her steak she gave up, and Glen finished it for her.

He wrapped her in his jacket before they left the restaurant and let his hands linger on her shoulders for a couple of seconds longer than needed.

She warmed instantly.

"If I knew I was leaving Southern California, I would have been prepared."

"If I had told you where we were going, it wouldn't have been a surprise."

And she did like the thrill of discovery.

When he opened the door to a waiting car, she slid in and said, "You've thought of everything."

He settled back in his seat as the car took them in the direction of downtown.

"I'm kinda shocked," he said.

"About what?"

"We didn't cross hairs once. I think that's a first for us."

"Oh, I don't know. I might have come to blows with the steak."

"You ate half."

She rolled her eyes. "At least you didn't order dessert."

He paused.

"What?"

"Nothing."

It wasn't nothing . . . he still had something cooking. He really didn't have a poker face.

"I hope you've had a good time."

She hadn't stopped smiling since he kissed her. A kiss he hadn't repeated. He didn't even reach for her hand or let his palm linger too long on the small of her back.

"Are you kidding? The face on the waiter when we told him where we were from . . . and that you flew to meet me, picked me up . . . flew us here, a helicopter. I think the guy thought we were full of crap. That alone was worth the tale."

"It is a little over-the-top," he admitted.

She wanted to question him more on why he'd taken such extreme measures for this date, but the car stopped at the curb of the building they'd flown to in the helicopter.

They walked along the now familiar path to the elevators, where an attendant greeted and escorted them to the roof.

Glen shook the pilot's hand and helped Mary into the passenger seat. She put on the earphones without being instructed. It was full dark, and the lights of the city directly contrasted the darkness of the bay.

"It's simply stunning," she said once the helicopter lifted into the air. "I understand Trent's affinity for choppers."

It was well known that Monica's husband, Trent, loved flying helicopters. According to Dakota, all the Fairchild men knew how, but unlike his brothers, Trent almost never sat in the passenger seat of a chopper.

"What does it take to learn to fly?"

"Study . . . practice. Why? Is that on the Mary bucket list?"

She shrugged her shoulders.

"Is that Alcatraz?" She changed subjects and pointed out the window.

"I believe so. Have you been?"

She quickly shook her head. "No, and don't care to. I do not need to see the inside of a prison."

Glen's laughter filled her headset.

They were no sooner in the air than they touched down on the tarmac and were shuffled into the plane they'd arrived on.

Instead of wine, Glen handed her coffee once the plane was in the air. Added to that, there was the warm smell of chocolate as he handed her what looked like a piece of cake without frosting. "You're killing me," she told him.

"It's small."

"I hate working out."

"Me too."

He still handed her the cake and didn't let her hand it back.

It was flaky and moist in the middle and practically melted in her mouth. "Oh, goodness . . . this is sinful."

He paused as he watched her take another bite.

She noticed his lower lip open and the tip of his tongue peek out before he realized he was staring and pulled himself together. A perfectly female part of her did a little happy dance. She hadn't meant to be enticing, yet here she was, capturing the attention of a charming, gorgeous man by simply eating her dessert.

Mary wiped the edges of her mouth and tried not to stare. "Why did you go through all this effort, Glen? I'd have been just as happy with a quiet meal in a nice place close to home."

Her question pulled his gaze away from her lips and onto his own plate. It was his turn to shrug. "I think we've both been wanting this for a while. I wanted to make it count."

Mary lifted both hands in the air. "Mission accomplished."

He grinned, flashed a dimple on the left side of his face, and ate half his dessert in one bite. "Besides . . . a nice meal close to home would have ended hours ago," he said around his food.

Mary actually put her fist to her chest. "How the heck can you be so charming and such a . . . a . . ."

"A what?"

She couldn't put to words what she thought. "You stole Dakota's monkey from me."

"I touched it first."

"I saw it first," she said, laughing.

"And you thought I'd just give it up."

"It would have been the chivalrous thing to do."

"On a date, maybe . . . but don't hold your breath . . . in a hospital gift shop. No way, babe. It's like a Bluelight Special at Kmart. Every man for himself."

She couldn't help but laugh. "You're too young to know about a Bluelight anything from Kmart."

He finished the rest of his dessert and continued to talk while waving his spoon. "I saw a movie."

Mary gave up on the chocolate, gave the rest to Glen, who happily devoured it. She enjoyed watching him eat and had to shake herself to look away.

"Did you get away with everything when you were a kid?"

"Trent got away with everything. Jason got away with nothing . . . I lingered in between."

"Middle child syndrome. Did you try and fix things between your brothers . . . make your parents happy?" She was analyzing him, but he didn't seem to mind.

"Some."

Hmm, the great negotiator. "So what exactly do you do at work?"

He hesitated and had a lingering smile as if he was surprised she'd asked. "I'm the CFO."

She didn't waver her stare.

"I work with a lot of finance in the company. I try and find ways of building the business, maintain parts that are lagging. Analyze what's working."

"Sounds like an imperative part of the company."

He shrugged. "Jason was always bossy, Trent had a hard time following instructions, I had the numbers and schmoozing thing down."

"It all worked out."

"Yeah . . . I like what I do."

Mary sat forward in her seat. "Did you pick it?"

"Chose my job?"

"Yeah . . . was it your decision, or did your father suggest that leg of the company to you at some point and you felt obligated to do it?"

Glen tilted his head as if questioning her question.

"You analyze everyone, don't you?"

She was doing it again. "Occupational hazard. Forget I asked."

This time Glen pushed his plate away and leveled his eyes to hers. "Shortly after our parents' death, Jason, Trent, and I sat down . . . we got shitfaced drunk, and we talked about what we wanted to do. Trent was the most torn. Couldn't do the desk. Said he needed to ease into the company. Jason spent the largest amount of time with our father in the office. He'd already been working with the company and knew more of the staff than any of us. I had a position, but it wasn't CFO. I'd worked with our head of operations, and with his help, took on the position I now run." He paused. "We all had a choice. Our father didn't force anything on us and we were more than happy to jump in when we needed to."

He delivered the information with very little emotion on his face. They were simply the facts that no longer bothered him to provide.

"Your parents must have been very proud of you all."

Now he smiled. "We gave them a fair share of grief, but I think we turned out all right."

It was after midnight when Glen walked her up to the front door.

She turned and smiled. "Should I invite you in?"

He tilted his head for a second in thought and gave a quick shake. "If you invite me in, I won't want to leave."

Her whole body shivered with the meaning of his words. "Are you flying home tonight?"

"I have a room at The Morrison."

"That's silly. You've slept on my couch before, you can—"

Glen stepped into her personal space and brushed her chin with the backs of his fingers. "I don't trust myself to stay on your sofa bed, Mary. And I don't want you to think this night was about that."

Mary wanted to analyze what the night was about, but her head was too fried to think that hard. "Okay."

"However, I do want to kiss you again."

It was as if he was asking. "Dessert before dinner, and after?"

"I like to indulge."

Mary tilted her chin higher and rested a hand on his chest. "I had a wonderful time."

"I did too." He leaned closer. "You're not nearly as uptight as I thought you'd be."

She couldn't help but chuckle. "And you're not nearly as annoying as I thought you'd be."

"A good start then."

"Hmm."

And then he was kissing her. The taste of coffee and chocolate mixed with Glen was edible. Unlike when he'd kissed her in the kitchen, this time he didn't back away when she traced his lips with her tongue. He accepted her invitation and explored. Even at the late hour, or maybe because of it, her body tingled to life and moved to get closer. She hadn't been kissed in a long time and enjoyed every second, every minute as he drew away and came back for more. She clawed into his shirt with one hand and felt the one holding her purse inch down his hips before Glen ended their make-out session on the porch.

They were smiling into each other's eyes. "You should probably go before I invite you inside."

"I probably should." Only he didn't walk away.

"Glen?"

"Hmm?" His hands tightened around her waist.

"Thank you, for tonight."

He pushed himself away and kissed her forehead. "It was my pleasure."

"Good night."

He took his cue and stood back while she opened her door. "Sleep well, Mary."

She closed the door behind her, leaned against it, and hugged herself with a completely adolescent smile.

Chapter Eleven

Mary's phone buzzed next to her bed. One glance at the screen had her rolling over and texting back.

`Yes, Dakota. I'm alone.`

She tossed the phone down and rolled over.

She'd no sooner fallen back asleep than Dakota's voice rang from downstairs. "I'm making coffee!"

Mary groaned. "I hate you," she yelled.

"Hate me later. I'm a gimp, remember? And what the hell is all this plastic down here?"

She forced herself upright in bed. The first thing she saw was Glen's jacket, which he'd failed to take off her shoulders before he drove away. She crawled toward it and brought it up to her nose. Everything twisted inside.

Mary pushed into a bathrobe and padded barefoot downstairs.

Dakota stood on crutches as she removed coffee cups from Mary's cupboard.

"What are you doing?"

Dakota turned and stared . . . she waited a few seconds and said, "You didn't get laid."

"Oh my God, Dakota." Mary expected nothing less from her friend.

"Why?"

"It was our first date."

"A long-awaited first date. And you haven't had sex since Jesus was a lad."

Mary moved to take the cups out of Dakota's hands. "Sometimes I hate that you know everything about my sex life."

"No, you don't."

No, she didn't. "We didn't have sex because . . ." *Why didn't we have sex?* "Glen . . ." How was she going to put this.

"Glen didn't want to?" Dakota's voice rose two octaves.

"Oh, no . . . he wanted to. We both . . ." Mary pointed to the kitchen table. "Sit. You're making me nervous."

She poured them coffee, mixed in cream and sugar for the both of them, and sat down. "He took me to San Francisco."

Dakota gave a full tooth grin. "I got your text."

"We flew from the airport into the city on a helicopter."

"Eeek!"

"I know. Seriously great moves. Oh, but wait . . . he kissed me before we left."

"What? Before you left here?"

"Yeah." Mary gave Dakota a play-by-play, they both squealed when she described things like how he gave her his jacket, ordered for her when she refused . . . and how he refused to come in because he didn't want Mary to think he'd spent all those first date efforts to get some horizontal naked time.

"Oh, man. I didn't realize Glen could be so romantic."

"Me either. We didn't even argue. We always argue."

"You two bicker like an old married couple. It's hysterical."

"We do, don't we?"

Dakota reached over and patted her hand. "This could be the start of something good."

Monica's words tossed around in her head. "I'm going to enjoy it, even if it's not a start. No regrets."

"Good." Dakota sipped her coffee. "So when will you see him again?"

"I don't know; we didn't talk about it."

"It's not like he can meet you for lunch."

"He would be a complete distraction if he lived here."

"Distractions are good."

They turned the conversation over to Dakota and Leo, and by the time they were finishing their coffee Mary's phone was ringing.

The girlie squeal thing would end eventually . . . but she enjoyed it now. "Hi, Glen."

"You sound wide awake."

And he sounded delicious. "That's because Dakota hobbled over here at the crack of dawn."

Dakota swished at her with both her hands.

"Good thing I didn't stay over then."

"Oh, she texted first to make sure I was alone."

Glen's laughter filled the line. "Glad you ladies have a protocol."

"Like a tie on the door at the dorms. Are you on the way to the airport?"

"Nope, already in the air."

"Makes me wonder how many hours a year you're up there."

"Probably about as many as you're in your car. Hold on." She heard him talking to the copilot.

"What's he saying?" Dakota whispered.

"What are we? In high school?" Mary giggled.

Dakota nodded with enthusiasm.

"You there?" Glen asked.

"Aren't there laws about talking on cell phones while flying?"

"No. We don't get pulled over for speeding either."

"Keeps your insurance rates down then."

Glen was laughing again. "So, next weekend?"

"This weekend isn't even over yet."

"Let me rephrase. Next Saturday . . ."

"That would be the day after Friday," she teased.

Dakota slapped the edge of the table and held in a laugh.

"You like pulling my chain, woman."

"I haven't pulled your chain yet." The words fell out of her mouth so fast she couldn't close it quick enough.

Dakota roared with laughter and Glen's silence on the line made her cringe.

"Who are you and what did you do with that innocent woman I took to dinner last night?" he asked.

"I told you my mouth got me in trouble."

"I'll remember that. We'll circle back to that chain a little later. Saturday at eleven in the morning."

She waited for more.

Silence.

"Are you asking?"

"Hell no. Why ruin what's working?"

True.

"What should I wear?"

"Casual. We'll be outside and it will be in the eighties. And bring a swimsuit . . . just in case."

"A swimsuit?"

Dakota's eyes lit up.

"Unless you like jumping in the water fully clothed."

"Not particularly."

"Glad we have that settled then. I'll text you later about that chain pulling."

"Good-bye, Glen."

He disconnected the call and Dakota and Mary squealed.

The plumber didn't show up Monday as scheduled. They'd broken the blade to the concrete saw they needed to use to open up the floor and a new one wouldn't come in until Wednesday, the day the job was supposed to be completed.

Monday was an evening work schedule for her. Not all of her clients were available to talk in the middle of the workweek.

Her routine for the past three years was to do her laundry on Mondays along with her grocery shopping. Wednesday afternoons were set aside for cleaning, which would have worked out perfectly if the plumbers were done, but that wasn't going to happen.

Instead of grocery shopping, she found herself at the mall searching out a new swimsuit. This was normally a job for her BFF to join her on, but alas . . . Dakota was a tad busy with baby Leo's first pediatrician appointment.

Thank God for cell phones.

With a dozen different bathing suits in hand, Mary stepped into the dressing room that had the worst invention known to man, fluorescent lights. She faced the three-way mirror and cringed. The first suit she tried on was a white one-piece with tiny black polka dots. She snapped a picture and sent it to Dakota, who was waiting to help her out.

`Please tell me you have bikinis to try on.`

`This one is cute.` She didn't have enough of a tan for white.

Mary slid out of the suit and into another one-piece.

Her phone buzzed. She glanced down, expecting to see Dakota chiding her, and instead found Glen.

`Hey, Counselor.`

`Hey yourself. This is a new way to communicate.`

The blue suit was strapless. She snapped a picture and sent it to Dakota.

Her phone buzzed twice.

I'm in a meeting and bored out of my head.

Mary leaned against the dressing room wall. Aren't you the boss? Can't you just leave?

She switched conversations. That one doesn't show your cleavage. BIKINI! Dakota shouted.

Another suit went to the *no* pile.

I called the meeting. Hence, I can't leave.

Mary went for the red bikini, stopped between the top and the bottoms to reply to Glen. Poor baby.

Well? Dakota had the patience of a teenager with the car keys.

Give me a second.

The bikini was right up Dakota's street. Skimpy with tons of cleavage. Mary snapped a picture.

Are you teasing me? Glen asked.

Yes I am! She enjoyed the banter. Even via texting.

Mary sent the picture with the question. Don't you think my ass needs more coverage? Dakota would be straight up if it was too small. She took it off and put on the black two-piece that she felt would be a better fit.

Her phone buzzed.

Well? Did your phone die? Dakota's question caught her off guard.

Didn't you get the...oh shit!

Mary's heart kicked in her chest when she switched back to Glen's screen. Sure enough, there she was, red bikini with a question about her ass.

Her phone rang, and she nearly dropped it.

Oh, God. Oh, God.

It was Glen.

Her hands shook. “That picture wasn’t meant for you.”

“Are you trying to kill me?”

“It wasn’t. I swear.” She sat on the dressing room bench holding her head with one hand, her phone in the other.

“My employees think I’ve lost it.”

Her embarrassment turned to laughter.

“It’s not funny.”

“It’s kinda funny.”

“So if that wasn’t meant for me, who are you sending bathing suit pictures to?”

“Dakota. I’m shopping and she couldn’t come with me.”

“Uh-huh.”

“I swear.”

“Well . . . in that case. If you’re shopping for next weekend, and you’re wearing that for me, no your ass doesn’t need more coverage.”

Oh, just kill me now.

“If you’re shopping for another weekend when I won’t be with you, then yes, it needs more coverage.”

She was holding in her laughter so hard she teared up. “I’m never going to live this down, am I?”

“Not in this lifetime.”

Her phone buzzed. “Dakota is texting me. She’s going to think I abandoned her.”

“I might have to post this on Instagram.”

She stopped laughing. “Don’t you dare.”

“Buy that one.”

“It’s too small.”

“Instagram is one click away.”

“Okay, okay . . . don’t, Glen.”

“Buy it and I won’t.”

“I’ll get you back for this.”

“Sounds like a promise, Counselor.”

"Aren't you supposed to be in a meeting?" she asked.

"Buy it."

"Good-bye, Glen."

He hung up.

She didn't even try to explain what happened to Dakota in a text. By the time she left the dressing room, the employees probably wondered if she'd used the space as a phone booth.

She put both the red and the black bikinis on the counter and offered a coy smile to the teenager at the register.

Mary glanced at her phone and the picture of her standing in the three-way mirror with too much of her butt sticking out and laughed all the way home.

—

"I met someone."

Mary's jaw dropped. "You what?"

"We both volunteer at the homeless shelter. I was serving the potatoes, he was serving the chicken."

Mary saw stars and dropped into one of her patio chairs, pressing the phone to her ear. "Okay, when you say you met someone . . . you mean you met someone, met someone?"

"What is that supposed to mean?"

"You know what it means."

"I don't know. You're going to have to spell it out for me."

"Sister Mary Frances!"

"She is not here, m'dear. Hasn't been for nearly ten years."

"Mary Frances!"

"That's better." To say she was shocked would be a vast understatement. "I didn't think that was possible."

"Believe me, I'm just as surprised as you."

"That isn't likely."

"He's very charming, Mary. You'd like him."

"You're dating." It wasn't a question.

"We've had coffee . . . and pie."

"Coffee and pie?" She was not hearing this. The woman who all but raised her . . . the *nun*—who'd all but raised her—was dating.

"He's a widower. His children are grown, has two adorable grandchildren—"

"Wait! You're . . . you're dating."

"I know it's a lot to take in."

"You don't date . . . you can't." Mary wanted to retract the words once she said them out loud.

"Technically, I can." Sister Mary's words started to clip.

"I'm sorry. I'm shocked. I'm not saying the right things."

"Perhaps we should speak another time."

"No. I'm sorry. Truly." Mary remembered how hard it had been when Mary Frances left the order. Only one of her sisters kept in touch, the others refused since the Mother Superior had forbidden it. It took nearly five years for the church to recognize she was gone, and even then, Mary Frances mourned what she'd given her life to as if she were a scorned woman divorced from the love of her life. Mary pulled in a breath. "Tell me about your widower. What's his name?"

Mary Frances paused. "Do you really want to hear this?"

"I do."

"His name is Burke. He's originally from South Wales."

"Does he have an accent?"

Mary Frances sighed . . . like a girlie sigh, and Mary had to hold back her tongue.

"He does! He sounds so astute. And he's funny. You'll really enjoy him, Mary."

Mary gritted her teeth and smiled as she spoke. "How long have you known him?"

"A couple of months now."

Mary punched a fist in the air. "And you're just now telling me?" She kept her voice slow and measured.

"I was afraid you wouldn't approve."

I don't!

"That you'd be upset," she continued.

Mary forced herself to calm down and speak the truth. "I am . . ."

"Is this because of the church?"

"No." And it wasn't. She was more self-aware than that. "You're the closest thing to a mother as I've ever had."

"Oh, Mary . . ."

"I'd imagine any child having some difficulty finding out their parent was dating after a long relationship."

There was a pause on the line. "I suppose that's true."

"But it's not because of the church. Please know that holds no weight in my feelings."

"Oh, c'mon." Mary Frances always cut the bull.

"All right. Perhaps a little." Mary didn't want to vocalize her concerns about Mary Frances having sex. Just thinking about it had Mary squeezing her eyes closed. "But only because I knew you for so many years as someone that didn't date."

"Coffee and pie is hardly dating."

"Pie could be the night before, and coffee could be the morning after."

"Mary Colette Kildare!"

Oh, the middle name came out.

"Sorry."

"I should think so."

Because Mary was who Mary was, she added. "But it could be."

"It isn't!" There was laughter in Mary Frances's voice.

This was going to take some time to get used to.

"Tell me about Dakota's son."

They spent the next ten minutes talking about Leo . . . about Dakota's "trip down the stairs" and Mary's plumbing problems. When she hung up she realized she hadn't mentioned Glen. She knew immediately why. Mary Frances's excitement about her own personal life didn't need any interference from hers.

Chapter Twelve

Ever since Mary's bikini picture, Glen could think of nothing else. In fact, he saved the picture and referred back to it several times a day.

And it was only Thursday.

He had every intention of flying out Friday after work but knew he wouldn't pick her up until the time he'd told her.

"You're flying back to LA?" Jason asked while they had their weekly lunch meeting.

Glen ate three french fries at a time. "I'm taking Mary out."

"The blonde."

"Is there another Mary?"

"What is up with my brothers and blondes?" Jason teased.

Glen simply shoved more fries in his mouth and grinned.

"She doesn't seem like your type," Jason said.

"Oh?" And what did Jason think was his type?

"You know. Too reserved. I thought you liked 'em a little more . . . I don't know . . ."

Glen removed his phone from his pocket and pulled up the bikini image of Mary and turned his phone around.

"Oh, wow."

When Jason grabbed his wrist to get a closer look, Glen pulled it back, suddenly feeling like showing his brother the picture had been the wrong thing to do.

Since when did he hold a moral code for that?

"That was Mary?"

"Yeah, forget I showed you that."

"Let me see that again."

"No." He put his phone away.

"Whoa . . . okay. Sorry. That didn't look like the Mary I know."

Glen shook off his unease. "She's the same Mary . . . just more playful than you'd think."

"Clearly."

Glen glared.

"Sorry."

"Anyway," he said, changing the subject. "I'm leaving tomorrow. I'll be back Sunday."

"Whatever works, bro. Tell me how the broker scrub meeting worked out."

Glen was happy to change the subject.

—

Mary stared over the counter, her mind completely lost in all things dating. Not her dating, but Sister Mary . . . she really needed to stop thinking of her as a nun. As soon as Mary had hung up the phone, questions started popping up in her head like mini balloons about the heads of cartoon characters. *Have they kissed? Has Mary Frances ever kissed a man . . . as in before she became a nun? Did she ever have desires when she was a nun?* Maybe Mary didn't want to know the answer to that one. But still . . . just because someone is married doesn't make them dead. The whole idea of her pseudomom sitting across from a guy eating pie and giggling produced equal parts ewh and aah.

Mary picked at her sandwich without tasting it.

"I was wondering if I'd see you in here again."

Mary blinked out of her distraction and looked over her shoulder. "Oh, hi." *Darn, what is his name again?* "Kent, right?"

He gave her a full-watt smile. "You remembered."

"Of course. How is the new job?"

"Bumpy, but it's good. Lots of personalities at a law office."

"I bet." She'd had clients who were lawyers before, they were a very literal fact-driven group overall. Emotions weren't an option, so cracking through them, in Mary's experience, wasn't easy.

"Are you going to eat that, or do I need to get you a bigger box?" Carla asked.

"A bigger box, I think."

"So, Mary . . ."

Kent was still standing behind her stool at the counter. The spaces on both sides of her were taken, not giving him room to sit.

Carla picked up Mary's plate and slid the sandwich inside the Styrofoam box.

"Yes?"

"I was wondering if you'd like to go out this weekend."

She saw the question coming from a mile away. "Uhm, the thing is . . . I have plans."

A strangled smile stuck to his face. "Maybe another time then."

What did she want to say to that? She didn't have a boyfriend, not technically, she wasn't married. Kent was an attractive man. A nice man. "Maybe," she found herself saying. To avoid more conversation, she dropped the necessary money on the counter and released her seat to the next hungry customer.

"I'll take you up on that," Kent told her.

Take me up on a maybe? "It was nice seeing you again."

Kent moved, but only a few inches, to let her pass. "I look forward to it."

The weight of his eyes followed her out.

—

Mary struggled with what to wear, what to bring with her, what to expect.

It was after ten thirty. Glen was due within a half hour and she hadn't gotten dressed yet. She had clothes pulled out over her bed. Denim shorts? Cotton? Daisy Dukes or something to hike in? Flip-flops or sandals? Or should she wear sneakers?

She pulled out tops for all the shorts and stood back to look at the mess. She tossed the Daisy Dukes on the floor. *Too skimpy.*

Denim? She glanced outside, felt the warm rays of the sun through her window. She considered the amount of food Glen had offered her on their first date. The denim met the Daisy Dukes.

Mary glanced at the time and compromised between hiking shorts and a simple cotton pair that hid a little more of her butt than the other choices. She shed her bathrobe and pulled on her clothes. In the bathroom, she pulled her unruly mess of hair back in a ponytail and applied a fresh coat of lip gloss. "Not bad."

She heard the doorbell downstairs and ran back into her room. Her new bathing suit, along with a wrap, was already tucked in a small bag. She tossed in the flip-flops and hopped into her white tennis shoes as she jogged downstairs.

The bell rang again. "Coming!"

After pushing through the plastic, she opened the door.

Glen wore a dark T-shirt, cotton shorts, and a smile.

"Where's the swimsuit?"

Her shoulders slid and she rolled her eyes. "In the bag!"

"Better be." Glen stepped over the threshold and pulled her close. "Hi."

He had a way of making her giddy. "Hi."

He kissed her. It was brief. It was hello . . . and it was hot!

When he released her lips he pulled on the back of her hair with a tiny tug. "This could be fun."

"Do you have a line for everything?"

He wiggled his eyebrows and then looked above their heads. "I thought this was suppose to be finished by now."

She stepped through the plastic and into her living room in search of her purse. "There was a delay." She walked into her kitchen and kept talking. "If you look down, you can see where they cut in, but they didn't have the jackhammer to pull out the concrete." She found her purse next to her phone. "Which turned out fine since the insurance company wanted to come and take pictures of the damage."

"I'm glad your insurance is paying for all this."

She hurried back in the living room. "Oh, no . . . my insurance is only paying for new floors. The five grand for the plumbing fix is on me."

"Ouch."

"Tell me about it. I just hope once the plumber gets in there he doesn't find more issues. Or I'll be back to eating Chinese noodle soup." She was teasing, but . . .

She stopped in front of him and sighed. *Sweater!* "Hold this." She shoved her beach bag and her purse into Glen's arms and ran upstairs. "I need to grab a sweater."

Glen laughed as she ran away.

She tossed a shirt lying on top of the sweater she wanted from her bed to the floor. The mess wasn't really her style, but she'd get to it later. Her eyes landed on Glen's dress coat from last weekend. Much as she hated giving it up . . . she removed it from the back of her door and brought it with her. "I believe this belongs to you. I probably should have had it washed." She *should* have had it washed. How unthoughtful of her.

Glen handed her back her bags and took his jacket from her fingertips and folded it over his arm. "But then it wouldn't have smelled like me."

She stopped in her tracks. "Who said anything about me smelling your jacket?"

"Are you telling me you didn't?"

She blinked a half a dozen times. "We're not talking about this."

He chuckled as he walked her out to the car.

Glen loved watching her laugh. He'd purposely rented a Jeep that didn't have a top to make sure Mary got over any *my hair has to be perfect* issues from the moment she got in.

As it stood, she held on to her ponytail and enjoyed the wind as he drove them to the pier.

"Aren't you going to ask where we're going?"

She shook her head. "I'll figure it out eventually."

A parking attendant took the Jeep and Glen walked Mary to their next form of transportation.

"A boat?"

It was a charter with a dozen other passengers. "To get to Catalina."

Mary's brows squeezed together. "Did I tell you I get seasick?"

Oh, no! "You get seasick?"

She held his stare and started to slowly smile.

"Oh, I'll get you for that."

She laughed with a shake of her head. "You're too easy."

It took less than an hour to get to Catalina. Mary might have smiled when they were in the air, but she was beaming now. The sea agreed with her. They sat toward the back of the vessel, where the sides were protected by shields to ward off the wind.

Two of the other passengers struck up conversations with them, from the weather to their occupations. Or, in the case of the other couple, what they'd done before retirement. They lived on Catalina full time and came to the mainland twice a month to shop.

Mary told them she was a therapist, and Glen said he was a pilot.

Mary watched him for a moment after he'd given half the truth to the couple but didn't elaborate about what he did for a living.

They parted ways once they stepped onto the small island. "How about some lunch?" he suggested.

"Let the feedings begin."

Glen took the liberty of placing his hand on her back as he led her through the dense crowd.

Catalina was only eight miles across at its widest point with one main city populating it. The city of Avalon, for the convenience of tourists, was one hundred percent walkable. Which worked out well since the main transportation on the island was limited to golf carts and bikes.

"We have an hour and a half before our next adventure," Glen told Mary as they walked the small city filled with shops, restaurants, and tourist traps.

"Did you have something in mind for food?" she asked.

"Leaving that up to you. I picked last weekend."

She glanced around before grabbing his hand and pulling him into a Mexican restaurant.

Mary liked her food spicy. She splashed hot sauce all over everything and didn't break a sweat when she popped a jalapeño in her mouth.

They had just enough time to walk to the launch ramp and grab a water taxi.

The sailboat was large enough to have a small galley and a place for Mary to change. A crew of three waited to take the two of them halfway around the island to where only the sound of the waves hitting the hull would distract them. Mary emerged wearing a cover-up over the patches of red material Glen had all but burned into his memory.

"If you two are ready," the captain said once they were both seated.

Glen rested his arm on the side of the boat and encouraged Mary to sit back. "You'll love this," he said so only she could hear.

"Good thing I don't turn green on boats or this day would have been ruined."

Glen placed a hand on her shoulder and pulled her into his side. She fit, perfectly.

The crew hoisted the sails and the material caught the wind. The wind also caught Mary's cover-up and Glen was treated with an up close vision that a camera couldn't do justice to. Mary tilted her face to the wind and the salt spray hit her closed eyes.

They spotted a pod of dolphins . . . or did they call it a school? Glen didn't know, and the two of them debated it for ten minutes before attempting to look up the information on their phones. But a signal was nonexistent, which had them both turning off their phones and putting them away for the duration.

Mary removed a tube of suntan lotion from her bag and distracted him by running a generous portion down her legs and over her arms. "Did you hear what I said?"

He almost said yes . . . then realized he had no idea what she'd just said. "No. I'm having a hard time hearing anything with you doing that."

She slid her arms out of her cover-up and let it drop around her waist, and Glen's brain fried. She was beautiful, curvy in all the right places, slender in all the others. His mouth watered. "You have a picture in your phone."

He let his eyes drop for a nanosecond and promised himself a longer look when she wasn't watching him. "It isn't the same."

"It's just a bathing suit."

"It's not the suit."

Maybe it was the reflection of the sun off the water, but he swore she blushed. "How is it you're not used to compliments?"

She continued with the lotion, this time higher on her thighs. The tips of her fingers moving between the material and her skin.

Lucky fingertips.

"I don't get them as often as you might believe."

He waited for her to struggle with the spaces she couldn't reach, and took the liberty of removing the tube from her hand. "Then you either don't wear a bikini when you're swimming or you're hanging out with the wrong men."

She pulled her hair over her shoulder and presented him with her back. Her skin was soft and warm . . . his hands covered her shoulders and rubbed the lotion in with slow, strong strokes. He figured as long as she was getting a massage out of the application, she wouldn't realize how much time it took for him to apply the SPF 30. So he used his thumbs up the edges of her delicate spine and rolled the tension up her neck and back down. Mary stopped talking and moaned.

That simple noise took his semi–state of arousal into high gear and had him sucking in a deep breath.

Get ahold of yourself, bud!

Talking to himself, in his head, wasn't new. In fact, it was becoming a necessary part of dating Mary. He promised himself he'd take it slow, not scare her off. They had too many mutual friends and too much chemistry to push this fast.

Mary was quickly turning to putty in his hands.

"How about I lie down and you do that for an hour."

"Because we have an audience and I don't trust myself to do this that long and remain a gentleman."

She passed a look over her shoulder of complete trust. "You surprise me."

He moved quicker to avoid his hard-on becoming more prominent. "Oh, how so?"

"Let's just say I didn't think you'd be so careful with me."

"What did you expect?"

She leaned back to say something in his ear when her arm brushed against his erection.

He didn't move a muscle and she delivered a knowing grin. "I expected you to think a little more with that."

"*That* has a mind of its own. I don't always listen."

Mary's hand dropped to his thigh. She nodded over the side. "The water's kinda chilly, you know . . . if you need to cool off." The woman loved to tease him.

Instead of asking the crew to lower the sail, he took Mary by the waist, not allowing her to put that damn wrap back on, and slid her close. "I have a better idea. How about you sit right here until this goes away so I don't embarrass myself."

She snuggled close. "Sometimes it's nice to be a girl. We can be turned on and no one knows it."

He glanced down the length of her body and let his fingers resting at her side squeeze her hip. "Your nipples are straining . . . and it's not cold out here."

He kept her arm from crossing over her chest. "Oh, no you don't."

"I am cold," she told him.

"That was a lie."

She shivered, but there wasn't an inch of gooseflesh on her exposed skin.

Chapter Thirteen

Mary woke from her dream still feeling the roll of the ocean under her from the day she'd spent on the water with Glen. And she was aroused. Painfully.

They'd returned to the harbor, caught the charter back to the mainland, where they'd enjoyed a casual dinner before he drove her home.

He walked her to the door and kissed her like a lovestruck teenage kid, his hands just shy of rounding all the bases, before his strangled words ended their night.

And Mary, as improper as she could be at times, didn't take matters into her own hands and pull him inside. Instead, she waved good-bye and ended the night with a cold shower of her own.

Only now, at two in the morning, she was hot and awake and completely frustrated. She flipped her pillow to the cool side, pounded it with her fist, and forced her thoughts away from the man whose smile made her body weep.

—

"I'm going to have a talk with that man if he doesn't step up!" Dakota's words first thing in the morning would have been appreciated if they weren't being delivered so early.

"And what exactly would you say?"

Dakota was moving around really well on the crutches. Walt and Leo were having a little father/son time bonding on a Sunday morning so Dakota could get the weekend scoop at the crack of dawn.

"I'd tell him that you are *not* the one to make the first move."

"I *can* make the first move."

Dakota deflated that with a stare.

"I could if I wanted to."

"How long have we known each other?" Dakota asked.

"Six years."

"And how many times in those six years have you made the first move?"

She cringed. "I was raised by nuns."

"It's a wonder—"

"Oh my God, I forgot to tell you," Mary interrupted her. "Mary Frances is dating."

Dakota's jaw dropped.

"I know! That's exactly what my reaction was. Dating, Dakota. Like having coffee and pie with a widower."

"Pie the night before and coffee in the morning kind of dating?"

Mary couldn't help but wonder if it was her BFF's influence that had her asking the same question earlier in the week.

"She denied that."

"You asked her?"

"I was stunned. I asked her all kinds of things I probably shouldn't have."

"I wanna meet him," Dakota announced. "What kind of guy dates an ex-nun? How old is Mary Frances?"

"Fifty-eight."

"That's not that old."

"I know."

Dakota dropped a hand over Mary's. "She's probably a fifty-eight-year-old virgin."

That put things in a different perspective. "What a sad thought."

"Tell me about the guy."

Mary didn't leave out one detail.

Glen didn't call from twenty-five thousand feet, he texted instead. `Your wrap was in the Jeep.` Truth was, he'd "accidentally" left it on the floor when he'd handed her back her bag. He felt a little like a panty snatcher when he'd curled the material in his hand and smelled her most of the night.

`You should probably toss it in the wash.`

`That is NOT going to happen.`

`It smells like suntan lotion.`

`It smells like you.`

There was a dot, dot, dot on the screen, until finally . . . `I like the image that jumped into my head.`

So did he. `I have to check my schedule about next weekend. When is a good time to call on Mondays?`

`Before two. Call my cell.`

`We'll talk tomorrow.`

`Fly safe.`

I always do, sweetheart.

"I'm leaving him." Nina Golf sat across from Mary with her hands folded firmly in her lap, dark-rimmed sunglasses hiding the emotion in her eyes. "I can't do this anymore."

None of this was news to Mary, she'd seen it coming for months. Instead of saying those things out loud, she sat back and waited to see if Nina was going to open herself up.

"He's too demanding. And crazy. He's been over the edge ever since I started staying at Bev's place."

"Beverly is your single girlfriend?"

"Right." Nina paused. "Just because she's single doesn't mean we're out trolling for men every night. It isn't like that."

Mary waited . . .

"Jacob calls me a slut. I'm his wife. He shouldn't call me names."

"I have to agree."

"He's such an asshole. He called my mother and told her I was sleeping around on him."

"Nina . . . did you ever tell Jacob what happened last winter?" It was time to remind her client of her infidelity, if in fact the last time she'd stepped out of her marriage was so many months ago.

"No. Of course not."

"Do you think Jacob might have picked up on anything? You were very conflicted over the holidays."

Nina removed her sunglasses and revealed dark circles from either a lack of sleep or tears.

"Do you think he knows?"

"What I think isn't important. Consider this. You had an affair. And not just a one-night stand, but something that lasted for several weeks. You told me yourself how guilty you felt, and when it ended, you dedicated yourself to your husband with renewed energy. Didn't you both go to Hawaii in January as a second honeymoon?"

Nina nodded.

"You returned and within a month you were both in here struggling again."

"That's because he is unreasonable when I want to go out with my friends." Her defensiveness was palpable.

"What happens when you go out with your friends?"

"We drink . . . we dance."

"Get picked up on?"

"If guys are attracted, I can't help that."

"I didn't say you could. How does it make you feel when guys come on to you?"

Nina started tapping her foot against the air. "It doesn't suck. It's nice to get dressed up sometimes and feel like a woman."

"Do you do those things with Jacob?" Mary already knew the answer to that but asked the question anyway.

"Jacob hates going out. Says he did enough of that when he was single."

"So you go out without him and men try and pick you up?"

"That doesn't mean I'm sleeping with them."

Mary sat forward. "We've talked about this. Being unfaithful in your marriage is more than just an act of sex."

"I'm not falling in love with them either."

"Nina, I'm not asking you these things to corner you into saying something, or believing something. I'm asking you these things so you can look inside yourself and ask some important questions." Because her sitting in front of Mary and denying everything was a massive flag of bullshit. If Nina was her friend and not a client, she'd call her on said bull in a heartbeat. Nina was doing her best to destroy her marriage on her end. "Do you wear your wedding ring when you go out, Nina?"

Her client lowered her eyes to her left hand and started to twist her wedding bands.

She didn't answer the question.

—

Mary walked out of her office after seven. It was nearly dark, and she was exhausted. She checked her cell phone for messages as she walked to her car. Glen didn't call her before she made it into work, but he'd texted her around three apologizing and saying he'd call her later that night at home.

She tucked her phone back in her purse once she realized there wasn't any pending message. The thought of her favorite Mediterranean takeout, which happened to be on her route home, put a smile on her face. Rotisserie chicken sounded perfect.

Then she turned the key and her car moaned with a weak response. The light in the cab dimmed and her stomach dropped.

She tried again.

The noise in the engine, or lack of noise, and the fact that the dash didn't light up, told her it was her battery.

The lights in her car automatically turned off and on so long as she didn't override the switch. So why had it drained? The car was only a few years old, with less than thirty thousand miles on her.

Mary pushed open her door and popped the hood. Not that she knew what she was looking at. Most of the engine in the car was covered by a massive shield. There were bits sticking out here and there, but nothing that she could see was obviously wrong. She glanced around the nearly vacant parking lot and wondered if there was anyone in the building still around to give her a jump.

"It had to happen on a late night," she said to herself.

With the hood still up, she leaned back into her car and removed her purse. Her AAA card sat behind her driver's license. She pulled it out and started to dial.

A pair of headlights turned in her direction and started to drive away. Probably for the best, she didn't like attracting strangers while standing alone in a parking lot.

"Triple A roadside assistance. How can I help you?"

"I think my battery is dead."

The car in the lot slowed to a stop behind her car.

"Where is your location?"

Mary rattled off the address, kept her eye on the car behind her.

"Do you need help?" The voice from the driver asked through a rolled down passenger window.

Mary leaned down to see the person. "I'm calling Triple A."

"Okay . . . wait, Mary?"

Mary peered closer. "Kent?"

"Ma'am?"

"I'm sorry, just a minute," she told the woman on the phone.

Kent left his engine running and got out of his car. "What happened?"

"I think it's the battery."

Kent thumbed in the direction of his car. "I have jumper cables."

"Do you? That would be great."

"Ma'am? Do you want me to send a driver?"

Mary turned back to the phone. "I think I'm good. Someone is here to help."

"Thank you for calling Triple A. Feel free to call back if you need further assistance."

Kent moved to the front of her car and unbuttoned the dress sleeves of his white shirt before rolling them up to his elbows.

"I don't know what could have happened. The lights are automatic. Even the dome light turns off after two minutes."

He fiddled with the cables that connected the battery to the rest of the engine. "Try turning it over."

She slid into the driver's seat and turned the key.

The car moaned again without turning over.

"Definitely sounds like the battery. Let me pull my car up to yours."

Kent backed up and swung his car around to face hers and popped his hood. She stayed where she was and waited for him to connect the cables.

"It's a good thing I was working late," he said.

"Great timing."

"I didn't realize this was your building."

"Yep, this is where I rent space to see my clients."

"Oh." He disappeared under her hood for a few seconds. "Try it now."

She got back in her seat. "C'mon."

The engine took a second to catch and then turned over. "Oh, thank goodness."

Mary left it running and stepped out of her car. "I can't thank you enough."

Kent set the jumper cables on the ground and closed her hood. "No problem."

"I really don't know what happened for the thing to drain."

He wiped his hands together. "I'd get that checked right away. Wouldn't want to be stranded in a less hospitable place."

"That's true. I'll take it in tomorrow. Really, Kent. Thank you."

He stepped a little closer and leaned against her car. "You can thank me by going out with me."

She kept her smile but found herself biting her lip. Last month she would have taken him up on the offer. "Uhm, the thing is . . . I'm kinda seeing someone."

"Oh . . . just kinda?"

"Well, we've known each other for a while . . ." Why was she explaining this to a stranger? "We just started dating."

"Sounds serious."

She lifted her shoulders. "I don't know. Could be."

"And you don't date two men at the same time."

Mary shook her head. "Tried to in college. It didn't work out very well."

His chest rose and fell with a giant sigh. "Well, if something changes, you let me know."

Thank goodness. "I will."

He pointed in the air in her direction. "I'll take you up on that."

He turned back to his car, closed the hood, and put the cables back in his trunk.

"Thanks again."

"My pleasure. Have a nice evening, Mary."

Alone in her car, she gripped the steering wheel and felt some of the tension leave her system. Kent followed her out of the lot and waved when they turned in opposite directions at the first intersection. Then Mary took a solid breath.

Chapter Fourteen

Glen listened to Mary's phone ring for the fourth time. He'd already left her a message on her house phone and considered calling her cell. But she'd told him she had clients into the evening and not to bother since she turned it off.

Here it was close to nine at night in California and he was starting to worry.

Since when did he worry about a woman missing his call?

He heard her message machine pick up and lifted the phone from his ear to hang up the call.

"Hello? Glen?"

"There you are." Her voice made him smile.

"Yeah . . . God, what a day. Can I call you right back? I just ran in the door."

"Of course."

"Okay. Give me five minutes." She hung up.

When she called back, he was sitting on his leather sofa in his den, his socked feet kicked up on the coffee table in front of him.

"Hey," he said.

"Hey, yourself. You're up late."

"I missed my call this morning, I couldn't have you wondering if I lost your number."

"I would hope you'd have memorized it by now."

He had . . . a long time ago, but he wasn't going to tell her that. "You're getting in late."

"Long day at work. Then my car wouldn't start."

"Why? What happened?"

"Battery. But I don't know why. I'll take it in tomorrow and have it checked. I'm going to eat in your ear while we're talking, hope you don't mind. I'm starving."

He chuckled. "Go on ahead. So was there someone in your building to give you a jump?"

"The one behind me, actually. Everyone in mine was gone for the day. I hate car problems with a fiery passion. Dakota is always telling me I need a stun gun in my purse for when things like this happen."

On this he had to agree with Dakota. Mary would be a beautiful, blonde target if she broke down in the wrong neighborhood. "I'm guessing you don't own a stun gun."

"No. After Dakota shocked the heck out of Walt last year . . . I don't know, seemed like that thing is too dangerous."

"Why would she stick Walt with a blast of electricity?"

"It was an accident. He approached her from behind in a dark parking lot. She didn't know it was him. She felt guilty for weeks. Didn't stop her from laughing about it, but boy was she guilt ridden over it!"

"That's funny."

"It was. Anyway, I didn't need one today, so I guess I'm good."

He heard her attempt to chew as they spoke. "About this weekend."

"Uh-huh?"

"There's a dinner party I've committed to going to on Saturday."

He heard her drink something before she responded. "I understand. I'm thoroughly enjoying our weekends, but can't expect to dominate every one."

He liked that she sounded sincere and a little disappointed at the same time. "I want you to be my date."

She cleared her throat. "In Connecticut?"

"The party is in Manhattan, but yes."

Mary was silent, and for a minute he thought she had her mouth full again. "Uhm, I don't know how to say this, so I'm just going to."

"Go ahead."

"I-I can't afford a flight back east right now. Not with all my plumbing issues—"

"Mary—"

"I'd love to join you. And it's only fair that I visit you instead of you making the trip all the time. I mean—"

"Mary—"

"And my car, who knows what's wrong with my—"

"Mary!"

"I'm sorry. I'm rambling."

"I'll send a plane. I wouldn't have asked you to come here without offering a ride. I have meetings on Friday and can't fly out to get you, but I do have a leg in LA that is coming back here Friday night. Or if you want to fly on Saturday, I can arrange that, too. Just tell me you'll come."

"It feels like I'm taking advantage."

He knew that was coming. "You didn't ask me, I'm asking you."

"I don't know . . ."

He needed to change tactics. "Dakota and you are best friends, right?"

"You're changing the subject."

"Just answer the question, Mary. You're tight, correct?"

He heard her sigh. No food in her mouth that he could tell. "Yes. She's my family."

"You two talk, right? About everything?" If there was one thing Glen knew about women . . . other than the need for chocolate on occasion, it was their ability to talk.

"Yes."

"Do you ever offer her advice?"

"What?"

"Like when she zapped Walt with the stun gun, did you talk about that?"

"Of course we talked about it, how could I have told you about it had I not talked about it?"

"You gave her advice," he asked.

"I told her she shouldn't feel guilty about buzzing anyone who walked up to her in a dark parking lot, even if it was her own mother. If you're scared, you need to protect yourself. It's natural."

Glen smiled in the darkness of his den. "So a professional observation on human nature."

"Fight or flight. So yeah, professional."

"Has Dakota ever given you one of her books for free?"

Mary hesitated with her answer. "I'm her best friend. Of course she gives me a copy."

Glen knew he needed to make the next words count or no matter how much the comparison worked, Mary would think he was full of shit.

He paused and spoke from his heart. "I miss my mom."

"You're changing the subject aga . . . wait, wh-what did you say?"

He felt his chest constrict with the admission. "I miss her. I miss my dad, too . . . but my mom . . . I don't know, we didn't have a lot of time together in those last years and I feel like I missed out on something."

He heard Mary pause. "Oh, Glen . . . it's natural. She left your life too early."

"I know. Still sucks."

"It does suck."

They were both silent for a moment. He didn't realize how hard the words were to say. He'd started out with this just as a way to get what he wanted, but now he felt better saying it out loud.

"I can come on Friday after five and need to be back Monday morning."

Glen found himself squeezing his eyes shut. "My mom would have liked you."

"You'll have to show me pictures."

"She was beautiful . . ." Glen went on to tell Mary how both he and Jason thought Trent was going to be a girl. And how they'd even put makeup on him when he was a toddler, teasing him. "Don't tell Monica . . . oh, who am I kidding, women can't keep secrets."

"We can . . . just not ones as funny and innocent as that. A wife needs to know if her husband was an involuntary cross-dresser."

"I'll have to dig up the pictures we took that day. Maybe have one framed for his birthday."

He did love the sound of Mary's laugh.

"I'll make all the arrangements for this weekend. The dinner is formal."

"Floor-length formal or closer to what I wore in San Francisco?"

"Ask me an easier question."

"Men! Are you wearing a suit or a tux?"

"Tux."

"All right then."

"That's it? No more questions?"

"Unless you're the best man in a wedding, a tux is only worn with superformal events. So instead of flat-out asking where you're taking me, I can safely assume that a floor-length gown would be appropriate."

"I didn't realize I was dating Little Miss Etiquette."

"I didn't realize I was dating Li'l Mr. Clueless. I would think with your dating portfolio you'd know what a woman should wear."

He should have been offended by the *dating portfolio* comment, but they both knew it was true. Glen moved the phone away from his face and yawned.

"You should probably go to bed," she told him.

"You heard that?"

"I did."

"It is after midnight here." He had to be in the office by nine.

"Then I'll say good night."

"Okay. I'll call you later in the week with details." He waited for her to end the call.

"Glen?"

"Yeah?"

"Don't think for a second I don't realize what you did back there . . . with the questions about Dakota . . . you telling me about your mom. I just don't want you to think I'm dating you for the perks."

"I don't think that."

"I'm glad we're clear on that. Now go to bed."

He laughed. "Yes, dear."

She ended the call without saying good-bye.

Glen couldn't be happier.

Noise from a jackhammer tore Mary from her bed. She twisted her head toward her alarm clock and slapped a hand across her eyes. It was seven thirty in the morning. And her neighbors were going to be pissed.

She grabbed her bathrobe from the edge of her bed and ran down her stairs calling the plumber's name. "Leroy!"

The noise grew louder closer to the source.

"Leroy!"

She saw the shadows of two men beyond the plastic tarp before she unzipped it. The back of the man controlling the jackhammer faced her. There was no way she was going to be able to get his attention without touching him.

Mary reached out and tapped his shoulder.

He didn't respond.

She used her whole hand the second time and he jumped away. His eyes were wide with shock until he realized she wasn't a threat.

Mary waved a hand across her neck indicating for the man to cut off the machine.

When the racket stopped, her ears buzzed.

"Did you look at the time?"

Both men stared at her. "My English not good."

"My Spanish is worse." She didn't recognize either man. "Leroy?"

The man standing outside her door responded. "Leroy come later." He waved his hand in the air.

"Okay."

The man with the hammer smiled and turned back to the giant noisemaker.

"No, no, no! People are sleeping!"

"No do?"

Both men looked thoroughly confused.

Mary pointed to her wrist. "Time," she said. Then she placed both palms together and leaned them against the side of her head as if they were a pillow. "People are sleeping. I told Leroy he couldn't do this until after ten."

They exchanged glances before talking to each other in Spanish.

The same guy tried again. "We done ten."

"No. Start at ten." This wasn't working. She lifted both hands in the air. "Hold on. I'm calling Leroy."

Thankfully the man had his cell phone on him and answered immediately. "Leroy! What the heck."

"Wait, who is this?"

"It's Mary Kildare. There are two guys with a jackhammer waking up my neighbors."

"I told you we were taking the slab today."

"And I told you not to start until after ten."

"My crew has another job after yours."

It was too early for this. "Then send them to the other job first and come back here later."

"They can't. The other job has a baby in the house."

She wanted to scream. "My neighbors have babies. Leroy, this is not negotiable. I cannot have these guys making *this* kind of noise at *this* time in the morning. I'm in a condo with a shared wall!"

"That will delay us."

Mary pinched the bridge of her nose to keep from cussing. "How long?"

"I might be able to get the crew back there by Thursday."

"This is getting ridiculous."

"If they come on Thursday, I can get over there on Saturday—"

"Saturday does not work for me." And she didn't want him around on the weekend she was out of town. She couldn't stop him if he showed up with a jackhammer then.

"It's your floor. If the guys can't make it Thursday, they can be back Monday morning."

"Monday *afternoon!*"

"Right, your neighbors."

Mary handed the phone to one of the guys standing in her doorway and waited while he fired off Spanish and grumbled. When he hung up, she was relatively sure she was being cussed at and smiled at simultaneously.

With all the chaos of the morning, Mary found herself running out the door with coffee in her hand to make her first appointment. Once behind the wheel she twisted the key and heard her car protest. Unlike the night before, it gave up its complaining and turned over. But the muttering the thing was making reminded her of what she was supposed to be doing. And it wasn't fighting with the plumber.

To make matters worse, her first client of the day didn't show . . . and didn't call. She had a two-hour window of time between eleven and one. Mary thought for sure she'd be asking someone in the building to jump her car, but it finally turned over on the third try.

By three, the mechanic had called to say they couldn't get her car up to check out what was draining the battery until the morning. By three fifteen, Leroy called to say he would bust the floor on Monday . . . afternoon. Sarcasm and disapproval laced his message. By three thirty Mary was standing outside her building waiting for her Uber ride to show up and texting Dakota. `I'm coming over and I'm bringing wine.`

Dakota was quick on the reply. `That bad?`

The Uber driver pulled up and she jumped in the back. He repeated the address she'd already put in the system and she confirmed it before returning her attention to her phone. `You have no idea.`

Mary heard the friendly "come in" from the back of Dakota's place after her knock. "I'm back here."

Leo crying told her where Dakota was in the condo.

"Look who is awake." Mary smiled at the two of them. Dakota was in the process of changing a diaper, and Leo was in the process of waking the dead.

"He doesn't like his butt cold." Dakota smiled down at her baby. "And when Mommy changes your diaper, it's cold . . . isn't it?" Her voice raised an octave as most adults' did when talking to infants.

Mary peeked over Dakota's shoulder and smiled for the first time that day. "He's growing so fast."

Dakota taped down the edges of the diaper and tugged on his tiny pants. All of this she did with one hand while leaning against a crutch.

"Where's Walt?"

"I sent him to the store." Dakota backed away. "Why don't you hold him while I wash my hands."

Mary stilled and found her palms itchy. Why was she hesitating?

Dakota found her other crutch and made her way into the kitchen.

Mary squeezed her fists and approached her nephew. *Careful with his head.* He fussed as he kicked but settled almost immediately when she lifted him. He weighed next to nothing. She settled him into the crook of her arm. "How you doing, big boy?"

Leo blinked and stared as he quieted his cries.

Mary's crazy day floated away with a blink of a tiny baby's eyes. When Leo let out a peep, she found her body moving side to side, and the motion made him smile. "Not bad for a newbie, eh?" she whispered.

"It's about time," Dakota said from the other side of the room.

Mary glanced up to see her BFF staring at them. "What?"

"You do realize this is the first time you've held him."

Leo watched her with trust. "Actually, I think this is the first time I've *ever* held a baby." She knew it was. "Maybe I should sit down."

"You'd never drop him," Dakota told her.

Mary slowly let her butt reach the sofa.

Dakota slumped a little less gracefully in the chair beside them. "You've really never held a baby?"

"When would I have had the opportunity? I don't have siblings. I didn't go with you when your sister had her last one. I was raised by nuns . . . and they don't have babies . . . so Leo is my first."

"Leo is almost three weeks old, Mary. I was starting to worry."

Mary released the tractor beams of Leo's eyes and looked at her friend. "I was afraid I wouldn't like it."

"What's not to like? Except when he's puking on you, he's kinda cute."

Leo gripped her fingers with his whole hand. "He's still cute when he's puking on you."

Dakota snorted, but Mary knew she was kidding.

"It's not hard to figure out, Dakota. My parents abandoned me. I can't help but wonder if they just didn't want kids. Maybe they didn't have a nurturing gene. Maybe they passed that on to me."

"That's stupid."

"Not necessarily. Some studies show—"

"I'm calling bullshit."

"Hey, language," she teased.

Dakota waved a hand in the air. "He's too young to understand. You're full of crap."

Mary denied Dakota's observation.

"Oh, I'm sorry . . . what was it you did for a living again?" Dakota asked.

"Helping people sort out their problems is not the same as caring for a child."

"No, it's not. But you care by nature. You can't help but care. You just told me to watch my language because you care. You're one of the most nurturing people I know, so if you think for one minute you will be anything but the doting aunt Leo needs, then you have your brain in the sand."

Mary swung her head and let her hair dangle in Leo's face. He closed his eyes and let out a tiny gurgle. "I don't think my brain is in the sand. Do you think I have a sandy brain, Leo?"

Dakota sat back in her chair and put her blue leg up on the coffee table. "I should probably text Walt and let him know he can come home."

It took Mary a moment to catch Dakota's words. "I don't get it."

"When you said you were coming over I asked Walt to leave and not come back until I called."

"What, why?"

"Because you haven't held our son and I knew you'd bugger out of it if Walt was here to help me."

Mary narrowed her eyes. "That's one sneaky mom you have there, Leo. You're going to have to watch out for her."

Hours later, after a couple of glasses of wine and a lot of baby talk and girl talk, Mary meandered across the street to her taped-up living room and garage without a car. She went straight up to her bathroom and turned on the water in the tub.

Once she was comfortable, with the lights dim and another glass of wine in her hand . . . she dialed Glen's number.

His hello made her smile.

Chapter Fifteen

Mary packed way too much for a weekend in the city, but she'd rather have too many options than not enough. And with Glen as her tour guide, who knew where they'd end up or what they'd be doing.

She Ubered to the airport and was met by one of Glen's pilots, who took her bag and shuffled through security as if they were living pre-9/11.

On the plane, Mary used her time to catch up on some reading and take a nap. The sun set through the window at twentysomething thousand feet. She wasn't sure how this had become her life . . . but she didn't hate it. All that Catholic upbringing made her feel guilty, but she didn't dare pinch herself for fear she was dreaming.

When the plane landed, Mary expected to be shuttled on to the hotel Glen told her he'd acquired for her. Instead, Glen stood at the bottom of the stairs descending from the plane with his hands in his pockets and the wind blowing his hair.

She jogged down the last few steps and tossed her arms around him. She tilted her head toward his and greeted him with a kiss.

"Well, hello to you, too."

"I missed you. I probably shouldn't tell you that, but I did."

Glen kept an arm around her when the pilot exited the plane. "Thanks for getting her here safely, Freddy."

The pilot placed her bag on the tarmac and shook Glen's hand. "Anytime, Mr. Fairchild."

"Thank you," Mary added as Freddy started to walk away.

She tucked into Glen's side and faced the wind. "I feel like I should tip them or something."

Glen stumbled and started laughing. "Please don't start something everyone else will have to follow."

"But that was the fastest trip across the country I've ever had."

"It's the same amount of time in the air."

"Yeah, but there was no security, the plane took off almost the second I got on board. People would fly more often if it was always that easy."

Glen rolled her bag beside him as they walked off the tarmac and into the terminal.

Mary glanced around. "Wait, how did you get in here? I thought only ticketed passengers made it this far."

He squeezed her shoulders with one arm around her. "Did you have a ticket?"

"Oh." She hadn't thought of that. "You live a crazy life, Glen."

"Can't argue that." He kissed the top of her head, and if she wasn't mistaken, sniffed her hair before standing tall. "I missed you, too."

Glen drove a Land Rover.

The drive into Manhattan wasn't bad. It helped that it was on the tail end of rush hour.

"We have a suite at The Morrison," he told her.

"Shocking." Dakota's sarcasm was really rubbing off on her.

Glen grinned. "Have you met any of Monica's family?"

"Just you and your brothers last Thanksgiving."

He nodded and changed lanes . . . not that one did that in Manhattan so much as attempted suicide by moving the car over with a hand on the horn and one finger flying in the air. Glen managed without the finger.

"Once you've met the Morrisons, you'll understand why you can't stay at any other hotel if they have one where you're going. Have you ever been to the South?"

"Not really. I don't think the Florida conference last year is what you're talking about."

"No. I'm talking deep Texas. Georgia . . . the Carolinas?"

"Bucket list," Mary told him. "I haven't even been to Dakota's hometown." But then, up until this last year, Dakota had avoided it like fish avoid dry land.

"Hospitality. There is no other word for it. Every person I've met from the South is deeply offended if you don't take them up on the offer of accommodations or a meal."

"Are you sure they're not just being polite?"

"Deeply offended."

Mary always thought Dakota had been kidding about that Southern trait. "So if I took a trip to say . . . Seattle, and didn't ask Monica to hook me up, she'd be offended?"

"Ah, no. Monica would completely understand. But after you meet her sister, Jessie, or more importantly Jessie's extended family, the Morrisons . . . oh, yeah. Offended might be an understatement."

"So I'm staying at The Morrison."

He huffed out a laugh. "You catch on quick."

The Morrison overlooked Central Park. The corner suite had a central living space complete with a living room, dining room, and kitchenette. Mary was drawn to the window the moment she walked through the door. "Wow! What a view."

Glen rolled her bag into a separate bedroom. "You're in here," he told her.

She did a tiny spin and took in the sleek gray tones of the space. An expansive marble entry melted into a plush Berber carpet. The splash of color came from the dark plum sofa and accents on the dining room chairs. Three oval glass chandeliers illuminated the ceiling. It was modern and very New York. "Where's your room?"

He pointed to a closed door on the other side of the living room. "Door locks on this side."

"You're very thoughtful."

"I'm a thoughtful kinda guy. Now grab your purse, I'm starving."

"I had a little something on the plane."

He grabbed her hand. "Then you can grab a little more something here."

She snagged her purse, which she'd just left on a hall table, as he dragged her away from the room. "You're pushy."

"I'm thoughtful and a pushy kinda guy. Especially when I'm hungry."

They rode the elevator holding hands.

When they exited the hotel, Glen held her hand tighter.

"What are you in the mood for?"

The beauty of New York City was that you could walk two blocks in any direction and find the flavors of the entire world, or close to it.

"I'm not the hungry one."

He ignored her and rambled off their options. "Burgers?"

She shook her head.

"Chinese or Thai . . . Korean barbeque?"

"Salty."

"Deli . . . maybe tomorrow for lunch," he suggested. "Fish tacos?"

"You pick," she said.

"There's a great Italian place around the corner. Pizza?"

"Ohhh, pizza."

Glen pulled her in a circle and started walking the other direction. "Pizza it is."

Mary sat back, holding her stomach, after eating not one, but two pieces of the giant pizza filled with dough, sauce, and cheese cooked to perfection. "You're trying to make me fat."

Glen was tearing into his third slice. "You eat like a bird."

She tapped a finger on her empty plate.

"Well, maybe not with pizza," he said with a wink.

The tiny pizza joint was loud and crazy busy. They'd ordered at the counter and brought their box to a small table by the window. They classed it up by drinking wine from a screw-cap bottle.

She pushed her paper plate aside, rested her chin in her hands and her elbows on the table. "Have you ever done this before?"

He had just opened his mouth to take another bite. "Eaten pizza in New York? Yeah, all the time." Glen shoved a fourth of the thing in his mouth.

"No. Not the pizza. Dated someone who lived on the West Coast?"

He finished chewing, picked up the red and white checkered napkin, and wiped his mouth. "Hmm, uh, no. Well, not as far as California."

She made a little rolling motion with her hands.

"What?"

"How far have you gone for a date?"

He stared up at the ceiling before waving his pizza in the air. "France." He popped more sauce, cheese, and dough into his mouth.

"France is farther than California."

Glen was not going to give up his meal for the conversation. "You asked how far I flew for a date," he said around his food. Talking with your mouth full was usually a complete turnoff for Mary, but Glen was the poster child for cute doing it. "That would be France. Dated . . . as in more than one date . . . Detroit."

"So you flew to France to get laid and Detroit for a relationship."

He cocked his head and stopped chewing when he took in her words. His slow nod of acknowledgment was followed by him shoving pizza in his mouth.

"What happened between you and Miss Detroit?"

He held his pizza but didn't bite this time. "Miss Detroit, as you call her, came from money . . . I thought great, someone who has it won't be using me to get mine."

"I guess that isn't how that turned out."

He waved his pizza. "Daddy was cutting her off." He took a bite.

He left the part that she was searching for someone else to support her unsaid.

"What about Miss France?"

He finished chewing, chased his food with cheap wine. "That was just fun."

Mary knew her eyes were wide.

"We both knew it was for fun," he quickly explained.

"Oh."

"Have you ever done that?"

"Flown to France for fun? Ah, no."

He smiled. "Flown, drove . . . taken a walk, just for the fun?"

Inside she cringed. She'd been asking personal questions, and Glen had answered with sincerity . . . she should probably follow his lead.

"College . . . once. It didn't work out well and I couldn't bring myself to do it again."

"So what was wrong with Mr. College?"

Mary tipped back the last of the wine. "I was seeing someone from my modern lit class . . . it wasn't serious . . . just college, ya know?"

"I went to college." His smile told her he had all kinds of knowledge on the subject.

"One day Mr. College came along . . . asked me out. I was interested, but I put him off."

"Because of Mr. Modern Lit?"

She shrugged. "Because I'd never dated two different guys at the same time. Eventually my girlfriends were in my face about how if Modern Lit and I didn't have a conversation about exclusivity, then why was I treating our time together as exclusive. Then they went on about how did I know if Modern Lit wasn't dating other girls. After all, we were in college."

"So you listened to the girls and went out with Mr. College."

"I did. Mr. College and I went out for fun, as you say it. Don't look so impressed," she teased. "It didn't end well."

"So what happened?"

She could almost see the inside of her dorm when she repeated the series of terrible events.

"Mr. College was leaving my dorm and Modern Lit was surprising me with Starbucks."

"Oh, that's bad."

"It was awful. In the end I didn't end up with either guy and didn't date for close to a year." She shivered. "Ugh!"

"I take it Modern Lit thought you were an item."

"Yeah."

"And Mr. College was . . . you were too much trouble for his time."

"That about nails it."

"So how is it you still like surprises after that?"

Good question. "I drank the Starbucks. It wasn't the coffee's fault I got caught in the walk of shame."

—

Mary was not wearing a coat suitable for an early spring night in New York. Glen kept his arm around her as they quickly walked back to the hotel.

The minute they reached the room, he took the phone and ordered room service. "Red or white?" he asked her.

"Stick with red."

"Chocolate, fruit, cheesecake, or ice cream?"

Mary shook her head. "I'll have a bite of yours."

She didn't pay attention to his glare and didn't answer his question. When room service answered his call, he ordered a bottle of merlot and then started ordering dessert. "We'd also like a slice of that triple chocolate cake and your chocolate covered strawberries . . . you have cheesecake, right?"

"Of course, Mr. Fairchild. Plain or with a fruit topping?"

"Plain . . . and do you have ice cream?"

"What are you doing?" Mary stepped in front of him, hands on her hips.

Glen simply smiled. "You didn't tell me what you wanted so I'll order it all."

Mary snagged the phone from his hand. "We'll take the chocolate covered strawberries. Only the strawberries."

"And the chocolate cake," Glen told her.

"And the cake," she told the attendant. "No, we don't need the cheesecake or the ice cream. The wine and two desserts will be plenty. Thank you."

He really did like getting his way.

"You're a brat."

"I am," he admitted. "And you're stubborn."

She grabbed her purse, muttered something under her breath, and walked into her bedroom. "I'll be right back."

Glen opened the blinds to take in the New York skyline.

When Mary returned from her room, she had twisted her hair back in one of those twists women do and shed her shoes. The fact she was relaxed enough to dress down in front of him had him smiling on the inside. A woman working hard to impress would have left the room to put on more makeup or slip into something sexy. If he was being honest with himself, he'd say he wouldn't mind the sexy on Mary.

"You do know you're staring," she said.

He'd be doing more than staring if he wasn't worried about blowing it. "You're easy to stare at." And Mary was surprisingly easy to fluster.

She moved to the window and turned her back to his stare. "This doesn't get old."

His gaze lingered on her before turning to the view beyond the room. "It makes the long elevator rides to the top floors worth it."

"Sounds like such a hardship," she teased.

"It is when the elevators break down."

She glanced over her shoulder. "And how often does that really happen?"

He couldn't remember . . . "It could happen."

Mary turned back to the view. "I'll take my chances for the view."

A knock on the door brought with it their nightcap and dessert.

A middle-aged balding man wearing a crisp white jacket and a smile delivered room service. After removing the lids from the food, he asked, "Would you like me to open the wine, Mr. Fairchild?"

"I'll take care of it." Glen tipped the man and thanked him.

He watched Mary from the corner of his eye. She was already checking out the food. Glen couldn't wait for her to dig in so he could tease the crap out of her.

"Those strawberries look good," he said as he twisted the cork out of the bottle of wine.

She snapped her gaze back to the lights outside. "Do they?"

He bit his lip to keep from laughing. Instead of taking the wine to her, he brought the open bottle and two glasses to the sofa before he poured. "How are Dakota and Walt doing with parenthood?"

His question brought her attention back into the room.

"They're a good team." She sat and accepted the glass of wine.

"When does she get that cast off?"

"Another couple of weeks. Poor thing." Mary sipped her wine and sat back. "Leo is adorable."

"Sounds like someone's clock is ticking."

Mary nearly choked on her wine. She leaned forward and coughed, holding the wine away from her to avoid spilling it. "God, no."

That was not the reaction he'd expected. "You okay?"

Mary ran her thumb under her lips and licked the end of it. "You obviously know little if you think my clock is ticking."

Now this he needed to hear. He'd yet to meet a woman pushing thirty who didn't have a ticking biological clock.

He took the plate of strawberries sitting on the table and set it between them before handing her a napkin. "Enlighten me."

Mary set her wine down and busied her hands with the napkin. "I don't plan on having kids."

"I don't think Dakota and Walt planned anything."

Mary didn't look at him while she spoke. Instead she removed one of the strawberries and examined it. "Let me rephrase. I'm not going to have children." She bit into the strawberry. The moan of pleasure almost distracted him from the conversation. Almost.

"How can you be so sure?" He'd heard some of his male friends say they didn't want to be dads, but he couldn't remember one woman saying the same thing with as much conviction as Mary.

"I never played with dolls. Didn't babysit as a teenager. I think babies are cute but when I see them I don't have any desire for one of my own. All the signs point to me not wanting a child. Heck, I didn't even pick up Leo until yesterday." She popped the rest of the strawberry in her mouth and set the stem on the plate.

"Our house didn't have dolls to play with and no parent in their right mind would have wanted me to babysit for them. Babies are adorable and I've never held Leo . . . but that doesn't mean I won't want to be a dad at some point." He hated that her conviction was so absolute. Any other woman and he'd be all *one less thing to worry about.*

Mary lifted another strawberry from the plate. "I wouldn't be a good mother."

"How can you possibly know that?"

"Genetics." She bit another strawberry in half before chasing it with wine.

So this was about her being abandoned. He wasn't about to argue the point that she could be the complete opposite of her biological parents. He simply sat on the information and watched her eat.

He brought the slice of cake from the table to the space next to what was left of the strawberries and set a fork on Mary's side of the plate before taking a bite. "I think I'd be the cool dad."

She smiled. "How so?"

He'd always pictured his kids in the copilot seat with big grins and complete control. He envisioned Christmas morning playing with Legos and family vacations to Disney World. "I like thrill rides," he abbreviated his thoughts. "Parenting will be one giant roller coaster."

Mary pointed a fork filled with cake in his direction. "That's if you have sons. How much thrill will there be when you're chasing away the boys from your daughter . . . boys that are a whole lot like you?"

His cake caught in his throat.

Mary laughed. "That's what I thought."

"I'm not that bad."

"I'm sure you were a saint as a teenager chasing girls."

She had his number. "I'm still a saint chasing girls."

Mary was laughing again and attempting to keep food in her mouth. "You are destined for daughters. Be prepared."

"I think you just jinxed me."

She took another bite. "I think I did."

He waited until her mouth was full to ask, "So is it good? Li'l Miss *I'm Too Full.*"

Mary pushed the plate to his side of the sofa. "It's awful." She licked her fork with the tip of her tongue. Thoughts of teenage daughters chasing away boys disappeared and all Glen saw was something else on the tip of Mary's tongue.

"Lucky fork." The words slipped out of his mouth before he could stop them.

Chapter Sixteen

Mary was convinced that Glen was not going to make a move.

He'd held her hand, bundled her close walking on the cool New York streets . . . he offered a warm welcome, poured her wine, and watched her eat strawberries like a porn star, but he was not inching closer.

She kept eyeing the closed door to the room he was supposed to sleep in with remorse.

For all the playing Glen had under his reputation, he was not playing her.

Maybe it was her.

Maybe he was studying for a new reputation and she was the control group.

A tiny voice said in a whispered shout, *maybe he's trying to be a gentleman.*

The tiny voice suddenly had a devil's smile. *Maybe you should make the first move.*

Mary wondered if Dakota had sent the message subliminally.

He'd brushed off his *lucky fork* comment and put the dishes back on the service cart and refilled their wine.

"Someone got very quiet," he said when he sat back down.

The wine was making her dizzy, but it didn't stop her from taking another sip. "This is good."

"So you're sitting there contemplating the wine?"

"Nope." She shook her head and gathered her courage. "I'm contemplating something else."

He leaned back with such ease, his wineglass dangled from his fingers and a smile inched up from the corners of his mouth. "Are you going to tell me?"

She took another sip. "I'm considering that option."

"Now you have me very curious."

Make a move!

"I'm wondering . . ." She forced her eyes to his. "I'm wondering if I should go to bed or force you to take me to yours."

The smile on his lips moved to his eyes as he met her admission with a moment of silence. "Force me?" The question slowly rolled from his tongue in amusement.

That was not the word she'd meant to use. "Forget I said that."

Glen started shaking his head. "Uh-uh . . . can't do that. I would really like to see what Mary forcing me to take her to bed looks like." He was still sitting back against the sofa, completely relaxed, while she was starting to tap her foot against the floor.

Mary wanted to channel her best friend right at that moment in the worst way. Dakota would know exactly what to do with a challenge like that, where Mary sat there and ate her words.

"Lose your nerve?" he teased.

"I'm thinking!" she snapped.

Glen sipped his wine and watched her.

"You're enjoying this."

"I am."

"I never make the first move." Why did she tell him that?

Glen said nothing.

She set her wineglass down and stood.

"Giving up?" he asked.

It was her turn to be silent. She reached for the top button on her shirt and pushed it through the hole.

Glen's eyes dropped to her hand.

She undid the second button, and Glen's grin turned into an open mouthed stare.

Mary pushed part of her shirt to the side and traced the edges of her bra before sliding away another notch.

Glen set his wine down when she reached the last button.

When she started to slide the shirt from her shoulders, Glen stood and grasped her hand.

Without words, he placed her head in his palms and kissed her. It wasn't slow, it wasn't hello . . . or even a good night. This was the kind of kiss that moved to something completely different. His lips were open and hungry.

Mary braced herself by placing her palms on his chest and holding on.

He tilted his head and enveloped her. Their tongues danced and Mary's body swayed into his for full contact. The roughness of his shirt against the bare skin of her chest had her fingers searching for his buttons. While she searched for more skin, with their lips fused together, Glen's hands slid down her back and over the globe of her bottom with a gentle squeeze. She saw stars. The simple touch was so welcome, so desired, her body scattered like rain being shaken off a dog in a storm.

She heard herself moan as she slid a button loose and moved to another.

Glen released her lips, gasped for air, and took them again.

Finally, she found his chest, his shirt slid from his shoulders, and she examined by braille. He was the most sculpted man she'd ever touched. For the amount of food the man ate, he should have held on to a few undesirable pounds. But no, he didn't.

She let her fingernails scrape over his shoulders and down his spine.

Glen rewarded her with a quick tug closer.

Mary felt her nipples harden and felt everything south open for more. Her body needed attention, needed Glen's attention. She released hold of his chest and reached around to unclasp her bra.

Through Glen's assault of her lips, he batted her hand away and did the job for her. He caught one breast in his hand and finally let her breathe.

With one hand around her waist, he bent her back and took her tight nipple in his mouth.

"Oh, Glen." Stars . . . there were so many stars. Her legs started to lose the ability to hold her up and her senses united with one purpose.

"Beautiful," he mumbled as he moved to her other breast.

He caught her when her legs gave way. Had she ever lost control like this? She knew the answer but couldn't concentrate on the question for more than a fraction of a second.

The man was good . . . so good at finding the right pressure, the right touch. Glen spun her around and in two steps had her back on the couch and his fingers working the clasp of her slacks. She lifted for him, felt cool air and his hot stare when she kicked her pants free.

Mary watched his eyes as she traced the inside of her thigh with one polished nail. He moaned, said something she didn't quite catch, and dropped to his knees. Like with the removal of her bra, he batted her hand aside from her thigh and replaced it with his tongue. Her hips lifted from the couch with a mind of their own.

Lovely agony described his touch. She wanted more, but didn't want this to stop. If this was what making love to a player was like, sign her up. Every touch was urgent and desired but nothing was rushed to the point of being forgotten. Her lips throbbed from his kiss, her nipples ached for more attention, and her core cried for his touch.

Mary yelped when he nibbled the inside of her thigh hard enough to leave a mark. She wanted to protest, but the stubble on his chin rubbed the burn away and his breath warmed the space between her legs. Even with her panties on, she thought he was going to offer some relief, but no . . . the man moved to her other thigh.

She raised a limp hand to the side of his face and helped him focus on what she needed.

Glen chuckled. "What do you want, Mary?"

The man was the devil. "I swear on all that's sacred, if you don't touch me . . ."

He continued to chuckle.

She braved an open eye and found him staring. "Glen!" Her voice gave warning, and thankfully, he wasn't going to make her beg.

He traced the back of a finger against her thigh and lightly petted her through the cotton layer of her panties. Her body shuddered. There was no way Glen could know how easily she orgasmed, but he was about to find out. "Take them off," she told him, no humor in her words.

"Demanding," he said with a smile in his voice.

Her hips arched, and he tugged the tiny fabric away.

"Mmm," he hummed as he leaned in.

Mary closed her eyes and waited.

His breath against her core had her wrapping one leg over his back and one hand fanning through his hair. Mary opened for him and arched, and he was there.

There was heat, and his tongue, and a gentle nip of his teeth, and Mary lost it.

She heard her own cries and couldn't bring herself to care who heard them.

Glen rode her orgasm with her until the stars stopped spinning and simply sparkled in the sky.

"Good Lord, woman."

"Loud? Sorry . . ." She wasn't. Sorry . . . she wasn't sorry.

Glen smiled up at her as he clasped her hips and tugged her farther down on the couch. "Now that we have the first one out of the way . . ."

"Someone needs to get naked." She leaned over and pushed her hands in the waistband of his pants and found his erection.

He leaned his head against hers and pushed into her hands.

Mary tried to wiggle out from under him. "Let me," she said as they changed positions.

Glen stood long enough to remove everything. His erection invited her to touch. So she did.

He'd freed his wallet before his pants hit the ground and flipped it open.

Mary took the condom from him and tore the wrapper open. She pushed him onto his back and in two strokes had him covered.

She liked this part. Where her body said, *yes, please, can we do that again, only this time with more depth?*

Mary kissed her way up his chest, lingered on the throbbing pulse of his neck, before reaching for his lips.

Glen lifted her hips and placed her over his erection.

She moaned, broke from his kiss. "Please," she whispered.

He pushed forward, slowly. His guttural sigh told her how much he enjoyed the feeling as he sank into her.

She kissed him while they found their pace. With the edge off, she could go farther. When she felt him pushing harder, she shifted position and took him deeper. Glen's palms grasped her breasts as if they controlled everything.

Mary clenched every muscle she had and heard Glen respond with an expletive.

She wanted to cuss herself. Instead, she tightened and took everything he wanted to give. And when she knew he was close, could tell from how tight he held his breath, how stern his jaw clenched, she brought her hands to his, which held her breasts and squeezed. He took her hint and pinched her nipples . . . and Mary found her release.

Glen had no choice but to follow.

—

She collapsed on top of him, her breath a rapid fire in his ear. This was not the woman he'd expected.

"We didn't make it to a bed." Mary giggled as she spoke.

"I'm surprised we made it to the couch."

She lifted her head and smiled down at him. He kept one arm around her waist and pushed some of the hair that had escaped the clip out of her eyes. "That was . . ."

"It sure was!" Mary's smile reminded him of the sweet woman he'd been dating, the body squirming on top of him reminded him of every fantasy he'd ever had rolled into one. "I was too loud."

"Never."

"We're in a hotel, people could have heard me."

"Who cares? Besides, I liked it." *Loved it! Wanted to record it and listen to it repeatedly!*

Her cheeks started to warm. "I don't have a lot of control."

"I noticed." He traced one of her cheeks with the pad of his thumb. "Why didn't you tell me you were fire in bed?"

She did a little eye roll and made herself more comfortable. "How would I have brought that up in casual conversation?"

"Oh, I don't know . . . 'Hey, Glen, I'm a wildcat in between the sheets. Prepare to have your mind blown.' That would work."

Mary squeezed her eyes shut. "Wildcat and mind-blowing are not words I'd use."

He slid one hand over her ass and gripped it until she opened her eyes. "I would," he said.

"Well, then . . ." She straightened her back, their bodies still intimately close. "It may take a little time to get me here, but once I am, I enjoy it."

"It?" he teased with a shift of his hips.

Her eyes widened. "Sex. I enjoy sex."

So did he, but this felt like more. "I think this is going to work out very well for both of us then."

Mary released the clip from her hair and let her curls roll over her shoulder. "I hope you're not tired."

"Never."

They didn't get out of the hotel room until afternoon the next day. Housekeeping would probably weep when they saw the suite, and the guests on either side would probably ask to switch rooms.

For the first time in what felt like forever, Mary didn't care. She was sore and relaxed at the same time. They left the hotel in search of food, both of them wearing grins the size of Texas.

The cold wind zapped her the second they stepped out of the hotel.

"I thought it would be warmer."

Glen signaled for a cab instead of taking the slow route. "We need to get you a coat."

"I brought a sweater."

Glen kissed her temple before opening the back door of the car. "That's cute."

They got out a few blocks later at Saks.

Mary couldn't remember if she'd ever walked into the department store, let alone bought anything there.

A doorman welcomed them inside and several painted-on faces smiled at them as they passed the cosmetic counters. An elevator took them to the desired floor where plenty of warm coats filled the racks.

Glen went straight to a designer label and removed a three-quarter-length wool coat. "Try this."

She didn't see a price tag but slid her arms into it anyway. "It's heavy."

He winked. "You're in New York."

Mary faced the mirror and did a little turn. How often would she wear it? One look at Glen and she hoped it would be often.

She tried on two more before finding the prefect fit and length. Mary removed it and searched for a price tag. When she found it, she thought for certain there was a misprint on the tag. "Glen?" She waved him over from another rack he was looking for her size in. He placed both hands on her shoulders and looked at the coat from behind her. "Does that say what I think it says?"

"Huh. Yeah, I think so."

Mary promptly put the coat back on the hanger and placed it back on the rack. "We're leaving."

Glen removed the coat when she twisted away. "Good, I'm hungry."

She stopped and pointed. "Glen!"

"It fits, you like it."

She stepped closer and lowered her voice. "I like the coat, not the price. I'll be fine."

He slung his arm over her shoulders and spoke close to her ear. "I'm all about chivalry, but it's butt cold out there, and I like my coat."

About that moment, an employee approached them with a careful smile and perfectly pressed clothes. "Did you find what you're looking for?" she asked.

Glen said yes when Mary said no.

The clerk batted her eyelashes and smiled toward Glen. He handed the lady the coat. "We'll take this."

Mary pinched his ass. "Glen," she warned under her breath.

"You're cute when you snarl."

Panic gripped her chest when the employee stepped behind a register and started ringing up the sale. Mary's lips were touching his ear. "I can't afford it."

He returned the lip to ear favor. "You're not paying for it."

The panic started to spread. "Glen, no. I can't accept that."

"You can. You just say thank you."

"Glen!"

The clerk smiled at them as if she saw this kind of under-the-breath argument daily.

Glen placed a finger in the air and turned his back to the employee. "Listen. I didn't tell you to bring a winter coat. It's my fault you're not prepared."

"It's not winter. I should have checked the weather report."

"I did check the weather report and didn't think to tell you. My fault, therefore I pay for the coat." His hand reached for his wallet.

She wanted to tell him she'd pay him back, but she knew a two-thousand-dollar coat was way outside of her budget. "I'm going to spank you for this."

He did one of those once-overs men did and winked. "Is that a promise?"

"Oh, God."

Glen laughed, turned, and handed the employee his credit card.

Snuggled into a coat that cost half of what her plumbing problem set her back, Mary walked beside Glen as they left the store. They stepped just outside the door when she swung around and clasped Glen's face with both hands. She kissed him hard, and when she pulled away, she said, "Thank you."

The doorman cleared his throat, bringing their attention to the fact that there were people behind them wanting to exit the building.

Glen put his now familiar arm over her shoulder and walked her toward their lunch.

And when he wasn't expecting it, Mary slapped his ass once . . . just because she told him she would.

Chapter Seventeen

"I can't believe you're here." Monica greeted Mary with a hug. "Why didn't you tell us you were bringing Mary?" The question was aimed at Glen.

Mary assumed they were going to be leaving the hotel for the black-tie event, but instead they took an elevator ride to one of the ballrooms at The Morrison, where guests had just started to arrive.

Glen gave a quick hug to his sister-in-law, saying, "No one asked."

Trent leaned in and kissed Mary's cheek. "Hi, Mary."

"You remember, Jason, right?" Glen asked.

Glen's older brother stood beside his siblings, wearing a similar smile and the same broad shoulders. Mary couldn't imagine the trouble these three had managed when they were younger. "Of course I remember Jason." She hugged him. "How are you?"

"Stressed, overworked, you know . . . the usual."

"Tell your boss you need a vacation," Trent teased.

"Bite me."

Mary loved the banter between the brothers. "So is this a Fairchild Charters function?" she asked.

Monica exchanged looks with her. "Didn't Glen tell you what this is all about?"

Mary shook her head, careful not to move it too fast or undo what the hairdresser at the hotel took thirty minutes to put up.

"It's a giant schmooze-fest," Trent said under his breath.

Jason nudged the youngest Fairchild. "We hold an annual black-tie dinner for our premier clients. Both those whose jets we charter and those who travel with our service."

Glen went on to say, "For the past several years we hold the event here at The Morrison and combine our efforts and *schmoozing*, as Trent put it, with The Morrison's elite clientele."

"There will be a lot of networking going on between these walls tonight," Jason said.

"There will be a lot of drinking," Monica added.

"And that."

Mary looked around the massive hall. "Does that mean your sister will be here?" she asked Monica.

"Jessie and Jack should be here any minute."

"Good, I can finally meet her."

Monica looped her arm between Mary's. "I'm stealing your date," she told Glen. "Let's go find Katie."

"Who's Katie?"

"Katelyn Morrison Prescott. She puts all this together."

Mary glanced over her shoulder as she walked away from Glen and his brothers. His reassuring wink told her he was watching.

The second they were away from the men, Monica leaned close. "So how are things going with you two?"

Mary squeezed the other woman's arm. "I'm having the best time."

—

"You're looking awfully content, Glen." The comment came from Jason's mouth.

"Well, look at her. Wouldn't you be?"

Jason watched the two women walking away. "She's beautiful, I'll give you that."

"So what's it been, a month now?" Trent asked.

"About."

"What's your track record, three?"

Glen wasn't liking where the conversation was headed. "I'm not that bad."

Both his brothers laughed.

He couldn't tell them things were different with Mary without a dump truck full of feedback, so he kept his thoughts to himself.

"Don't we have some schmoozing to do?" He tugged on the cuffs of his shirt so they peeked from under the long sleeves of his tuxedo.

She was a beacon in a sea of beautiful people. It helped that she stood slightly taller than many of the women in the room, and that amazing head of hair that sat on top of her head was second to nobody in attendance. Glen spotted her the second he lifted his eyes above the crowd. She'd been away from his side for less than twenty minutes and he was slowly working his way back.

He was half listening to Chuck and Mr. Widden, a man who chartered several flights a month for his financial firm.

"With the market so damn fragile, I'm surprised any of us are doing a damn thing." Mr. Widden's words half registered.

"I know . . ." Looked like Jay, the newest senior broker, was stepping into the conversation with Monica and Katie. "If you'll excuse me." Glen didn't wait for approval before leaving the conversation.

All Glen heard was laughter . . . Mary's laughter, when he approached the small party. Jay saw him approach first and stood a little taller.

Glen did something he seldom did. He took the space beside Mary and Monica and slid an arm around Mary's waist. "There you are."

She did a little take back and grinned.

"Hello, Katie."

Katie Prescott, or Katelyn Morrison, as the majority of the room knew her, was a true debutante. Her porcelain skin and designer everything always turned heads when she entered the room. The six-inch stilettos that were an extension of her already model-long legs helped her stand above many of the men in attendance. She pushed in and kissed his cheek. "You bear! Where have you been hiding Mary? She's delightful."

"Mary keeps herself in California."

Glen extended a hand to Jay. "Glad you could come, Jay."

"Even if it was an option, I wouldn't miss this." Jay glanced between Glen and Mary and excused himself. Message sent, and message received. Glen felt like he could take a deep breath. "What are you ladies drinking?"

"Something white," Mary said.

Katie shook her head. "I'm waiting for dinner."

"Not me, I'll take a white wine, too."

Glen looked around the room and signaled a waiter with a tray filled with glasses of wine.

A commotion that could only be created by someone with celebrity status focused their attention to the front of the room.

"Oh, Daddy."

The larger-than-life Texan was a man Glen had never seen without his Stetson or his confidence. Gaylord Morrison was a force, a man he'd met briefly when his father was still alive and had come to know even more with Trent's marriage to Monica. The world of money was smaller than one would think.

Katie lifted a hand in the air and grabbed her father's attention.

Gaylord patted backs, smiled, and wove his way through the crowd. When he reached his daughter's side he lifted her clean off the ground. "Look at my baby girl."

Katie tolerated his attention and adjusted her dress when her feet touched down.

"Really, Daddy!"

"Where is your husband?" Gaylord asked.

"Dean was meeting Jack and Jessie in the lobby."

Gaylord turned his attention to Glen and quickly skipped over to Mary. "And who do we have here, Glen?"

"Mr. Morrison, I'd like you to meet Mary Kildare. Mary, this is the iconic Gaylord Morrison."

"Iconic? Good Lord, man, you make me sound old." Gaylord laughed and tilted his hat in Mary's direction.

"I've heard a lot about you," Mary told him.

"You have me at a disadvantage."

"Daddy, behave," Katie scolded.

"Monica and I are friends."

Gaylord glanced beyond their heads. "Where is our resident nurse?"

"She's around here somewhere," Katie told him.

"Such a sassy one, Monica. You." He looked directly at Mary. "You look about as innocent as they come."

Glen couldn't help but think of the moments before they'd dressed for dinner . . . the shower . . . her screams.

"You can't always judge a book by its cover," Mary told him.

Glen let his fingers dig into her waist and she smiled up at him.

Gaylord nodded his head once. "Probably a good thing you have some fire behind you, dating this one." He pointed at Glen.

"I'm not sure if that's a compliment."

"I'm not sure either," Gaylord told him.

Before anyone could comment further on Gaylord's assessment of Glen's character, the rest of the Morrison clan joined them.

Glen made the introductions.

Jessie hugged her like they knew each other. "Monica has told me all about you."

Mary told Jessie nearly the same thing and the conversation spun around to Dakota and Walt . . . How was the baby? And how was Dakota doing with a broken leg?

It didn't take long for the waitstaff to shuffle the party into the dining room that seated close to three hundred guests. A podium sat on a small stage with a single microphone.

Once everyone was seated, Jason and Gaylord moved to the podium to welcome their guests. Luckily Jason wasn't a rambler of bullshit, and Gaylord always had a way to cut to the chase.

Jason started before dinner was served. "On behalf of my brothers and everyone at Fairchild Charters, we want to thank you all for continuing to call on us when you need to fly. I'll skip the PR portion of my speech and suggest everyone drink up and enjoy the evening."

Glen leaned over to whisper in Mary's ear. "Always had a way with words, that one."

Gaylord took the podium. "Not a bad looking group we have here."

The audience laughed.

"Years ago when Jason's father and I met . . . I remember a bottle of Kentucky bourbon being involved . . . we both brought out our phones to show off the faces of our children. It didn't occur to either of us to bring our client pool together. It took those young children to find lives of their own to bring the idea to fruition." Gaylord slapped a meaty palm to Jason's shoulder. "Your father would be proud of all of you."

Jason nodded his thanks.

"Now I had some Texas beef flown in for this shindig, so eat up. Those of you who ordered the fish . . ." He shrugged. "Can't help you there."

The applause was minimal and the waiters descended on the room with the first course.

The tables where the Fairchilds and the Morrisons sat were spread among their guests. This was an event to make the customers feel special, not for the families to pull into themselves and ignore everyone else.

Still, Glen had a hard time concentrating on anyone other than Mary.

Their table was a mix of business executives and their wives or dates. It wasn't uncommon for Glen's table to house a bachelor or two, but nearly no one arrived at this event dateless. The bachelors seldom returned with the same date unless they were on the fast track to remove their bachelor status.

Hugh Darnell sat beside his flavor of the year. He'd started dating women who had sleek black hair and olive skin and who wouldn't be caught eating pizza in public. Glen never did understand the pencil thin look, but Hugh leaned that way. Glen didn't bother putting to memory the name of Hugh's date. He was talking with the Lowtons, the token married couple at the table, about his dot-com, which he'd created in the frenzy and managed to keep relevant and lucrative ever since. Hugh's date looked bored with the conversation and started talking fashion with Irvin Murray's date . . . someone who Glen had met one time before . . . but her name still evaded him.

At one point during the meal Mary leaned close so only he could hear her. "How well do you know these people?"

"The Lowtons did business with my father. Hugh's been a client for half a dozen years now . . . new money, spends it, and isn't afraid of sharing it either. He's generous with his executive management. Charters planes for his team constantly."

"I would think most of the people in this room would do that."

Glen did a quick shake of his head. "Businessmen are the worst about sharing. Our celebrities and sports figures, they share and play often."

Mary reached for her wine and spoke over the rim of her glass. "What about Irvin?"

"Don't know him well. Trust fund," he said, as if that explained everything.

"What about Delilah?"

"Who?"

Mary nudged her head to the opposite side of the table. "Hugh's date."

"Never saw her before."

The waiters moved around the table removing salad plates and replacing them with the main course.

"And Pnina?"

Glen made the deduction that Pnina had to be Irvin's date.

"We've met, but I don't know her."

"Hmm."

From what Glen could tell, Mary was deducting things inside her head with the little bit of information he'd given her. He wanted to quiz her on her observations but knew that would have to wait until those he wanted to talk about were more than a dinner plate away.

"Is your therapist hat on?" he asked.

"Is it ever off?"

Yes, he wanted to tell her . . . when she was in bed.

Dinner felt like it took forever to get through. Once the plates were cleared, Glen took the liberty to excuse both himself and Mary from the table with the ploy that he needed to introduce Mary to a few people. He did make a show of stopping at Jason's table, where some of the guests were already up and mingling before the second half of the evening took place. The stop was brief before Glen pulled Mary to an outside patio.

The cold instantly slapped him in the face.

"What are we doing out here?" she asked, folding her arms around herself.

Glen answered her question with his lips.

Mary answered back.

Chapter Eighteen

Dinner moved on to dancing and a raffle.

Mary watched the rich and famous elbow rub. She'd been dragged from Glen's side a couple of times by either Monica or her sister, Jessie. As Glen had told her, the Morrisons were some of the kindest people she'd ever met. And yes, Gaylord made it very clear that she'd best not even think to stay in a hotel that didn't have his name on it unless she was in a remote part of the world where he didn't have a hotel. "There's always empty rooms, so don't feel like you're putting anyone out."

Glen swept her onto the dance floor twice, then said he needed to put some distance between them unless he wanted to end the evening too quickly or embarrass himself with a teenage hard-on all night.

Just after midnight they made their way to the room, made it as far as the door to Mary's room before clothes started falling like rain on a Seattle night.

Later, Mary laid her head on Glen's bare chest, one leg draped over his. "We didn't cut out too soon, did we?" she asked.

"We cut out just in time."

She let her eyes drift closed. "You have a wonderful family. I don't want to offend them."

"You don't have to worry about things like that."

Mary's eyes opened with his words. Did she not have to worry because her time in his life was limited? Offending his family, his colleagues, didn't matter if she wouldn't be around next year during this event?

Enjoy the moment, Mary.

—

The sound of her cell phone, plugged in on her side of the bed, pulled her from her sleep.

Glen rolled to his side and laid an arm around her bare waist.

Her cell rang again and had her wiping her eyes into focus. The blackout curtains in the room did a great job of hiding the time. It was after eight but felt like the middle of the night.

"Hello?" Her voice sounded as foggy as her head.

"Mary? Hey, it's Dakota."

"I recognize your voice . . . is everything okay? It's early there."

"Who is it?" Glen asked with one eye open.

"It's Dakota."

"Hmm . . ." Glen closed his eye to match the other and swept her hips closer to his.

"Is that Glen?" Dakota asked.

"Yes, Captain Obvious. We aren't out of bed yet . . . late night. If this is a social call, I'll call you in a couple of hours." Mary switched the phone to the other hand. "Dakota?"

"Sorry . . . no, uh, it's not, social. Not a social call."

Mary leaned up on one arm and attempted to wake up. "What's up?"

"I'm not sure how to say this." Dakota's voice wavered.

Dakota's voice never wavered.

Mary scrambled to a sitting position. "What's wrong?"

"Your house . . . uhm. I was putting Leo back down after his feeding and caught light outside. A couple of lights were on at your place. I thought it was strange. I called over . . . you didn't answer."

"I'm not there."

"Right, right. So I told Walt to check it out. Make sure the plumbers didn't come by and leave stuff on, doors open . . . ya know."

"Cut to the reason you're calling, Dakota."

Glen had opened his eyes, concern on his face.

"Someone broke in, Mary."

Mary physically shook as a chill burned her bones. "Broke in?"

"The police are over there now with Walt."

Mary envisioned her living room as she left it. Tarp still separated her front door from the living space, but everything was in its place.

Glen placed a hand on her shoulder. "What's going on?"

Mary found Glen's eyes. "Someone broke into my house."

"What?"

Dakota continued to talk. "Whoever broke in trashed things. Hard to tell if stuff is missing."

"Damn."

"Double damn," Dakota replied. "How soon can you get back? The police need to know what's missing."

Mary lowered the phone. "I need to go home."

Glen smoothed her hair and kissed her forehead before slipping off the bed and reaching for the hotel phone.

Who would break into her place? Why? She didn't have expensive stuff. Her life wasn't bargain basement, but break-in worthy? Mary didn't think so.

"I'll text you when I'm on the plane."

"Okay. Love you, Mary."

"Love you too."

Mary was dressed, packed, and en route to the airport within an hour. Glen drove through the city in his own thoughts.

"I'm sorry our weekend is cut short," Mary said when she saw the airport come in focus.

Glen reached over, grabbed her hand, and kissed her fingers. "You have nothing to be sorry about."

Somewhere over the Midwest Mary broke her silence. "You didn't have to fly home with me."

He lowered his chin and met her stare. "If I'd been in LA, received the call you did this morning . . . would you have come back with me?"

Of course.

"That's what I thought." Glen wove his fingers with hers throughout the remainder of the flight.

The ride from the airport to her condo took less than thirty minutes on a Sunday without traffic.

The squad car in her driveway somehow made Dakota's call more real than it had been all morning.

Mary slowly opened the door while Glen talked with the driver.

The front door was open, the tarp from inside kicked out with the wind.

The sound of footsteps running across the street accompanied Walt's voice calling out.

"Mary!"

From her peripheral vision, she saw Glen and Walt do a quick handshake as they both walked beside her.

"Thanks for checking on the place." The words were autopilot from Mary's lips.

"No problem. Listen, it's a wreck in there."

Yeah, she got that from Dakota's conversation. "I'm okay."

Walt's expression told her she wouldn't be.

She crossed the threshold, moved back the tarp, and caught the edge of the wall with her shoulder.

Her condo was trashed . . . there was no other way to describe it with one word. Everything that stood upright was on the floor. Her lamps tossed across the room, her couch was upside down with the cushions slashed and the stuffing pulled out. The few pictures she had were smashed and lying on the ground, shards of glass scattered all around.

"Mary." Glen said her name from a fog.

"I'm okay." She wasn't. But saying she was somehow gave her the strength to move through her home.

Two uniformed police officers stood in her kitchen . . . a kitchen that looked a lot like her living room. Drawers had been opened, dumped out. A pile of white powder . . . sugar, if she wasn't mistaken, had been poured from the container she kept it in directly onto her stove, the container tossed to the side.

"Officers, this is Mary Kildare. The homeowner."

Mary spun in a circle. "Does everything look like this?"

Walt looked her in the eye. "Just about."

Glen stood at her side, his jaw a tight, unreadable line.

"Miss Kildare, we have some questions—"

She held up her hand.

Their questions could wait.

She walked out of the kitchen and up the stairs.

Her bedroom was worse. The bed had been torn apart. Feathers from the pillows looked like a sixteen-year-old's slumber party after a pillow fight. It didn't look as if any of her clothing was still inside the dresser. She slowly moved into her bathroom and gasped. Like in every Hollywood movie that contained a break-in, lipstick had been used on her bathroom mirror.

BITCH!

Bold print.

Exclamation point.

She trembled.

The shaking started at her feet and she felt it slowly rise and hit her knees. When the ripple had her catching her breath, she felt her body slump.

Glen kept her from sliding to the ground.

"I got ya. C'mon . . . let's get you out of here."

She didn't remember walking down the stairs, didn't remember crossing the street. When she looked up, she was sitting in Dakota's living room with her best friend's arm around her, repetitions of *everything is going to be all right* drifting in the air.

The police were in Dakota's kitchen, talking with Glen.

"Who would do that?" Mary's words didn't require an answer. She knew Dakota didn't have one.

"I don't know. Walt and I've been asking ourselves that all morning."

"Did you see it?"

Dakota nodded. "They wanted to know if I saw anything missing."

She knew she'd have to go back and look at everything . . . sort it all out.

Glen and Walt accompanied the officers back into the living room. Glen handed her a cup of what looked like hot tea and took the seat beside her.

"Miss Kildare . . . I know it's difficult." The older of the two policemen addressed her first.

In slow, controlled measures, Mary felt the thoughts of a victim rise above the fog and those of the therapist start to take hold.

Analyze.

Conclude.

Predict.

"This was personal," Mary muttered.

The senior officer nodded. "That's what we believe."

"Not a random act?" Glen asked.

Mary shook her head. "*Bitch* was personal. Everything else . . . ransacking the house, tearing it up . . . could have been anyone looking for valuables." Joke was on them; she didn't have any to speak of.

"Exactly." The officer, whose name eluded her, sat on one of the opposite chairs. "Does anyone's name pop in your head who would do this?"

She shook her head with a shrug. "None."

"Your friends tell us you're a therapist. What about your clients? Anyone unhappy with your advice? Anyone unstable?"

Mary rested her head in her hand. "Many of my clients are unstable. Not clinically . . . well, maybe some. But . . ." She couldn't start blurting out names. She had a confidentiality clause and edict that she had to hold herself to. "I haven't had any threats."

"What about that crazy guy who called your house a few weeks ago?" Glen asked.

Mary hesitated and caught herself. "No . . . he was upset—"

"The guy was crazy, started calling you names."

"What was this man's name?" the second officer asked.

Mary put her hands in the air. "Speculation. And not something I can divulge."

"The man sounded insane enough to check out."

She narrowed her gaze to Glen. "You play pilot, I'll play therapist. You're barking up the wrong tree." Only as the words left her mouth she wasn't completely sure they were true. Jacob Golf had presented a few unstable behaviors in the past couple of months. Behaviors consistent with bipolar disorder or borderline personality disorder. Could she add psychotic behavior to the list? None of that guaranteed he was capable of tearing up her home.

The officers exchanged glances. "If your opinion on the subject changes, or you come up with someone you think might be responsible, we'd appreciate your cooperation."

"I'm happy to cooperate, Officer . . ."

"Taylor," the senior officer reminded her.

"Officer Taylor. You can understand my position. I have a long list of clients, none of which know where I live unless I missed one of them following me home, and I cannot simply hand out their names. I might not be a doctor, but I hold the same ideals of client confidentiality."

"Even if one of them destroyed your home?" the second officer asked.

"If I believed one of my clients was involved, I'd happily give you their name." She heard Glen grunt behind her. "I'd have to have more than one upset event to justify breaching my ethics."

"Someone broke into your house!" Officer Taylor said once again.

Walt stepped forward. "I have to agree with Mary on this. And I *am* a doctor. I tick off a lot of patients when they come to my ER wanting something I'm not going to give. Drug seekers, hypochondriacs, psych patients wanting meds. Shelling out an endless list of names will simply have my license suspended. If Mary doesn't have a name to give you . . . a viable threat . . . she doesn't."

Mary welcomed the voice of reason, even if Glen appeared to steam on the outside of the conversation.

Officer Taylor put the pad of paper he held in his hand back into his breast pocket and stood. "Okay. We need you to go through your house and tell us if anything is missing."

Mary ignored the feeling of liquid in her knees and stood.

Chapter Nineteen

Watching her walk back into her house brought physical pain to Glen's chest.

Mary held her chin high, pushed through the plastic a second time, and managed not to look like she'd been sucker punched in the gut like she had when they'd arrived an hour before.

"Do we know how they got in?" she asked as she picked up a lamp and put it upright on a table.

"Forced entry from the back."

"I'm surprised my neighbors didn't hear this happening."

"We already questioned them. They said they heard a few things after midnight, but with all the workers you've had around, they ignored it and went back to bed."

Officer Taylor's remote radio held a continual feed of noise as Mary walked around her condo setting her belongings upright. It was as if she was cleaning as she went.

"I assume you've had someone in here dusting for fingerprints?" Glen asked.

"We have. We concentrated on the point of entry, the bathroom upstairs, and the car."

Mary stood abruptly. "My car?"

Another round of cops looking at each other, and Walt checking out his shoes, gave Glen another pull in his gut.

Without words, Mary marched toward the door to her garage from the kitchen. The fluorescent lights flickered to life, revealing the damage.

The hood was open, splashes of dark powder revealed where the police had looked for the culprit's prints. Scratch marks, as if the car had been keyed, ran the length of her compact car. From where Glen stood, it appeared as if someone pulled plugs and belts from the engine just to create damage, and two of the four tires were flat.

"Why not just steal it?" Mary asked.

"You said it yourself. This is personal," Officer Taylor said. "I'll be surprised if you find anything missing."

Mary twisted back into the condo with forceful strides. Unlike the first trip through the living room, when she carefully picked things up and set them back down, she shoved her hands into the mess and searched. She found a set of keys and tossed them on the counter. "Extra car keys."

She spun in a circle, gave up on the kitchen, and marched up the stairs.

Back in her bedroom she used her foot and kicked through the clothing on the floor. There was a picture of a middle-aged woman and Mary in a cap and gown. The glass was broken, but the image was unscathed.

Glen's eyes found the bathroom mirror, the word scribbled there burned into his brain. Mary ran around the space on autopilot. She sifted through jewelry, picked out a few things, and set them aside. "The only real pieces I have are still here."

Glen fisted his hands. He'd feel a whole lot better if she found something missing.

The next trip was to her home office.

"Son of a bitch." Mary's words were angry. And considering how seldom she cussed, they struck home.

The room mimicked the rest of the house.

"We dusted in here, too. In case a client of yours is responsible."

"This will take time to go through. But if they were looking for something, joke is on them."

"How so?" Officer Taylor asked.

"I shred my notes after I enter them into my computer."

They all looked at the upright computer.

"Passwords and encryption make it difficult for just anyone to access."

"It didn't stop someone from trashing the space," Glen said.

Mary stepped over a pile of papers spread all over the floor and reached into one of the drawers on her desk in search of something. When it appeared she didn't find what she was looking for, she knelt down and sifted through the mess. She found an envelope and looked inside. "I had some cash in here." She kept sifting and shook her head.

"How much?" Officer Taylor asked.

"Maybe five hundred." She tossed the empty envelope on the desk.

"It's obvious there is a lot to go through to determine if anything else is missing. We'll need you to sign the police report. I'm sure your insurance will want a copy. We have pictures, but the red tape for you to get copies I'm told is a pain. I suggest you take photos yourself for your insurance claim."

Mary faked a smile. "Thank you. I appreciate your advice."

"You live alone, is that correct?" Officer Taylor asked.

"I do."

"You might consider installing an alarm system. Beef up your locks."

Mary folded her hands over her arms and rubbed them. Glen moved behind her and placed his hands on her shoulders. "Do you think whoever did this will come back, when Mary's here?"

"It's hard to say. Whoever did this took a bit of time . . . like they knew you were gone. Destroying property and not stealing it suggests this guy is angry and wants to piss you off."

"Mission accomplished," Mary said.

"They might be too much of a coward to confront you personally."

"Might be?" Glen asked.

"It's hard to profile a suspect on one incident. The guy could have come looking for Mary, didn't find her and trashed the place."

Glen's fingers squeezed Mary's shoulders. Her hands on his reminded him she was under his grip. "She's not safe here."

"No more or less than she was last week. Only now you'll be watching, locking things tighter. We'll beef up patrol in the neighborhood. And if the prints come up with any possible suspects, we'll call. If you come across anything you think we should investigate, we will."

Mary removed herself from Glen's grip and extended a hand. "Thank you, Officers. I'll let you know if anything presents itself."

Glen and Walt walked the police out the door, leaving Mary in her office.

Before they left the house, Glen stopped them. "Gentlemen . . . one more question."

They both turned and gave him their attention.

"If Mary was your sister, your cousin, girlfriend, wife . . . what would you do?"

Officer Taylor spoke first. "I wouldn't leave her alone. Not right away. Whoever did this was angry. Ripping up the furniture, destroying everything, messing with her car. This isn't the act of some snot-nosed kid getting some kicks out of ruining someone else's day."

"It's personal," Walt said.

"When it's personal, and the effect the perpetrator desired isn't achieved—"

Officer Taylor finished his partner's sentence. "It's often repeated."

Glen ran a hand through his hair and turned to the door behind him.

"What if we're wrong?" Walt asked. "What if it was a random act?"

Officer Taylor released a sigh. "You said you're a doctor."

"ER. Pomona."

The cop shook his head. "Then you should know better than most to believe none of what you hear and half of what you see."

Glen watched a play of emotions pass Walt's face.

"Ask yourself what you see," Officer Taylor's partner said.

"What *do* you see?" Glen asked.

"I see a beautiful, single woman living alone. These are the facts. She holds herself as someone who doesn't make enemies but has a profession that digs into the past of others. There may be an endless list of possible suspects, but I believe that Miss Kildare does have a name or two swimming in her head."

Glen had one and he didn't know of any of her other *clients*.

"Single woman . . . does she date a lot? Could she have an ex-lover who's upset with her?"

Glen looked to Walt.

"You're the only guy she's dated since I've known her," Walt said to Glen.

"Keep your eyes open," Officer Taylor told them. He removed a card from his breast pocket and handed one to each of them. "Call anytime. Nine one one works, too."

When Glen and Walt stepped back inside, they both sighed like old men with a losing poker hand.

"What a mess." Walt righted a chair that needed to find its way to the curb since half the stuffing had been removed from the back.

Glen glanced up the stairs. "I'm going to check on her."

Walt nodded toward the door. "I need to update Dakota before she attempts to find out for herself."

"Go! I'll help Mary here."

"I can call some friends to help with the mess."

"Maybe. Let's see what Mary wants to do." Glen wasn't sure more hands in the mix were wanted.

Glen found Mary standing over her desk, her hands anchoring her weight, her head hung low.

"Hey."

She pushed away from her desk without looking at him. "Hey."

"Are you okay?"

She huffed. "No . . . yes. I'll be fine." She knelt down and grabbed a handful of papers from the floor and brought the edges together by slapping them against the desk.

"Walt said he had some friends who could come over and help with the mess."

"I don't know. I need to sift through all this crap and find what might be missing before I invite people to help me throw stuff away."

Glen pushed up his sleeves. "Where do you wanna start?"

Her smile humored him. "You don't have to—"

His glare stopped her from continuing.

"Okay. I guess we should take some pictures." She lifted a handful of papers from her desk. "I'm looking for my insurance information to put in the calls."

"I'll grab your insurance from the car, start taking pictures downstairs. Then I'll help you up here."

"All right."

She didn't look all right to him. Instead of harping on her opening up about how she was feeling, Glen left the room.

He heard Mary talking under her breath to herself once he was out of sight. "Things were just going too good . . . something had to happen."

He hesitated at the top of the stairs, glanced over his shoulder.

—

Mary felt as if a freight train had run over her by the time the sun had set.

The homeowners insurance took about an hour on the phone, with the promise of more time in the morning during normal office hours. The car insurance didn't give her fifteen minutes of conversation before letting her know that her homeowners policy would be responsible for her car because it was parked in her garage at the time of the vandalism. When Mary called the home insurance people back about her car, they couldn't confirm or deny coverage on it.

While she sat on the phone, Glen swept up broken dishes, put anything that survived the crash into the dishwasher or washed it by hand. Mary kept the phone to her ear and helped him put things back where they belonged. Not that there was much left. The sugar everywhere made it even more fun when their shoes started sticking to the floor.

It looked like she'd be doing some serious shopping just to replace her essentials.

She started one of the many loads of laundry needed. The thought of wearing anything that the man who had done this might have touched gave her hives.

Mary made the necessary calls to her Monday afternoon clients last. Stating a personal emergency, she apologized and rescheduled three of them, leaving messages for the other two. One being Mrs. Golf. Even though she couldn't point a finger at Jacob directly, he was the only person who came to mind when the police started asking questions about people in her life acting irrationally.

The crazy thing, even for her, was that some of her clients had priors in the past . . . two she could name who had vandalized an ex's home . . . but she didn't think for a minute either of them had done this to her.

She stood in the entry to her living room with her hands on her hips. "I'm going to need a huge garbage can." The couch was slashed, along with the chairs. Refinishing them would cost more than replacing.

The lamps were busted, well, one of the two . . . and the coffee table had glass in the center that was spread all over the carpet.

"I haven't lived on cardboard boxes for years," she said with half a laugh.

Glen pulled the garbage can he had rolled into the kitchen beside her. "Builds character."

He was attempting to make her smile . . . and she did.

She knelt with a dustpan as Glen swept in the glass. "Did he have to smash all the glass?"

"Apparently."

"Probably a good thing all this carpet is going. I'm bound to find glass in it for years if I kept it."

"Good way to look at it."

She had to, or she'd be in tears.

And she didn't cry.

A knock on the front door had Mary jolting upright.

"Hey, guys?" The voice belonged to Walt.

Mary slumped. "Come in."

Walt opened the door, pushed back the tarp, and waved his thumb out the door. "We have dinner in about ten."

Mary started to protest.

"Dakota said, and I quote, 'Don't let her say no. She doesn't like to cook on a good day, and today sucks.'"

Mary found her smile. "Fine."

Walt waved a hand in the air. "Ten!"

"We'll be there," Glen said.

Walt closed the door behind himself.

Mary scooped another tray of glass into the trash and dusted her hands on her pants. "I guess this is as good a place to stop as any."

They walked out the door eight minutes later, locking it as they left. "Seems useless," Mary said, looking behind her.

"Unlocked doors invite problems." He placed his arm over her shoulders. She took the moment to lean her head into his shoulder.

"I didn't invite this . . . and the doors were locked."

Glen kissed her forehead. "I know, hon."

Mary soaked up his support while she had it.

Dakota and Walt's home felt like heaven compared to her own. Everything was in its place; nothing was broken or sticky. The police hadn't left smudges of black dust just about everywhere.

And there was baby Leo.

If the scattering of baby paraphernalia didn't remind her he was there, his tiny cries would.

"Perfect timing." Walt handed her the baby the second she stepped into the room. "I'm pouring whiskey. Glen, what are you drinking?"

"Sounds good to me."

"Mary, white or red?"

Mary wiggled her face in front of Leo's, letting her hair feather up beside his cheeks. His cries turned into tiny giggles.

"Mary?" Walt asked again.

"Oh, white."

The sound of Dakota's gimpy gait walking down the stairs approached. "Now look who is holding the baby."

"He's a bright spot in a bad day."

Dakota came to sit beside her on the couch. "How are you holding up?"

She glanced away from Leo and tried to shake off the unease the entire situation mandated. "It's just stuff."

"Have you found anything missing?" Walt asked from the kitchen.

"Just the cash." Mary once again tickled Leo with her hair. "Good thing I don't have a lot of that sitting around, huh, Leo?" Her voice kicked up an octave.

Their informal dinner was eaten around the coffee table with Dakota and Walt tag-teaming Leo. The conversation about the mess across the street eased into a discussion about what needed to happen next.

"A security system is never a bad idea. Seems they only go in after someone is robbed."

"This has always been a safe community. The most trouble we've had is when those boys up the street threw weekend parties," Dakota told them.

"Thank God for college," Mary said.

"Glen, when are you going home?" Walt asked.

Mary drank her wine and waited for the answer.

"I told Jason and Trent not to expect me anytime soon."

Anytime soon? What did that mean? "You have a job, too, Glen. I can't expect you to stay here and hold my hand."

"You not expecting it makes me want to do it more."

She set her wine down. "I'm going to have to go to my office on Tuesday."

"We should have the majority of the place cleaned out by then."

"Dating me doesn't mean you have to share my problems," she told him. "You have a life."

Glen stared her down. "You go to work on Tuesday, and I'll supervise the security company when they wire your place."

"I don't even know what that costs . . . or if I can afford it."

He titled his head just like he had when he'd bought her the coat.

"Oh, no . . . the coat, okay. I did that. But no way am I letting you foot any bills related to this garbage."

Glen shrugged and forked the last bite of his dinner in his mouth. "Then I guess you're stuck with me until we find out who did this."

"What?"

Mary was vaguely aware that Walt and Dakota were silently watching this entire exchange.

Glen lifted both palms in the air. He dipped his right hand and said, "Security system . . ." Then he dipped his left hand. "Me as your roommate." His grin told her he wasn't kidding. "Your choice, hon."

"That's ridiculous." She glanced over at Walt, who seemed just fine with his ultimatum. And Dakota, the traitor. "You're all ridiculous."

"Pretending everything can go on as normal is preposterous, Mary, and you know it," Dakota said.

Mary's psychology hat snapped into place and her words flew out of her mouth. "You're feeling guilty."

"Excuse me?" Dakota asked.

"Guilty you didn't notice anything until after it was all over. Probably even more so because you're considering moving altogether and wouldn't be able to walk across the street to check on me."

Dakota didn't argue.

Mary turned toward Walt. "Ditto for you."

She found her eyes on Glen. "You want to play hero. Kinda stuck in the role since the call came through while we were together. The male ego kicks in with *nothing bad can happen if I'm there*, takes over, and all your normal responsibilities blow away. I have news for you . . . something bad can happen right now and you might not be able to do anything to stop it. Or worse, get hurt trying." She twisted back to Dakota. "And what if Walt had ran over when that guy was still there? What if he chased Walt back here with you and Leo?"

The room was silent until Glen challenged her. "All your what-ifs do not change the fact that you have friends who want to help, *Counselor*."

She understood that, but she also knew, on a level that only she could, the risk she took in counting on someone else for her well-being. She'd been going at life nearly alone since she was brought into this world, depending on others now was not an option.

"Help. But don't dictate what will and won't be in my life based on your needs."

"I'm basing it on your needs."

She shook her head. "Every good dictator makes the people believe they are making all the decisions for the people's own good."

From the look on Glen's face, she'd managed to tick him off. He set his drink down and stood. "Believe what you want, Mary. I'm not going anywhere. Walt, Dakota . . . thank you for dinner. I have a few calls to make." Then he was out the door.

Walt handed Leo to Dakota and followed Glen.

It took a few minutes for Mary's heart to stop pounding in her chest.

"You're wrong on this one," Dakota said quietly.

Mary started to protest.

"No, don't. Yes, I feel bad that we didn't see the asshole who did this. Maybe even a little guilty, but that isn't driving my desire to see you safe. And I have no doubt that Glen's ego is puffing his chest out saying he won't let this happen if he's here to stop it. It's not testosterone driving Glen to his actions either. Anyone else would be booking his flight home after what you just said."

Maybe he should go.

"You know what I see?" Dakota asked.

Mary didn't trust herself to speak . . .

"I see someone hurt who is too afraid to open herself up and let others in to heal her."

"I don't need someone else to heal me."

"You don't *want* to need someone to heal you. You only *want* to depend on the only person in your life who has always been there . . . yourself."

"You and I both know Glen is temporary. Depending on him for more than what we have right now would be a mistake on my part."

"Maybe. I don't have a window into that man's brain and he hasn't asked me for your ring size, so maybe he is transient. But he is a good guy who wants to help a friend out."

"Help . . . don't demand."

"In case you haven't noticed, you don't accept any help without the other person demanding it."

Chapter Twenty

The rag Glen was using to remove the word *bitch* off of Mary's bathroom mirror did a great job of smearing the lipstick instead of taking it off.

Mary walked in during his efforts and leaned against the doorframe. "I'm sorry."

"Forget about it." He kept scrubbing, making the mess bigger.

"No, Glen . . ." She approached from behind, placed her hands on his shoulders. "I was way out of line."

He caught her reflection in the mirror and dropped the towel on the counter. "You're under a lot of stress."

"Doesn't excuse bad behavior. I know you just want to help."

He turned around, placed his hands on her hips.

"Let me help you."

Mary closed her eyes.

"Please. I have the means, Mary."

"Glen—"

"I can't stay here indefinitely, I do have a life at home. But leaving you here less than protected would be impossible. Especially if there is something I can do."

"I don't know."

"I'm asking." He reached for her chin and forced her to look at him. "I'd want to do this even if I lived across the street. The fact I'm so far away makes it even more important. I don't think I'll be able to sleep in my own bed if—"

She cut him off with a long-suffering breath. "Okay. Put in the locks, the security system."

He'd won.

He tried not to smile.

"It's the right thing to do," she said.

Glen pulled her in for a kiss. He didn't mean for it to be anything but a thank-you, but she reached around and latched on.

A simple meeting of lips quickly turned into lava.

His heart kicked in his chest and his body responded.

When he pushed away from the counter, Mary jumped up and wrapped her legs around his waist. Glen caught the globes of her ass in his hands and walked the both of them over to her bed.

They fell together, Mary pulling at his clothes. Her struggles were desperate and needy, and this was where Glen knew he could help and she wouldn't protest.

The floor of the room was still a mess, but the bed had been remade before they'd gone to dinner.

Mary clawed her way past his clothing, making quick work of her own.

Only when Glen pushed into her did she still. While her desperation to get to this point had been frantic, now that turned to a slow, steady gait to heaven. "I have you," he whispered in her ear.

"Yes," she whispered back.

Glen stopped asking permission the following day.

He called a local service to remove the trashed furniture. The only thing left in the living room was a lone surviving lamp and the TV. Even the cable box had been destroyed, but the man hadn't touched the television. The cords to the speakers of her stereo system were cut in half, the console itself thrown on the floor.

They kept a running list of everything that ended up in the Dumpster for the insurance company.

They passed through the empty room to her kitchen. One of the two bar stools had been slashed like her sofa, the other was intact. The wooden kitchen table and chairs had survived. Thankfully he hadn't bothered with her washer and dryer, which had been running nonstop since they'd started cleaning the place up.

Mary's bedroom was starting to smell like a brothel. All her perfumes and cosmetics had been dumped on the floor, many of the bottles broken and leaking onto the carpet. While they had made the bed the day before and slept in it, there was a massive slash in the mattress, which would need to be replaced sooner than later.

Her dresser survived and most of her clothing.

Glen called a tow service to take Mary's car in for repairs. The insurance companies were haggling over who was ultimately responsible for the bill, and at one point the mechanic vacillated on starting the work. Glen pulled him aside, handed him a credit card, and told him he was covered. Mary hadn't seen the transaction when he'd done it, and he resolved himself to the fact he'd have to ask her for forgiveness later.

They went from the mechanic to rent her a car. All the questions remained the same . . . will the auto insurance pay for the rental? They didn't know, and Mary ended up using her credit card to drive away.

Her home office was intact, just in such disarray it would take her weeks to put everything to rights.

By the time they were ready for dinner, Glen had scheduled a professional service to clean the carpets upstairs the next day and a contractor to come and give an estimate for repairs on three of the walls, which took the brunt of the force the bastard who'd done this had inflicted when he threw her belongings around the room.

Mary was taking a shower before they left for dinner, and Glen was on her back porch talking with Jason on the phone. "Damn, Jase . . . you should have seen it. The only thing intact was her TV and computer."

"Any idea on who could have done this?"

"I think the police need to check out her clients."

"I can't imagine Mary would appreciate that."

Glen pinched the bridge of his nose. "No, she didn't agree to releasing any names."

"How is she holding up?"

"Like a rock. The woman gives stubborn a whole new meaning. Her entire home is all but destroyed and she just keeps moving forward. Not one tear. I don't know any other woman who would hold up like she is during all of this."

"When do you think you'll be back?"

Glen rubbed the tension out of the back of his neck. "A few days. I can work remotely while Mary's seeing clients." He knew his brother wasn't asking about work, but he felt the need to tell him he was thinking about it.

"We're good here. Just make sure your girl is safe."

Glen ran a hand through his hair. That was the problem. All the precautions in the world wouldn't assure her safety.

It took Mary four hours and three sets of clients before she felt her head was in the game.

Two of the three clients were married, working on their relationships, and the other set was a mother/daughter situation where they were just as codependent on the other as a married couple. And the daughter was in her forties. Mary had to keep from letting her mind wander during their sessions . . . asking if it was at all possible she was sitting across from the person who had trashed her home.

A text from Glen came in as she was finishing her notes. `Can I bring you lunch?`

`Meet me at the Hansen's deli?`

Twenty minutes later she sat at the counter, placed her purse in the seat beside her for Glen.

Carla swung by, dropped off the iced tea, and glanced at the vacant seat. "Meeting someone today?"

"I am."

"The cutie from the law firm?" Carla wiggled her eyebrows.

Mary was quick to shake her head. "No. He's not . . . no."

Carla didn't ask for details, just winked and moved on down the counter.

Mary checked her phone to see if Glen had texted with a need for directions.

"Hey, Mary."

She twisted in surprise. "Hi, Kent."

"I'm pleasantly surprised to see you here."

Mary blinked a few times without responding. The comment felt out of place.

"I didn't see your car in the parking lot. I thought maybe you'd taken some time off," he clarified.

She released a breath and smiled. "Oh, no . . . I had another problem. It's back at the shop."

His smile fell. "Nothing serious, I hope."

"Well, yes . . . but no. It's okay. Nothing I can't handle."

"That sounded suspicious."

Mary glanced toward the door. "It's been a crazy week."

"And it's only Tuesday," he said. He looked down at the empty seat. "Saving this for me?"

"Uhm, no. I'm actually meeting someone today." And sitting there talking to a man who had asked her out while waiting for the man she was dating started to feel as awkward as it looked.

When Glen walked into the deli she waved with a smile.

"I see."

Glen moved to stand behind the saved seat, cut off from taking it by Kent's presence.

"You found the place," Mary said.

"Google." Glen's one-word answer had universal meaning.

It was obvious that Kent wasn't moving, so Mary made an introduction. "Glen, this is Kent . . ." She'd forgotten his last name. "I'm sorry, what was your last name again?"

"Duvall." Kent watched Glen as if sizing up the competition.

"Right, Kent Duvall, this is Glen Fairchild. Kent is the man who helped me when my car wouldn't start last week."

Glen extended a hand. "I appreciate you helping Mary out."

There was a bit of a power struggle with the handshake. "Anytime. I hate to think chivalry is dead."

"The act, no . . . the men willing to participate . . ."

Kent finally stepped back. "I'll let you two get to your lunch. See you around, Mary."

Glen moved into her space the moment he could and greeted her with a kiss. She caught him glancing over his shoulder at Kent's receding back.

She bit her lip to keep from laughing.

"What?" he asked when he noticed her struggle.

"Male chest-bumping if I've ever seen it."

He didn't bother denying her claim. "Who is that guy?"

"Like I told you . . . he jumped my car the other night."

Glen lifted a menu. "Uh-huh! His eyes were all over you."

Mary gave up and started to laugh. "I told him no."

"Told who no?"

"Kent . . . he asked me out. I told him no."

Glen put down his menu, did a double take to find the man they were talking about. "Good."

She sipped her iced tea, smiling.

"Why did you tell him no?"

Glen was not letting this go. "Because I'm dating you. I know we haven't talked about being exclusive, but I can't bring myself to date two men at the same time." She quickly realized how that sounded and added, "My issue, not yours. It's just how I am."

He twisted back to the counter, looked at the menu. "So you said no, not because you weren't interested, but because we're dating?"

Mary rested both hands on the counter. "Could you be more jealous?"

He shrugged. "Probably."

She was laughing when Carla walked back around.

"And who do we have here?" Carla asked, winking at Mary.

Mary stopped giggling long enough for introductions. "Carla, best waitress in this place and overall wonderful woman, this is Glen."

Glen set the menu down with a smirk. "Mary's boyfriend," he added.

She stopped laughing.

"Is that right?" Carla asked.

"Mary's *exclusive* boyfriend," Glen said as if his first proclamation wasn't enough.

It was Carla's turn to laugh. "Well, Mary's *exclusive* boyfriend, what are you having?"

"What's good here?"

"The Reuben," Mary and Carla said in unison.

—

By Thursday the plumbers had finally fixed the pipe in her floor and hadn't found anything past the point where the roots had interrupted the flow of sewage. Mary tried not to enjoy the fact that Glen had taken the task of directing the work on her home, but she had to push all her clients into three days and couldn't dwell over drywall and paint. She spent most of her spare time talking to insurance agents and mechanics.

At night she fell asleep in Glen's arms, asking if he was flying home the next day.

Each time he met her question with *not yet*.

Friday morning the security system went in. Mary had only one client on Friday. By design, she'd been moving her clients around to give her the option of leaving for long weekends.

The technician stood beside a control panel pressing buttons and explaining the system.

Mary mimicked his motions. "So when I'm at home at night, I set it with this button?"

"Right, and when you leave for the day, or night . . . you set this. Giving you more time to turn it off when you come home before the alarm calls the police."

"Seems simple enough."

"Then we have a distress mode."

"What's that?"

"Let's say you're on the way in the house and someone comes up behind you . . . tells you to turn off the alarm."

She shivered. The thought hadn't occurred to her.

"The code you put in turns the alarm off and notifies the alarm company that you're in need of the police."

"So the alarm turns off and whoever is with Mary has no idea the alarm triggered the authorities?"

"Exactly!"

Mary wrapped her arms around herself. "Sounds thorough."

"Designed to keep you safe when you're here and when you're not."

Mary stood by the control panel, prepared to program her codes, while Glen showed the technician out.

When he returned, he placed an arm around her shoulders, his hand dangling on the other side.

"Thinking of a code?"

She nodded. "Something I'll remember."

"Not a birthday."

She rolled her eyes. "Of course not."

"Not your address."

"I wasn't born yesterday."

"When were you born?"

She huffed and started pressing buttons. "Good question."

He noted the code, and her answer. Glen couldn't help but feel for the meaning behind her words. Mary had no idea when she was born. Something as simple as a birthday Mary couldn't relate to.

"Now the distress code." She tapped a nail against the wall in thought, then chuckled before programming it in.

"I'm sure there is a meaning behind that."

"Danger to self . . . danger to others."

"Easy to remember?"

"Yeah," she chuckled.

"Looks like you're all set."

Mary leaned into his shoulder. "I can't thank you enough for all your help."

"I didn't do a lot."

"Says the man who gave up his life this week . . . managed to get the plumbers to take down all this tarp and finish the job. Says the man who fixed the holes, had the walls painted, the floors finished, and managed to get an alarm system that monitors my window, my doors . . . my life in just a few days. No. You didn't do a lot. You did everything."

Glen placed a playful smile on his face and looked at the ceiling. "Well, when you put it that way."

She punched his arm.

He grabbed it, pretended pain. "All I do and you beat on me."

"Poor baby."

He took her hands, pinned them to the wall, and kissed her.

She liked this part . . . the playful part where things could get hot and sweaty or simply move on to dinner.

He broke his kiss, stared into her eyes. "So, what are we going to do this weekend?"

She shook her head in amazement. "Don't you have a life to get back to?"

"Monday. That's soon enough."

"I actually had plans this weekend."

Glen leaned back. "Really?"

"I did. A long weekend. I had to cancel . . . in light of everything."

"Is that right?"

She could tell by his tone he didn't believe her.

"I didn't sit at home every weekend before you came along."

He pressed his body against hers, distracting her. "So what did you have planned?"

She closed her eyes, trying not to think of how perfect he felt like this. "Out of town trip."

His teeth grazed her earlobe.

"Without me?"

"Planned months ago," she told him.

"Sounds serious." His tongue replaced his teeth.

She wrapped one of her legs around his and leaned against the wall he was pressing her into. "Very."

He kissed down her neck, the tops of her breasts. "I think you're bluffing."

"I don't lie." And what he was doing with his tongue felt amazing.

"What was it?"

"Important . . ." She arched into him.

"What was it, Mary?" His hand slid up her frame, took her breast with a gentle squeeze.

"I'm not telling."

"I can stop doing what I'm doing until you tell me."

She reached around and grabbed his ass, pulled him closer. "Don't you dare."

"Tell me." One hand moved down her torso, played with the space between her jeans and her skin.

Just when she was sure he was going to dip lower, his hand stilled, his kiss stayed just outside of reach of her lips.

"Tell me."

She attempted to capture his lips. He pulled away.

"Brat."

"Tell me."

Mary grabbed the back of his head. "Arizona. Mary Frances . . . my spring trip."

Glen laughed before he resumed her desired position and possessed every sensitive spot on her skin.

First thing in the morning he pulled her out of bed and dragged her to the airport.

Looked like her *exclusive* boyfriend wanted to meet the only claim to family Mary had.

And he wasn't taking no for an answer.

Chapter Twenty-One

Mary Frances lived in a two-bedroom, two-bath bungalow in a quiet neighborhood outside of Phoenix. The front porch was designed to sit on and watch the neighbors, the cars, the kids playing in the street. Not that Mary Frances did a lot of that. The woman held a part-time job at the library and volunteered for just about every organization she could to fill her days.

Glen and Mary pulled into the driveway in the rental they'd picked up at the airport.

"Are you sure we shouldn't book a room at the hotel?" Glen asked for the millionth time.

"Mary Frances would be offended."

"I'd think she'd be more offended that we're sleeping together . . . her being an ex-nun and all."

Mary shook her head. "And we won't be sleeping together in the hotel?" She pushed the door open. "C'mon . . . she doesn't bite."

She made it three steps before Mary Frances, all five feet nothing of her, let the screen door slam behind her. Mary paused and let all the stress and worry of the past week float away.

She flung her arms around Mary Frances for a soothing hug. "It's so good to see you."

"You have to stop hugging me to see me."

"Shut up." Mary kept hugging.

When she did pull away and take a good look, her jaw dropped. "What is that on your lips?"

"Just a little lip gloss. It's dry here."

Mary ran her thumb over the other woman's cheek. "Blush?"

Mary Frances batted her hand away. "I am allowed, you know."

She wanted to squeal. Since when did Mary Frances wear makeup?

"Aren't you going to introduce me?"

Mary turned to find Glen standing at the edge of the walkway, enjoying the reunion.

"Mary Frances, this is my friend, Glen Fairchild."

Mary Frances looked him up and down, kept a snarky smile on her face. "When Mary called to say she was on her way and bringing a friend, I half expected a woman. I was starting to think my Mary was a lesbian."

"Oh, my—"

Mary Frances cut her off with an evil eye.

"Word! How could you think such a thing?"

"Because I haven't met someone you're dating since you were in high school." Mary Frances turned toward the house. "Let's go inside. It's getting hot out here."

Glen walked in beside her, chuckling. "Lesbian," he said under his breath.

Mary elbowed his ribs.

The house hadn't changed. Sparse furnishings, very few knick-knacks. A young picture of Mary on the mantel along with her college graduation picture with the both of them in it.

"I have iced tea or lemonade," Mary Frances said as she led them toward the kitchen.

Mary walked around the familiar kitchen to help with the refreshments.

"Lemonade would be great," Glen said.

The cupboard where the glasses normally lived now housed a half a dozen vases.

"I moved the glasses to the one on the left. Reaching that high was starting to hurt my back." Mary Frances took the seat opposite Glen. "Tell me, Mr. Fairchild . . . how long have you known my Mary?"

"We've known each other for about a year. And please call me Glen."

Mary Frances released a disapproving click of her tongue. "A year and I've not met you?"

"We haven't been dating that long," Mary explained. "We met when I went to that conference in Florida with Dakota. The one where she met Walt?"

Mary Frances nodded. "Yes, yes . . . the one where you and that sassy friend of yours ended up in a police car. I remember the story."

Glen started laughing. "How could I have forgotten that? I had to circle the airport. They wouldn't let me land due to some woman saying there was a bomb in baggage claim."

"I did *not* say there was a bomb! It was Dakota, and she said the luggage was taking so long you'd think they were searching for a bomb . . . or something like that." Then a little old woman practically yelled "bomb" and pointed her finger at the two of them. So yeah, they were both in the back of a squad car for the better part of three hours explaining the situation.

Mary Frances turned back to Glen. "So you're the pilot . . . I believe I have heard about you."

Glen smiled, and Mary cringed . . . she knew what was coming next.

"You're the arrogant player with commitment issues."

Mary wanted to bury her head in the sand.

"This is him, right?" Mary Frances asked with the sweetest smile a nun could have.

Glen locked amused eyes with Mary.

"My summation before we started dating," she explained.

He sipped his drink and said, "Arrogant? I'll go with confident. Player? We all have a past." He winked at Mary Frances when he said it. "As for commitment issues . . . maybe I just haven't found the right person to be committed to . . . until now."

Mary Frances slapped a hand on the table, laughing. "Oh, you'll do just fine."

Mary took a seat beside Glen.

"Now tell me what was keeping you from coming this weekend."

Mary stiffened. "Nothing. We're here, aren't we?"

"Don't start that with me, child. I heard your voice when you called on Tuesday. You were upset. So spill."

She needed to downplay this to keep the woman from worrying. "I have those plumbing issues."

Mary Frances just stared.

"And my car is back in the shop."

Glen kept silent beside her.

Mary picked up her drink and held out as long as she could. "Someone broke in while I was away last weekend. Not a big deal, just needed to clean the place up a bit."

Mary Frances blinked a few times, her face unreadable. Then she turned that gaze toward Glen.

"Her plumbing issues are now fixed."

The stare of death was heightened by the fact that it was difficult to tell if Mary Frances was breathing.

"Her car *is* back in the shop . . ."

Glen was going to cave, Mary felt it in her bones.

". . . because the person who broke into her house trashed the car, trashed her house. We've spent this week cleaning it up and installing an alarm system to keep your girl safe."

Mary reached over and pinched Glen's thigh.

He gently placed his hand over hers and removed the grip of her fingers without breaking eye contact with Mary Frances.

"Do the police have anyone in custody?"

Glen shook his head.

"It might be a random act."

Mary Frances turned that death stare on Mary.

She squirmed in her chair. "I'm fine. My house is safer than walking into a bank now. I didn't want you to worry, so I didn't tell you."

Mary Frances leaned forward. "You listen to me, young lady. It is my right to worry. I'm not so old that I'll fall into some kind of fit with bad news. Please don't treat me as such."

Mary lowered her eyes. "Yes, ma'am."

—

The mother figure in Mary's life was pure amusement. Glen could picture her in a nun's habit forcing confessions from the congregation with her stare.

Mary was in the kitchen helping the senior Mary with dinner while Glen was in the back of the house . . . on a ladder, no less, removing leaves from Mary Frances's gutter.

It wasn't like the woman asked. She told him where the ladder was and encouraged him to make himself useful so she could have a few words alone with her girl before dinner. Dinner that was going to include Burke, Mary Frances's beau.

Getting his head gripped around the ex-nun was one thing, thinking of her dating was quite another. And from the tight expression on Mary's face when Mary Frances announced that Burke was coming for dinner, she was less than excited.

Which was probably why Glen was hanging off the side of the single-story bungalow cleaning gutters, something he didn't even do for his own home, while the women were in the kitchen talking in hushed whispers.

Everything aside, Glen couldn't think of a better way to spend his weekend.

Staying at Mary's would remind him of her troubles . . . going home he'd be worried about her alone. Here, he could enjoy her company, learn more about where she came from, and find distraction in cleaning gutters.

Mary Frances ducked her head out of the back sliding door. "You can come down now, we're done talking."

Glen laughed, reached for another set of leaves. "Almost done."

"It's not like we get a lot of rain here."

"I'm up here, might as well finish the job."

She chuckled and left him to it.

He was positioning the ladder to the final spot on the roof when Mary stuck her head out. "He's here!" Her rough whisper said she meant business.

"I'm almost done."

"You're done *now*!"

Glen didn't bother holding in his laughter. "Yes, ma'am!"

Mary dusted off his shirt. "I can't believe she's dating."

"I can't believe how upset you are."

"I'm not upset!"

He laughed harder. "You don't lie, remember?"

She growled, pulled him into the house, squeezing the circulation out of his hand the entire way. Her fingernails dug in when she caught sight of Mary Frances's guy.

"Here they are," Mary Frances said when they walked into the room.

"My goodness, Mary . . . just look at her. She's just as you described."

"Burke, this is my girl, Mary . . . and her friend Glen."

Glen pried Mary's hand free of his and extended it. "Glen Fairchild. Mary's boyfriend."

"Oh, is it boyfriend now?" Mary Frances asked. "It was just friend when you arrived."

Glen winked. "We move quickly in the city."

He liked watching the older woman blush.

"A pleasure." He shook the other man's hand. "Burke Perry, Mary Frances's boyfriend."

Mary clenched at his side, the physical weight of his words and their meaning hitting her like a truck.

"I take it you weren't ready to hear that," Burke said, his English accent somehow softening the blow.

"Nope. Can't say that I was. First there was pie . . . then makeup . . . now a boyfriend."

Glen wished he had this on film. He couldn't remember ever seeing a woman so amusingly torn.

"It might take some getting used to."

Mary nodded like a bobblehead doll. "Yep. Probably."

"Changes make life interesting," Burke told them.

Mary kept nodding.

Glen kept laughing.

"If it makes you feel any better, Mary and I dating is like it was for you in secondary school. Quite innocent." Burke placed an arm on Mary Frances's shoulder. "Wouldn't you say, m'dear?"

"Well, of course it is . . . you're dating a fifty-eight-year-old virgin."

Glen lost it.

Mary tossed her hands in the air, twisted around, and said, "I'm out."

Glen followed her into the kitchen while the older couple giggled behind them.

"She's delightful." Burke's words carried through the house.

—

It was a damn good thing Jesus drank wine.

Mary handed a second bottle to Glen for opening before they started on the main course.

Burke was actually really nice.

It was Mary Frances who'd somehow morphed into something other than what she was when in the man's presence.

She blushed, giggled, and held his hand even after they said grace.

Watching Mary Frances, Sister Mary Frances, being a woman and not just a motherly type or a nun, was sensory overload.

Halfway through the meal Mary realized she'd all but removed herself from the conversation. She listened to Burke talk about his career before he'd retired. He spoke of his children and his late wife.

Glen touched on Fairchild Charters and explained that his parents were gone.

It was during a discussion of loss that snapped Mary out of her unease.

"The past is what molds you, it's what you do with that mold that counts," Burke said. He lifted Mary Frances's hand from the table and kissed the back of it.

There was happiness in the woman's smile that Mary hadn't seen before.

"Mary Frances says you have grandchildren."

Burke seemed pleased with her change in the subject. "I do. Would you like to see pictures?"

"Of course."

Burke pulled a phone out of his back pocket and placed a pair of reading glasses on the edge of his nose.

Mary Frances met her eyes from across the table.

Mary mouthed the words *I love you* and turned her attention to Burke's pride and joys.

When the evening wore down and Burke took his leave, he kissed each of Mary's cheeks and told her she'd been a delight.

The older couple walked out of the house to say good-bye without an audience, and Mary stayed in the kitchen cleaning up.

"Feeling better?" Glen asked when they were alone.

"Yes. It's just strange."

He moved in behind her, dropped his lips to the side of her ear. "I think he's good for her."

"So do I. It would be easier if I didn't like him."

"I doubt that."

Glen pulled up his sleeves and started in with the dishes.

"Mary Frances is precious. I think she kept talking about her virginity just to get you used to the fact she may not always have it."

Mary couldn't help but laugh. "Probably. It must be crazy strange for Burke to know that if they do . . ." She tried to picture it, winced, and squeezed the image from her brain. "Never mind."

Glen bumped her shoulder, handed her a clean dish to dry. "You'll survive."

The front door opened and closed.

"Oh, good. I dislike doing dishes." Mary Frances sat at the table and finished her wine. "Burke thinks you're lovely. I told him he had great taste."

Glen jumped in. "How nice of him, tell him I liked him, too."

"Always the charmer, this one."

"He's everything you said he would be," Mary said. "I'm sorry I wasn't more social when he first arrived."

"No worries. We both expected as much. With all the change you've had in your life, this one was bound to toss you down the rabbit hole."

"That didn't mean I needed to be rude."

"Nothing twenty Our Fathers won't remove."

They both laughed.

Mary Frances jumped up. "Oh, before I forget. The property tax bill came directly to the house. I'm not sure why." She pulled the papers from her stack on the small workspace that sat on one end of the tiny kitchen. "I didn't want you to miss it. I considered taking care of it myself."

"Don't even think of it."

"I do make some money."

Mary noticed Glen watching her during the conversation.

"We've had this discussion. Just put the bill in my purse. I'll take care of it."

"Okay, dear."

Mary Frances left the room and Glen leaned over. "What's that about?"

"I, ah . . . I take care of it. This." She looked over their heads.

"The house?"

"When she left the order she left with nothing. Her real sister helped her out those first few years, once I graduated and started to make a living, I took over."

"You bought her a house?"

"Prices are nothing here."

Glen stopped washing dishes. "No wonder you've been so concerned about the cost of everything. You're supporting two households on one income."

Mary dried the last dish and put it away. "I try to put some away for emergencies. I just didn't expect so many in one month. I'll recover."

He leaned over, kissed her fully. "You're a beautiful person."

She felt her cheeks flush. "Ah, you're just saying that to get lucky."

He kissed her again and Mary Frances walked back in the room. "Well that's one way to whistle while you work."

"She keeps attacking me, Mary Frances. You might have to talk to her about that."

"For Pete's sake!" Mary pushed away from Glen.

"It's about my bedtime," Mary Frances exclaimed. "Glen, I put a blanket and pillow on the couch for you."

Mary and Glen exchanged glances.

"That isn't necessary," Mary said.

"Oh yes it is. Boyfriend is not the same as husband. Glen sleeps on the couch."

"But you know that we've—"

Mary Frances stopped her with a wave of her hand. "Oh I'm sure that you've . . . but not in my home." She turned and patted Glen on the shoulder. "Besides, abstinence is good for the soul. I'm sure Glen won't mind."

Glen eyed the sofa. The small couch that didn't pull out into a bed.

"You kids get some sleep. We leave at seven for church."

Glen's eyes got wider.

Mary Frances hugged Mary, kissed her cheek.

Glen didn't go unhugged and kissed too before she left them alone. "Separate beds."

Mary flopped on the couch. "You weren't going to get any anyway."

Glen sat beside her. "Oh?"

She shook her head. "Started my period."

"Ah." Glen put his arm around her and pulled her close beside him. "Doesn't mean we can't cuddle."

She toed off her shoes and tucked her legs under her bottom. "It doesn't bother you to know about my cycle?"

He played with the edges of her hair. "I'm the exclusive boyfriend. I need to know about these things."

She closed her eyes and snuggled closer. "Feels strange telling you."

"Get over it. Now, about church . . ."

Chapter Twenty-Two

The first night back on the East Coast while Mary was on the West Coast was the hardest.

He made an hourly check-in once he knew she was home from work. First was a text . . . then a call. He stopped at midnight, then tossed and turned until two in the morning.

By Wednesday he managed to get some significant work done, distracted in the middle of his day by a brief phone call from Mary.

"Is it me, or does it feel quiet after all of last week's excitement?" she asked.

"It's not you."

"As the days go on, I can't help but wonder if maybe everything was random. If someone had something personal against me, wouldn't they be back for more?"

"I don't want to think like that." But the answer was yes. "What about that Jacob guy?"

"I haven't seen him. His wife said he took off to a cabin they used to visit every summer to regroup."

"Any idea how long he's been out of town?"

"I have no idea. He has a job, so I doubt it's been long."

Glen glanced out his office window. "Might be why it's been quiet around there."

Mary sighed. "I've thought of that."

"So you think he might be behind this?"

"I think I've put every client I know in the position of vandal in my head. Jacob being the most recent person who's been belligerent with me makes him an easy target."

"I think you should tell the police about him."

"That isn't going to happen without something more than just one outburst. Besides, it isn't always the loud ones that are the problem. It's the quiet ones who can't vocalize their feelings who take it out in passive-aggressive ways."

"Like trashing your place when you're not there."

"Exactly."

"And who is on your list that fits that profile?"

"Oh, I don't know . . . everyone else."

"Great!"

"Anyway, how is your day? Have your brokers come up with any new marketing plans?"

Glen leaned against the glass, grinning. Mary actually listened and remembered. "We actually have a few plans to target for the summer travel season." He bounced a few ideas off of her, found her genuine interest warming to his soul. When he hung up, she was running off to lunch and he had a meeting to attend.

Seemed to him, the East Coast–West Coast relationship was working out really well.

—

Mary was sinking her teeth into her Reuben when Kent pulled up to the empty space beside her.

"Hey," she said around her food.

He pointed down. "Am I good here?"

She nodded and wiped her mouth, washed the food down with her tea. "You're fine."

He glanced around. "I thought maybe your friend was joining you again."

"Glen? Ah, no. He's not here. He's doesn't actually live here."

Kent accepted the ice water Carla set in front of him. "Is that right?"

"He's on the East Coast."

"That doesn't sound terribly convenient."

She lifted her sandwich for another bite, hesitated before saying, "He's a pilot, so . . . it works. Except when my car breaks down. Thanks again, by the way." She filled her mouth.

Kent seemed to take in the information slowly. "I suppose if you're both committed to making it work, then good for you."

She smiled, tried not to look smug. "So far."

Carla set a Reuben in front of Kent. "Thanks, hon."

Carla winked, moved on down the line.

"Is your car still in the shop?"

Mary set her sandwich down and shook her head. "The guy did a number on it. It won't be running for another week and then it goes to the body shop."

Kent just stared at her. "What guy?"

"Someone broke into my house . . . ripped it up a bit. Messed up my car."

"What?" There was outrage in his voice.

"Someone with a Napoleon complex, I'm sure. Anyway . . . yeah, my car won't be back with me for a while."

"That sounds awful. Any idea who did it?"

"No clue."

"Are you concerned . . . living alone?"

"I'm not going to let this person win by living in a bubble. I'm being more careful. The police have been in the neighborhood more since the incident."

Kent reached into his suit pocket and removed a card. He took a pen and wrote on the back of it. "Here is my number. If you need someone to walk you to your car, just check on you . . ."

Mary hesitated. She didn't want the man to get the wrong idea.

"For your safety, Mary. I know you're dating East Coast guy. I can't help but wonder if that will work, but I get the hint. I'd like to think we're friends. If I had a girlfriend as gorgeous as you, I'd like to know there was someone watching out for her when I couldn't be there."

When he put it that way, it felt wrong not to take his number. "Thank you, I appreciate it."

—

"I think I need a drawer," Glen said from her bathroom the following Saturday morning.

He'd arrived in time to take her out to dinner Friday night, made love to her until one in the morning, and now stood in her bathroom brushing his teeth.

"A drawer?"

"You know . . . the boyfriend drawer."

She hid a smile behind her palm with a tiny squeak she knew he couldn't hear. She'd never been in a relationship long enough to warrant a drawer. "What makes you think you're drawer-worthy?"

She stood over the very place his drawer would be, removed a pair of panties, and slid them on.

"I think the exclusive boyfriend is entitled to a drawer."

Mary found a matching bra, hooked herself in, and dropped the bathrobe she'd put on after her shower. "Does that mean I can have a drawer at your place?"

"Of course . . ." He had a toothbrush in his mouth, so *of course* sounded more like *ah cus*. The water in the sink was turned on, then off. "But you might wanna come over at least once to see if you even want a drawer at my place."

It was kind of strange that she'd yet to step foot in Glen's home. "I have to be invited."

"Oh, sweetheart . . . you are always invited."

She smiled into the thought and walked to the doorway to the bathroom. Glen had a towel wrapped around his waist, his bare, sculpted chest stared at her in the mirror. "Have you ever had a drawer at a girlfriend's house?" she asked.

Through the mirror, he let his eyes fall up and down her frame. He licked his lips. "I've never had a girlfriend before. The drawer never came into question."

She found that hard to believe. "You've dated a lot of women."

"Dated. Some of them more than once."

"Not one girlfriend?"

"I don't count high school. And drawers weren't an option back then."

"Someone in college, surely?"

"I can give you Jason's number if you don't believe me."

"So I'm your first real girlfriend?" It sounded strange coming out of her mouth.

"Some might claim they were, but none that I would agree to."

She ran a hand through her wet hair in thought. "What is your definition of girlfriend?"

He pointed at her through the mirror.

"C'mon . . . that sounds like a line. Seriously, why me?"

Glen turned around with disbelief in his eyes. "Why *not* you?"

"I can think of a hundred reasons. Geography alone makes it difficult."

"I've seen you more in the past two months than either of my brothers, and we work in the same building. Give me another reason."

"I'm independent."

"A complete turn-on. I like you needy in bed, however."

"I'm opinionated and demanding."

"Women who roll over to please a man nauseate me. They're fake and it's only a matter of time before they let their true self come out. Then it's usually ugly."

She still wasn't convinced.

"You're beautiful," he told her.

"Beauty fades."

"You challenge me." His smirk deserved a place on the billboards of snarky smiles. "I like that!" He stepped closer. "You surprise and inspire me."

"Inspire?"

"Shocking, huh? Well, you do. Your honesty is refreshing and out of character for nearly everyone I know. You don't deliver your honesty in any way other than constructive."

"Side effect of my job."

"Don't care how you came about it . . . it's a wonderful quality . . . and girlfriend-worthy." By now he was standing over her, his hand on the side of her face.

"And one more thing."

"Yes?"

"My mom would have liked you."

The mom card nailed it. "Okay, fine . . . you can have a drawer."

He grinned like a kid who'd just scored ice cream for free.

Monday afternoon, she arrived home to find a bouquet of flowers on her doorstep. There wasn't a card, but she knew who they were from.

She set them in her kitchen and smiled every time she passed by.

The following weekend, Glen flew her to Connecticut.

—

Glen picked her up from the airport and drove her straight to his house. His gated community offered a layer of security that he'd always taken for granted until the day he walked into Mary's trashed condo.

His house sat on over an acre of land, with enough distance from his neighbors to not know when they were arguing or cooking fish. The house was temporary; he'd known that when he'd bought it shortly after his parents had died.

He always thought he'd land in Manhattan. Avoid the commute . . . but owning a company with things like airplanes and helicopters had its perks. And Glen wasn't opposed to public transportation. He avoided driving at peak hours in the city. Many would argue there was such a rush-hour monster in Manhattan. The city was a twenty-four hour driving nightmare. And if things got hairy and business demanded attention, there was always The Morrison not far away.

He had it good.

And he knew it.

He gave Mary the nickel tour of his home before sweeping her out the door with the promise of showing her more later. "We have somewhere to be," he told her.

"Everything is so green," she said as he drove her toward their destination.

"You can blame the snow and rain for that."

She glanced out the car window. "Not today."

He smiled. "Perfect day for what I have planned."

Glen drove past the gates of his family estate . . . the home he'd grown up in . . . the house where Jason now lived. They'd all been given the option to live there after their parents' death. Trent had immediately moved to Jamaica, where he spent several years drowning in his own sorrow and guilt. Glen couldn't bring himself to stay there, and Jason couldn't bring himself to leave.

So the house went to Jason. The estate sat on over fifty acres. It had its own airstrip and hangar. There were two guesthouses and an equestrian barn with half a dozen horses. A passion of his mother's that all of them worked to keep alive after her death.

Glen heard Mary blow out a breath as they passed through the gates. "Wow!"

"It's a lot to take in."

"You grew up here?"

"Yep."

He wondered exactly what Mary saw as he drove through the tree-lined drive, past the gates, and onto the property.

"It's amazing."

And she hadn't seen the house yet.

"We'll have time for the house later," he said as he detoured toward the hangar.

"I think it would take weeks to see everything."

"Maybe longer."

He parked his car outside the hangar. "Ready for an adventure?" he asked.

"I'm finding life with you to be one continuous adventure."

"Good answer. Leave your purse, you won't need it." He grabbed her hand once they left his car and led her onto the airstrip.

Nathan stood outside the Piper, smiled as they approached. Glen shook the man's hand.

"Nathan, this is Mary."

"Lovely, lass." His Scottish brogue always did a number on the ladies.

"Nathan has been here since . . . I don't know."

"I think you were in nappies. If that helps at all."

"I was young."

"Wet behind the ears, he was." Nathan had a good thirty pounds of extra around his waist but stood at least six two and had enough muscle under all that extra to back up anyone in need of backing up.

"Best mechanic and pilot I've ever met."

Mary seemed to understand what that meant and smiled. "A pleasure to meet you, Nathan."

"And such a beautiful voice. Do you sing, lass?"

"Like a duck, I'm afraid."

Glen walked over to the Piper, patted the wing. "Is she ready?"

Nathan shook his head in offense. "You asked, lad . . . here she is. See for yourself."

Mary caught on. "We're going to . . ."

Glen gave the single propeller a good tug. "Yep."

Mary sucked in an audible breath.

"This is the plane I learned to fly in. She's the plane we all learned in."

"You mean Jason and Trent?"

Glen nodded as he walked around the wing. "That's what I meant. As soon as we were old enough to reach the pedals, our father took us up."

"It's that old?"

He laughed. "Airplanes aren't the same as cars. The maintenance and care are meticulous enough to keep them in the air."

"It's small."

"Is that worry I hear in your voice?"

Mary shook her head. "Just an observation."

She didn't lie well.

Then again, a woman who didn't lie . . . even a little white lie, shouldn't be that convincing.

"C'mon."

He showed her where to step before rounding the plane and taking his seat. Inside the cramped cockpit, they brushed shoulders.

"This is crazy."

"You said you wanted to learn."

Mary grabbed her head with both hands. "But we're in . . . *this*."

Glen looked around. Saw the very basics of controls and navigation. Something to be flown on clear days with little concern for nasty weather, but that could also land safely with a skilled pilot in any condition.

"Where is Miss Adventure?"

"She's right here . . . just—"

"Good." He didn't give her any time for second-guessing. "Put those headphones on and the mouthpiece close to your lips."

Mary did as she was told and Glen went through the steps of firing up the Piper.

He waved out the window as he put the plane in motion.

—

The enclosed cockpit was meant for two. There were controls on each side that Mary kept her hands far away from. Unlike any other aircraft she'd been in, even the small space of a helicopter, this felt more intimidating.

"Can you hear me?" Glen's voice came through the earpiece with a tinny squeal.

"I hear you."

"It can get loud in here once we get going."

"One propeller means one engine?" Mary's question sounded ludicrous, even to her ears.

"I have you, Mary."

She looked over the wing at the runway as they rolled over it. "Good, cuz I'd like to eventually enjoy my cougar years."

Glen busted out laughing. "You have time for that."

He flipped a few switches and the sound in the cockpit increased. The plane followed a white line on the pavement almost as if a massive string were pulling it, increasing in speed as it went.

"See that thing in front of you?"

"The steering wheel?" It wasn't a wheel, more like a double-handled control for a video game.

"Yeah. Place your hands on it."

"Okay."

"Now pull back, slowly."

She pulled as slow as she could but still moved her hands.

"A little more."

The plane was speeding down the tarmac now.

"More."

Mary pulled with a little more effort and the ground beneath them disappeared. She gripped the controls a little tighter. "Oh my God! Did I just do that?"

"Yes you did, Counselor. Now let me have the controls for a minute."

Glen was smiling from ear to ear. He banked the plane to the left as it ascended into the blue sky.

Mary looked at the ground below as it slowly pulled away. "Feels like a slow-moving car."

"I remember thinking the same thing the first time I came up."

"So different from when you're in the passenger cabin of a jet."

Glen adjusted a few controls and leveled the plane out. "You ready for your first lesson?"

Mary grinned like a silly schoolgirl. "Seriously?"

"It won't really count toward a pilot license, but you will see if it's something you might want to explore."

"Kinda like driving a car before you get your permit."

"Exactly. Only up here, it's hard to get pulled over."

Mary placed both hands on the steering wheel, joystick . . . whatever the thing was called, and said, "I'm ready."

Glen let go of his side and Mary took control. The plane dipped and she pulled back on the wheel. "This is crazy. I don't know if I should keep my eyes on the sky or a dial."

"Both." Glen pointed at a dial. "This one tells you if you're ascending or descending. Try and keep it steady for now."

Mary found herself watching the dial like a speedometer on a car. She overcorrected the controls a couple of times before forcing her shoulders to relax.

Surprisingly, she wasn't nervous.

Glen sat beside her explaining more of the controls in simple terms. She knew there was more to flying, really flying the plane, than what she was doing, but this felt easy.

For the next hour Mary soaked in Glen's world and fell in love with his passion.

Glen landed the plane in Boston for an early dinner, which blew Mary's mind. Who flies to Boston for dinner, gets in a private plane, and flies back? Once again, Glen let her pull them off the ground, but she was in no way going to try landing.

They headed down the coast in constant conversation. Every once in a while Glen would interrupt her to talk to some radio control tower as they flew through the airspace of an airport. Even though there wasn't a highway in the sky, they still had to pay attention to other aircraft up there. Out over the ocean Glen programmed their course and engaged the autopilot function.

"Like cruise control on a car," she said.

"Only this aircraft steers."

"I can see why you like it. It's peaceful up here."

"And private."

"What stops people from engaging autopilot and falling asleep?"

Glen leaned back. "I'm sure it's happened. More likely autopilot is used for a couple to join the mile high club."

Mary glanced around the small space. "In this?"

"It's possible. Not comfortable, but it's been done."

She pointed a finger at him. "You?"

He shook his head. "Not in this plane. The four seater has more room."

"You're serious."

"I had a friend who offered a service in college. He put a curtain up between the cockpit and the back, made sure the seats reclined back. People paid good money to join the club."

Mary shook her head. "What people will do for sex."

"The beds are always used on our private charters."

"I feel like I'm constantly flying these days and I haven't used the bed."

Glen regarded her with a tilt of his head. "We need to change that."

His look alone had her pushing her knees together. "I think we do."

He leaned over, tilted her mic away from her lips, and kissed her.

Oh, yeah . . . they definitely needed to change that.

Just not in a plane with less space than a smart car.

Chapter Twenty-Three

It felt like she was always saying good-bye. This time was made worse because Glen needed to go to London on business and wouldn't be back until after the following weekend.

Before she left his home, she moved some of his clothing around while he was in the shower and placed one pair of panties and a bra in a lone drawer.

It was meant as a joke, but during her flight home Glen had sent her a text after discovering it, telling her she could have all the space she wanted.

It was dark when she stepped off the private jet at the now familiar airport and walked over to the waiting car that would take her home.

"Hello, Miss Kildare. I hope you had a pleasant trip."

"I did, thank you." She turned to wave at the pilots before climbing into the back of the sedan.

Mary kept thinking over her weekend. How crazy her life had become, and not all of it in a bad way. Even the recent break-in and plumbing troubles couldn't darken the energy she found to face every day. When she looked back on the weekend, all that had transpired, and tried to point to what she enjoyed most, she thought about the silly underwear she left at Glen's house. The feeling of belonging in his life, his world. She was almost afraid to say it, even to herself . . . but their relationship was going really well. She enjoyed teasing him about his lack of ever having a girlfriend but didn't turn that lens back on herself. A few men had floated in and out of her life, but none drawer-worthy. None she would have trusted to take her up in a single-engine airplane with no escape hatch. None who whispered her name when they made love to her. None she missed the second she stepped onto the tarmac to fly home.

Glen was turning into the real deal, and Mary wasn't sure if she should just abandon herself to the feeling of belonging to someone, even as a girlfriend, or keep the walls she'd constructed years ago up to save her the heartache if it didn't work out. Her two minds were fighting on which path to take, and her heart stood in the middle of the tug-of-war.

The driver pulled up to her condo and let her out.

She expected him to pull her luggage from the back and hand it to her, but instead he encouraged her to let him walk her in. "I was told you had a bit of trouble a while back. Mr. Fairchild asked that I see you were safely inside before I leave."

She smiled. Even without Glen there, he was trying to take care of her.

Mary turned the key in her door and let the driver walk in first.

Inside the alarm let out a steady buzz, waiting for her to disarm it.

She punched in a series of numbers and stood back.

The living room was the same. The new floors had gone in but the replacement furniture had yet to be purchased. Indeed, her lone lamp stood on a cardboard box and the fresh coat of paint made the place smell and look like she'd just moved in.

"Looks like you're okay."

Mary thanked the man and locked the door after he left.

She reset the alarm, telling it she would be walking around but to blast her ears off if someone opened a window or an external door.

Mary fell into bed thirty minutes later after a brief text from Glen.

```
I miss you already.
```

—

Jacob Golf called to schedule an appointment, one without his wife, the day Mary picked up her car from the body shop.

Mary's first thought was to tell him she couldn't see him. Call it a conflict of interest or some such thing. Then she wondered what the chances of him scheduling an appointment were if he'd actually been the one in her home messing it up. His appointments almost always took place after five to accommodate his work in the past. It wasn't a surprise that he asked to see her after six. They negotiated a five thirty time slot the following evening.

She considered telling Glen but then realized he'd just worry, probably do something stupid like fly out just to sit outside the door waiting to pounce on the guy.

The decision to treat Jacob as any of her other clients was made. That still didn't stop her from pacing the small office up until the minute he knocked on her door.

Her hands actually shook when she opened it and greeted him with a smile. "Good to see you, Jacob." The lie wasn't easy but needed to be said.

"Thanks for working me into your schedule."

"No problem. Have a seat."

Her office had a small love seat and two side chairs for her clients and the chair she sat in during the sessions. On one side of the room sat a desk that she used on occasion, but most of her work went home with her.

She sat across from him, placed her notepad in her lap, and waited.

He held a water bottle and continually twisted the cap.

"Nina's leaving me. Left me."

Mary acknowledged him with a soft smile.

"I guess you already knew that."

"I still see Nina every week."

"Yeah, she told me that. I'm guessing you know more about how she's feeling than I do right now."

"You know I can't talk to you about what we discuss."

Jacob twisted the cap off, took a drink. "You probably know what she's been up to, why she's so distant."

It was time to divert his attention to his own feelings and break away from Nina's. "How are you feeling about the split?"

"Like shit. It isn't what I want. I was here, wasn't I? Working on shit . . . all the shit we've swept under the carpet for years. We'd come here, dig it all up, fight about it for a week, and then come back for more."

Mary couldn't deny that had been their routine. Unfortunately all her advice in the world about her clients working on one thing at a time was seldom practiced outside of her office.

"It did feel as if you both had a lot of *shit* under that carpet to work through." She used his words.

His nervous hands kept twisting the bottle. He drank the water almost as an afterthought. "Didn't matter. You know what I think?"

"No."

"I think this was a distraction. This whole counseling crap was her way of showing me she wanted to stay in our marriage when she really didn't. She's having an affair, isn't she?"

Keeping her face neutral was a task worthy of an Oscar. "What makes you believe she's unfaithful?"

"You didn't answer my question." This was the part of Jacob that always made Mary uneasy. He didn't get what he wanted out of the question and his eyes pinned her down as if she would break and spill every detail she had.

"Even if I knew about an affair from either one of you, you know I can't discuss it."

"The bitch . . . I knew she'd been fucked by someone else."

Hearing the word she'd seen written on her mirror renewed the tremble in her hands.

"That is not what I said, Jacob."

"You didn't *not* say it either." He stood with such force the couch hit the back of the wall.

Mary dropped her pen.

He pointed the water bottle in her direction. "I told her we needed a male counselor if this was going to work. No, she picked you. Someone she could have agree with her."

"Jacob, please sit down. That's not how it is." Her voice wavered.

"I'm not a dog. I don't sit when someone tells me to."

He took another step toward her and Mary gripped the side of her chair to keep from backing into a corner. "You're making me uncomfortable, Jacob. I'm going to have to ask you to calm down or leave."

Jacob took another step toward her and she flinched. "I pay you to listen to me. You'll listen." He was yelling now.

"I need you to leave."

Steam practically radiated off the man's head. He stared at her for half a second, threw the water bottle he had in his hand at the opposite wall, and stormed out of her office.

Her heart kicked hard in her chest. It took ten minutes for her to stand, and when she did her hands shook to the point that when she reached out to close and lock the door, she couldn't grip the knob.

"That wasn't smart, Mary," she scolded herself.

She waited until she was sure Jacob had time to leave the parking lot.

The water bottle sat empty beside the wall. She reached for it and stopped just short of picking it up.

The man was unstable, upset . . . blaming her, to some extent, for his failed marriage. She found a box of tissues and used one to pick up the bottle without smearing her fingerprints all over it. She set it on her desk and picked up her phone.

Officer Taylor's phone went to voice mail.

"Hello, Officer Taylor. This is Mary Kildare. I have a name. A client." This could destroy her career. Or this man could be the one who'd destroyed her home, and it was only a matter of time before he did more than yell at her and throw water bottles. "I also have something that has his fingerprints on it. I'm in need of your advice on how to proceed." She left the message with her home phone number for the morning.

She hung up and put the officer's card with her others before tucking it back in her purse.

Kent's card sat below.

She called his cell number, hoping he was in his office.

A precaution.

Smarter than inviting the only suspect in her head into her office alone.

"Hello?"

"Kent?"

"This is."

"Kent, it's Mary."

"Oh, hey. This is a surprise."

And she didn't need him getting the wrong idea. "You said I could call if I needed someone to walk me to my car."

"Jesus, are you okay? You sound upset."

"A client left angry. If you're not in the office, it's fine—"

"No. I'm here. Give me three minutes." He hung up.

Mary felt some of the tension leave her shoulders. Even though she expected his knock on her office door, she still jumped.

"Mary? It's me."

She flung the door open and the shakes she'd had before became nearly uncontrollable now. Like all the adrenaline in her system dumped out all at the same time.

Kent reached for her shoulders with gentle hands and she slumped. She was safe.

"It's okay."

She leaned her forehead on his chest.

"Whoa . . . do we need to call the police?"

"I already did."

His hands squeezed. "Do you want to sit while we wait for them?"

"No . . . no. They aren't coming. It's hard to explain. I just need to get home."

Kent offered a soft smile. "Do you need me to follow you?"

"No. My friend is across the street. I'll be fine." She twisted away from his supportive hands, grabbed her purse, and locked the door behind them.

It was still light outside, but the parking lot was nearly empty.

She felt silly in the broad daylight hiding from shadows.

She unlocked her car door, taking a good look around. "Seems ridiculous now."

Kent didn't seem to mind. "What's this guy look like?"

"Six foot, I guess, thinning hairline, Caucasian."

"Did he threaten you?"

"No . . . he was angry . . . inappropriately so." She didn't want to go into details. "I don't want to take any chances."

"You shouldn't. When are you done tomorrow?"

"Four."

Kent placed his hands in his pockets. "I'll meet you in the hall."

"I can't ask that—"

"You didn't."

She placed a hand on his arm. "Thank you, Kent. You're a good friend."

He tilted his head. "Always. Drive safe."

Mary kept one eye on the rearview mirror, the other on the road. Before she pulled onto her street, she called Dakota and Walt.

Walt answered.

"Hey, Walt . . . I need you to do me a favor."

He met her in the street, walked her into her silent house, and encouraged her to join them for dinner.

Mary declined, said she had too much work to catch up on.

She had a microwave dinner with a glass of wine and an open laptop.

She'd sent a text to Glen, asking him to call if he was still up. The time change and busy weekend might have resulted in him going to bed early, so she didn't call.

By nine she thought he'd gone to bed and gave up on waiting for him to respond. She put her phone on the charger and left it on her kitchen counter before turning all the lights off and moving upstairs.

She attempted to read, find a happy place for her brain, and couldn't concentrate long enough to finish a page.

She considered a bath . . . then remembered every horror movie she'd ever watched as a kid and decided that would be the worst idea ever.

A pair of pajamas and a second glass of wine helped her get through one chapter.

Falling asleep was a challenge, staying asleep was impossible.

The phone jolted her out of bed at six in the morning.

Chapter Twenty-Four

Glen caught Mary's text before he went to bed the night before, attempted to text her back only to find silence on the other end.

He arrived at the office with a message from Walt asking him to call.

"Hey, Doc. What has you up so early?"

"Fourteen pounds of screaming love."

"I'm sure he's worth it."

"He is. I'm calling for a flight."

Glen grabbed a pen on his desk. "Finally convinced Dakota that she's not putting anyone out?"

"No, Dakota was booking a commercial flight. I reminded her that babies on airplanes make for lots of unhappy passengers. To which she said, screw them."

Glen laughed. "Sounds like Dakota."

"I told her I'd call you, see if you have any empty legs to Denver."

"Empty legs . . . she really doesn't get it, does she?"

"I think once she realizes that flying with Leo will be much better on a private plane than in a cabin with two hundred other people, she'll stop fighting it."

"Give me your dates, I'll put someone on it."

Walt told him when they planned on traveling, went on to give a time for them to visit Dakota's family in Savannah.

"I wouldn't have to fight her if you'd let us pay something," Walt told him.

Glen had heard this before. His first reaction was an absolute no. But Dakota wasn't one to take charity for long. "Tell her we can work something out."

"Will we?"

"Maybe . . . but in the meantime, let her taste how peaceful it is to bring a baby on a private plane. Then maybe one trip on a commercial jet. She's smart. She'll figure it out."

Walt sighed. "You're good."

Glen leaned back in his chair. "I've been doing this for a while."

"Thanks, Glen. I appreciate it."

"No problem."

"Listen, about Mary. That guy really scared her last night."

It took a moment for Walt's words to register. "What guy?"

"She didn't tell you? I thought she would have called you last night."

"We played tag with texting. What guy? What are you talking about?" Glen tapped the pen he'd been using against his desk.

"She called us on her way home from the office. She said one of her clients got a little out of hand, scared her enough to call that cop who wrote up the report after the break-in."

The pen in Glen's hand snapped in half. "Out of hand? Is she okay?" Damn it. Why didn't she call him?

"Scared her. And she doesn't scare easy. She asked that I come out and walk her into the house."

"Jesus." He ran his hand through his hair, glanced at his watch. *It's six in the morning there.*

"She's all right. Just shook up last night."

"Thanks for watching out for her."

"You don't need to thank me. I'm glad she called."

"Thanks for the heads-up. I'll get someone on these flights for you."

Glen hung up with Walt and speed-dialed Mary.

It was obvious he woke her up.

"Tell me what happened!"

—

Mary met Officer Taylor at her office before she saw her first client. He brought someone from the department who dusted for prints. They packaged the water bottle and went ahead and took samples from the doorknob of her office and that of the glass door leading into the building.

She went into detail about the encounter with Jacob and how he'd presented with this instability before her home was vandalized.

Much like with Glen that morning, she second-guessed herself, her reaction, but both men didn't think she was overreacting at all. They were going to see if any prints matched and bring Jacob Golf in for a little chat.

Once the police left, Mary took a few minutes to clean up the mess they left behind and made the phone call to Glen she'd promised.

"Ten o'clock and all is well," she teased when he answered.

"You're not funny."

"I have to laugh. But all *is* well. The police just left, I have ten minutes before my first client. Other than the zillion questions that will come from the people in the building I'll be answering all week, I'm good."

"It's good people know something is wrong."

There was a knock on her door. "My client is early. I have to go."

"Call when you leave."

"At four, I know. We already talked about this."

"Be safe."

"Good-bye, Glen."

"Four o'clock."

"Yes, sir."

"The prints on the water bottle weren't the best," Officer Taylor explained over the phone. "I have forensics checking those we picked up on the door. But I have to tell you, it's a low priority."

Mary didn't like the sound of that. "Why?"

"Honestly, because no one was hurt. Breaking and entering and petty vandalism—"

"There was nothing petty about what happened at my house!"

"I understand that, Miss Kildare, but in the eyes of the law. This isn't at the top of our list. Yes, we're invested in solving the case, but forensics is completely bogged down with violent crimes, homicides, and felonies. I'm sure you understand. A family counselor spooked by a man who finds out his wife is having an affair doesn't compete. Not in our imperfect system."

This was not the news she wanted to hear twenty-four hours after Jacob left her office.

"Have you brought Mr. Golf in for questioning?"

Office Taylor paused.

His silence answered her question before he uttered a word. "He wasn't at his place of business today and the estranged wife hasn't seen him in a week."

"Great. Just great."

"I'm sorry I can't do more. If you're threatened directly, or something else occurs, notify me."

"I did that." *And it isn't helping!*

"Miss Kildare, do you own a firearm?"

Yet another question about having a gun. "I didn't think I needed to."

He let the question about owning a gun alone, apologized again, and hung up.

Glen was expecting an update. Considering how upset he'd been about learning what had happened via Walt, Mary went ahead and called his cell when she got off the phone with the police.

"Hey!"

"You don't sound happy," he said.

"I'm pissed." She relayed the conversation, which left both of them seething.

"So they're waiting for blood to do anything."

"Don't say it like that!" But Mary knew he was right.

"I'm canceling my London trip."

Mary stopped pacing her kitchen. "The hell you are!"

"I can't be on the other side of the ocean with this going on."

"Glen, no! I told you I'd keep you up to date on what's happening to make you feel better, not for you to put your life on hold."

"Well, I don't feel better. Making sure you're okay is not putting anything on hold, it's prioritizing what's important."

She toned down the anger in her voice. "Thank you. You're important to me, too. But you're going to London."

"Mary—"

"I'll buy a gun." The decision was off the hip and not really what she wanted to do.

Her words were met with silence. "That should make me feel better."

"Then I won't buy a gun."

"No. That makes me feel worse."

Mary leaned against the counter. "Well, at least you're open about your feelings."

"I'm really not happy about all this."

"I would hope not. I'm the one who is starting to cuss about it almost daily."

"And you don't swear." His voice started to lose its edge.

"Nuns. They had rulers and Mary Frances wasn't opposed to washing mouths out with soap."

"And Our Fathers."

She started to relax. "Don't forget the Hail Marys . . . but those always felt wrong, considering my name."

A long, audible sigh met her joke.

"Listen, Glen. I know our geography is not quite perfect. I think we both knew that going in. But for this to work, we need to trust each other on every level."

"I trust you, Mary. It's the dirtbag I don't trust."

"I don't trust him either, but I'm not going to let him control my life. I'll be smart. Have someone walk me to my car after dark, keep an eye over my shoulder. I'll buy the darn gun and make sure I know how to use it. Maybe I'll even get one of those stun gun things that Dakota has."

"And a self-defense class," he added.

"Probably not a bad idea."

"I miss you, Mary." His words were like a hot knife in butter, and they kicked her heart in all the right ways.

"I miss you, too. But you know something?"

"What?"

"Just knowing you're there, that I can call you and if I really needed you to be here, you'd come—"

"Say the word."

"It means everything." She cradled the phone in her hands and imagined his face on the other end doing the same.

"Be safe."

"I will . . . good-bye, Glen." She started to hang up.

"No!"

"No, what?"

"Don't say good-bye."

She gripped the phone. "Why?"

"Just don't. Say good night, or talk to you tomorrow. Just stop saying good-bye."

The sadness in Glen's voice brought unexpected tears to her eyes. "Why?" She knew there was something behind his lack of saying those words.

A long gap in conversation made her think he wasn't going to explain.

"My parents said good-bye."

Mary covered her mouth to keep from gasping. Two solid tears fell from her eyes. "I'll call you in the morning."

"Okay. Until then."

Mary listened as her client, who was attempting to fix her marriage without the support of her husband, told her about her nonexistent sex life.

"Yes, I've gained some weight, but three kids will do that."

"Does your weight make intimacy difficult for you?" Mary asked.

"We've always made love with the lights off. Even before kids."

"What about—" A loud banging on her office door brought her question to an abrupt stop.

"Mary!" A woman yelled. The handle on the door jiggled, but the lock kept it from opening.

"Excuse me." Mary opened the door to find Nina fuming on the other side.

"You told him!"

She should have seen this coming. Mary stepped out of her office, glanced down the empty hall of the office building. "Nina, I'm with another client."

"I don't give a shit about your other client. You told him I had an affair."

With the volume of Nina's voice, she'd just told the entire building.

"I told him no such thing."

"He told me he came to you. That you confirmed it." Nina tossed her long dark hair over her shoulder.

"That isn't what happened." Mary hoped that her low voice would prompt the other woman to lower hers.

"You're lying. And to cover your tracks you've called the cops on him. Who the hell do you think you are? Jacob is an asshole, but he doesn't break into houses and fuck them up."

"Nina—"

"That's what the police said happened. Are you going tell me that's not true, too?"

By now two of the doors down the hall had opened, and more than one head popped out to watch the confrontation.

"We should discuss this in private."

"I'm done talking to you. I can't believe you betrayed my trust." It hurt to hear the words, even though Mary knew they weren't true.

"I don't know who I report people like you to, but I'll find out." Nina turned on her stiletto heels and stomped out of the building.

That didn't go well.

Mary tried to smile when she walked back into her office.

"I think I should go." Her client stood to leave.

"I'm sorry for the interruption. We can continue."

"I don't think . . ."

Mary pulled out her appointment book. "I understand. No charge for today. I'll see you next week."

"No. I think I'm good. I'll . . ."

Mary wanted to explain but knew that would just make things worse. "If you change your mind."

Mary stared at the closed door before burying her face in her hands.

The flowers on her doorstep at home put the smile back on her face. There wasn't a card, a habit she was noticing about Glen. Maybe there was something to that . . . like him not saying good-bye.

Instead of asking, she sent him a text. `I miss you, too.`

Chapter Twenty-Five

The cockpit of the Challenger was nothing like the plane Glen had taken Mary up in the previous week. In the copilot seat, Jason kicked back as they cruised at thirty-two thousand feet somewhere over the Atlantic.

The phone in Glen's pocket buzzed and he took a second to look at Mary's update.

He expected a time stamp and an *all's well* message. Instead he warmed into the words, `I miss you, too.`

He glanced over to find Jason staring at him.

"What?"

"I've seen that look before."

"What look?"

Jason pointed in his direction. "That one. The one Trent wears whenever Monica texts him."

"I like the attention, what can I say." He put his phone back in his pocket.

"It's more than that." Jason turned his gaze back to the controls in front of him.

It *was* more than that.

"Have you ever been in love, Jason?"

He looked out the window as if the sea had the answer. "My inability to give you a name suggests the answer is no."

Glen closed his eyes and saw Mary's smile, smelled the shampoo she used on all that hair. He pictured the single drawer in his home with her underwear.

"You love her, don't you?"

He did . . .

Jesus, he did.

"How did that happen?" he asked to the sky in a whisper.

Jason unbuckled his belt and climbed out of his seat, patting Glen on the shoulder as he left the cockpit. "You could do worse."

Before his brother disappeared into the cabin, Glen asked, "Do you think Mom would have liked her?"

"Are you kidding? Mom would be decorating a nursery and promising the first grandchild a pony. Not to mention Mary's tamed you. A task even Mom and Dad couldn't achieve."

Glen texted Mary back once Jason left. `Thirty-two thousand feet and all is well.`

It took a while for the dot, dot, dot to turn into words. `Texting while flying is dangerous! Stop it.`

`I'll text when I land, call you in the morning.`

`Looking forward to it.`

Yeah . . . Glen had it bad.

—

Mary walked out of her office at just after three.

Kent had taken the duty of walking her to her car when she worked late, but she didn't ask him to on early days.

That didn't stop the man from showing up anyway.

"You don't have to keep doing this."

"Someone has to keep an eye on you."

He walked her across the parking lot with a smile.

"I think I scared him off, or the police did. Everything is quiet here . . . quiet at home. I think the cloud has parted."

"It's when you stop watching that bad stuff happens. I work with lawyers, I know this stuff. I'll just keep this up if it's all the same to you."

She unlocked her car. "That's sweet. I don't want to sound ungrateful, I just don't want to keep putting you out."

"You're not putting me out, Mary."

"Okay. I'll let it go then."

"See you tomorrow."

She placed one foot in her car, talked with him over the car door. "I'm not coming in tomorrow."

Kent's lips twitched. "Big weekend?"

"Quiet weekend, actually. Glen is in London on business."

The information seemed to please him.

"You have my number if you need something."

"I should be fine, but thanks."

He stepped away from the car when she closed the door.

In the rearview mirror, Kent stood watching her drive away.

"This is getting awkward," she said to herself.

"Go! We are going to be fine." Mary sat with Leo in her lap.

Dakota's cast had come off the week before, and she and Walt were wearing something other than sweatpants and shorts and ready for a couple of hours away from the house.

"It feels strange . . . doesn't it feel awful?" Dakota tugged on Walt's arm when she asked the question.

"Two hours, Dakota. Leo and I will survive." Mary dangled her hair in Leo's face and watched him smile. "Won't we? I think we should invite all the neighborhood kids over and get pizza. Isn't that a great idea?"

"C'mon, Baby Mama. They're going to be great." Walt dragged Dakota out of the house.

Mary giggled at Leo. "We finally got rid of them, didn't we? Silly parents."

A list of possible reasons Leo was crying sat beside the list of instructions and every possible phone number Mary might need if there was an emergency.

It was comical watching Dakota squirm about leaving.

It was Dakota and Walt's first date since Leo's birth, and overdue according to everything Mary had read on the subject.

Mary moved from the couch to a spread out baby blanket on the floor and lay beside Leo, entertained by his smile. Colorful toys surrounded them, some played music, others flashed lights, two did both.

Thirty minutes after Dakota and Walt had left, her phone rang.

She found her phone in her purse and answered it without looking at who was calling. "We're fine!"

"We? Who are we?" The sound of Glen's voice made her heart skip.

She sat down next to Leo and continued to dangle a soft toy out of his reach.

"You found me out, Glen. I have another man in my life." She wiggled her nose at Leo. "Don't I?" she said in a high-pitched voice.

Glen laughed. "So Dakota finally caved."

"I thought for sure you were her calling."

"How is babysitting time?"

"Leo and I are just hanging . . . waiting for the pizza and beer delivery."

"I don't think he's on solid food yet."

"The pizza's for me . . . Leo has a hankering for something other than milk."

"It sounds like you're having fun."

"Leo's a really good listener, and I have lots to talk about." She had him giggling with a swish of her hair. "How was the flight?"

"Uneventful. I like flying with Jason. We don't get enough time together."

"I'd imagine he's a captive audience in a cockpit," she said.

"I think that's part of the appeal for this trip. That and the fact that our London affiliates need to see our faces more than once a year."

They talked about how often he went to London.

She told him she'd never been.

He told her he'd take her there soon . . . that she'd better update her passport.

To which she let him know she didn't have one.

And then Leo became a little upset that he wasn't the center of Mary's attention.

"I should let you go," Glen decided.

"I think there is diaper duty in my immediate future."

"And as awful as that sounds, I still wish I was there with you."

"Careful what you ask for. Next time you're changing diapers and I'll order the pizza."

"You're on!"

Leo offered a louder protest. "I'm being summoned."

"Go. We'll talk tomorrow."

"Sounds good."

He hung up without saying good-bye.

Mary couldn't be happier.

She set her phone to the side and picked Leo up. "Just you and me, bud."

He kept lifting his head from her shoulder as she walked up the stairs to the nursery to change his diaper.

Her first time at the plate, and Leo was good to her.

She sat in the glider with him on her shoulder after the task and rocked his sleepy eyes to rest.

Mary let him sleep on her for quite some time. The rise and fall of his little chest put a flutter in her belly she never thought she'd have. She couldn't help but wonder if her own mother had ever held her, ever thought about the tiny heart with its rapid beat inside her chest. Did her own father wish to change her diaper instead of being away on business?

Stupid thought. The chances of her biological parents ever *being away on business* was slim to none. Kids not ready for kids was a more likely scenario.

Her thoughts moved directly to Glen. He'd had such a different life, loving parents, stable home. Yet they were both just now entering a committed relationship for the first time.

Mary lifted Leo into his crib and watched him sleep.

It wasn't until she saw lights from a car outside that she walked toward the window overlooking the street below.

A dark sedan slowed to nearly a stop in front of the house. Mary wondered if it was an unmarked police car, something Officer Taylor said to expect. It didn't stick around long before it drove away.

Mary crept out of Leo's room thinking of how lucky she was to have what she did.

Mary found her phone and sent a quick text to Dakota. `Leo is asleep and everything is fine. Enjoy your evening.`

A smiley face was Dakota's reply.

—

Glen talked to Mary every day, texted her constantly . . . and yet he still missed her.

Their winter trip to London hadn't happened, so this one was longer than normal. Jason and Glen were due to fly back on Wednesday, and it was only Sunday.

Jet lag alone kept them a half a step behind for two days.

"Did Dakota survive a few hours away last night?" Glen called Mary as early as he could without waking her up. He'd just come off an afternoon lawn party that took place in tents because of the London rain. He had an hour to shower and change for the next round of shoulder rubbing on his Sunday.

"Two hours and twenty minutes . . . and yes. It was good for them. I saw it in their faces when they walked in the door."

"I would imagine the first time is the hardest, and after that it gets easier."

"I hope so, or she'll be sitting on a therapy couch in ten years asking what happened to her own identity . . . how did she become just a mom."

"What's on your agenda today?" Glen liked the idea of picturing what Mary was doing. It made the distance more tolerable somehow.

"Furniture shopping. There are a few wholesale warehouses in the valley I'm going to check out."

His mind flashed to the week of all the chaos. The first thing that needed to be replaced was her mattress. Glen didn't consider himself a shopper, but hopping from one mattress to the other with Mary by his side changed his mind. "Make sure there's a comfortable armrest on the couch," he told her.

"Why?"

"For when we don't make it to your bedroom."

He felt her blushing through the phone.

"Good call." Her giggle made him smile.

"I need to go. I'll call before I go to bed."

"I'd tell you that isn't necessary, but I'd be depriving myself of your voice. And I'm becoming addicted to it."

He knew the feeling. "I wonder if there's a twelve-step program for that?"

"Probably. Have fun schmoozing."

"Have fun shopping."

He heard her blow him a kiss through the line.

—

The problem with furniture shopping on a budget was everything you liked you couldn't afford and everything you could afford you hated. The salesman at the second store she went to followed her around like a puppy. He had doe eyes that lingered on her butt every time she walked in front of him. Still, he seemed harmless, just enamored. "There is a hotel surplus store a couple miles from here. Gently used furniture from some high-end places."

Mary thought about the sofa she and Glen had made love on. At the time she didn't consider how many others might have gotten naked on the furniture. Now she cringed. Bringing that into her home . . . not gonna happen. "I think I'll pass on that."

The store she was in was filled with hard, contemporary edges and glass.

After cleaning up glass in her condominium for two weeks, she decided wood would be a better option.

"Any stores close by that have more traditional furniture?"

The butt-watching employee happily told her about several places to shop. He seemed to understand her budget restraints and guided her to those he thought would be best. Then he asked her for her phone number.

"I'm sorry. I have a boyfriend."

"Boyfriend, not husband?" The guy was still smiling.

"More like a fiancé." She wasn't sure where that stretch of the truth came from, but after Kent, she didn't want there to be any misunderstanding.

"Fiancé is not a husband."

She laughed and his enamored smile gave way to total player status. "You're persistent. But I'm not interested."

His eyes did the full body scan. "Can't blame me for trying."

"You have a nice day." She turned to leave.

He called out after her, "It would have been if you'd said yes." He was still flirting with her.

Mary waved a hand in the air but didn't turn around as she walked out the door.

The next store leaned toward what she wanted but wasn't perfect. Unlike the last one, with flirty player guy, this store had very few salespeople on the floor. Every once in a while, Mary felt someone watching and thought for sure a salesman stood in the wings just waiting for her to show interest in something.

By the time lunch rolled around, she stood in the sixth store of the day. Maybe it was the heat that was climbing up into the hundreds or the fact she was hungry . . . or perhaps the sheer desire to get the job done, but the sixth store was the one she found her furniture in.

Full, rounded armrests and sturdy wooden end tables along with great prices. Sold!

It took over an hour to complete the paperwork and schedule a delivery, a delivery that cost twice as much since she lived in Orange County. Still, the furniture price offset the delivery charge.

She ate lunch at one of the many small fast food Mexican restaurants the valley offered. The dollar tacos were always good, but she always felt a little out of place when eating them. As much as Mary attempted to tame her hair, by the middle of the day it took on a life of its own. And when a fair-skinned, blue-eyed blonde walked into an eatery that often only had dark-haired, brown-eyed patrons, she stuck out. Even the menu was only written in Spanish. Good thing she knew her way around the language enough to order food.

She took her steak tacos and chips to a table and checked her e-mail on her phone while eating. Mary ignored the feeling of being watched while she ate.

On her way home she kept an eye on her rearview mirror a little more than normal.

Calling herself stressed, Mary did what she hadn't done in a while. She detoured toward the beach, which was filled with people beating the heat of the valley. With a floppy hat, a beach chair, a paperback, and a bottle of water, Mary found her Zen. She took a quick picture of her feet facing the waves and sent it off to Glen. She teased him with the message: `Hope the rain isn't too bad.`

He sent a text a short time later of a dark sky and rain pouring in front of a streetlight. `No such luck.`

Mary dipped her toes into the sand and her head into the pages of the book.

She liked her life. Loved having Glen in it. Loved the simple enjoyment of babysitting for her BFF. Loved knowing that someone cared if she was at the beach or at work or home watching TV.

She finished her day grocery shopping and missed a call from Glen while she was in the store.

His message made her smile.

"Sorry I missed you to say good night. I'm exhausted and have to be up early tomorrow. I'll dream of you."

If his message wasn't enough, the flowers on her doorstep when she got home had her smiling all night.

Chapter Twenty-Six

Mary met her Monday with a headache and a scratchy throat.

She was supposed to have breakfast with Dakota and Leo while Walt took the morning to check in with the ER.

"I just don't want to get the baby sick, and I feel like I'm coming down with something."

"All that shopping yesterday," Dakota suggested.

"I think it was the number of door handles I touched going in and out of stores."

"Do you have clients today?"

"After one. I'm probably fine, just a head cold."

"If you need anything just holler. I'll send Walt over with a biological warfare suit and some Tylenol."

Mary couldn't help but laugh with the image that came to mind. "I'm guessing the old Dakota is coming back." Dakota had always been a closet prepper. Someone who stocked enough food for four months and medical supplies for a year. During her pregnancy some of that waned.

"The old Dakota needed to remove the cast and the ten pounds of baby in her belly. Do you have any idea how good that first shower felt when I came home cast free?"

"You've already told me." About a dozen times.

"Feel better. If you plan on staying home, give me a call so I know it's you running around in your house."

"I will. Talk to you later."

"Bye."

Mary almost asked her not to say good-bye, but didn't.

She took a nap around ten, had some hot soup for lunch, and left for the office at twelve thirty feeling marginally better.

Right as she pulled into the parking lot at work, her phone rang.

"I was wondering if I'd hear from you today." The eight-hour time difference between her and Glen was not something she wanted to get used to.

"Meetings all day. Dinner with clients. How are you?"

Mary rubbed her forehead as if it was going to ease the ache inside. "I'm actually kinda sick."

"Oh, no."

"Yeah, think I picked up something shopping yesterday."

"Poor baby. I hate being ill."

"Don't we all. And I'm about to go into the office so I'm going to have to cut this short."

"You go. I just wanted to tell you I was thinking about you."

She cradled the phone as she sat in her car talking on it. "I miss you, too."

"I'll be flying back Wednesday and flying out again on Friday to come see you."

"I can't wait. I should be better by then."

"And Mary?"

"Yes?"

"I'm really glad you said yes to our first date."

"I'm really glad you asked."

He disconnected the call and she forgot about her headache.

—

"I have some good news." Officer Taylor had left a message when she was with a client, and when she called him back, this was how he started the conversation.

"I'm listening."

"We have a partial match from the prints we took off your office door to that inside your condo."

"Which means that whoever was in my condo has been in my office."

"And that is enough of a reason to find Jacob Golf and bring him in."

Mary wrapped the bulk of her hair in her hand and tossed it behind her back. "I thought you were looking for Jacob already."

"Sending a car to his residence and work when you called was the extent of our search. We'll bring him in, see if we can get him to consent to fingerprints to see if they match."

"If he's guilty, he won't consent."

"Maybe he'll say something that gives us the right to run him through the process. We'll get the prints."

Mary leaned the phone away from her mouth to cough. "This is good news."

"You sound sick."

"I am sick."

"I'll give you an update as soon as I have one."

"Thanks, Officer Taylor."

"You watch yourself, Miss Kildare. Once we heat things up, the guilty often get active."

"I'm picking up my shotgun next week. The guy at the store said it's the best for home defense." She held the thing once, went through the motions of loading it for the sake of buying it, but still wasn't sure she should have it.

"Shotguns do the job. Every woman in my family owns one."

Somehow, she knew he'd say that. "We'll talk soon."

"Feel better, Miss Kildare."

Mary barely made it through her last client before feeling like she was going to fall asleep on the drive home.

The lights in the parking lot did a fair job of lighting her route to her car. Not that she paid much attention to them.

Halfway around the building, she saw Kent walking her way.

"You're off early."

She coughed twice and lifted her hand holding her briefcase. "Finishing at home tonight."

"You look a little pale."

"Head cold," she said, even though she knew it was more than that. She used the remote on her keychain to unlock the door of her car.

Kent shuffled around her to open her door.

She muttered a thanks and climbed inside. "You're working late tonight."

"I told you I'd walk you to your car. I keep my commitments." Kent leaned in as he spoke.

Mary turned her head to cough. "I appreciate your help. But don't let me put you out." Her head was splitting.

"You're not putting me out."

She offered a weak smile. "I should get home."

"Good night."

Mary waved as she pulled away and counted the red lights on her way home.

It was the middle of the night in London, so she texted Glen instead of a call. `I heard from Officer Taylor. They have a match on fingerprints. I'll give you details tomorrow...I'm fighting more than a head cold. Ugh!!!`

—

Glen woke to Mary's text. He had a hundred and one questions about the match on the fingerprints but got stuck on the image of Mary laid up in bed with a Kleenex to her nose and cough syrup at her bedside.

He had a secretary that he never used for personal things . . . but there was a first time for everything, and he was half a world away. "I want a monkey . . . a teddy bear will do if you can't find a monkey, but the monkey is better."

"With a thermometer?"

"Yes, with a thermometer in its hand or mouth."

"You're serious." Sylvia was in her late forties and had worked as the CFO's secretary since before he took the position.

"It's above and beyond. I'll make it up on your birthday."

"My birthday was last month."

"Christmas then. I want the card to say . . ." He rattled off his sentiment with a smile.

"How much do you want to spend on this *monkey*?"

"I don't care."

"A hundred bucks?"

"I don't care."

"A thousand?"

"I. Don't. Care."

"Do you want balloons with this?"

His eyes lit up. "Great idea."

"I was kidding." The sarcasm in her voice made his smile bigger.

"Today. If she's not home, leave it at her doorstep."

"You don't pay me enough, Fairchild."

"Yes I do. Thanks, Sylvia."

"I draw the line at *breakup flowers*."

He imagined Mary picking up the monkey and reading his card. "I don't think you'll ever have to worry about those."

"I'm holding you to that."

"You're the best."

"Yeah, yeah . . . you owe me."

He liked his sassy secretary.

Chapter Twenty-Seven

Mary crawled out of bed the next morning long enough to call her clients and tell them she wasn't well and needed to reschedule or risk making them ill.

Walt showed up just before noon. "I left the bio suit at home."

Mary opened the door, wrapped her bathrobe a little tighter around her waist. "Dakota won't let you back inside until you've gone through decon."

"She's not that bad."

Mary laughed. She knew his wife better than he did sometimes.

He had his doctor bag and looked her up and around, asked her a bunch of questions.

"I think it's viral."

She knew what that meant. "No antibiotics."

"Nope, just good old sleep and crap to make you feel better. Dakota has a ton of decongestants, nighttime stuff. Daytime stuff. Don't drag yourself to the drugstore when you have one right across the street." He suggested a few things by name. All of which she had.

Mary rested her head in her hand. "I'm stocked. But let Dakota know I'll have her leave it in the middle of the street if I need something."

She walked him to the door as the bell was ringing.

A delivery boy, not much older than eighteen, stood with a stuffed something and a half dozen balloons.

"Ah, Miss Kildare?"

Mary lifted a hand.

Walt stood back when the kid handed her the toy.

It took a minute for her to recognize what the mass of fake fur was. Then she started laughing until she was coughing.

The kid stood back and looked around.

"It's a monkey."

Walt blinked, stared, and blinked again. "Yep. It's a monkey."

"That's funny." She kept laughing. The boy at the door looked behind him toward his delivery van.

"Oh, a tip." She twisted around, wondered where she'd left her purse as another coughing fit stopped her progress up to her bedroom.

"You know, lady . . . it's okay."

Walt removed a five-dollar bill from his wallet and helped her out.

In the back of her head it registered that the kid drove away and Walt said his good-byes . . . but all Mary could see was a silly stuffed monkey with sad eyes, holding a thermometer.

This time, Glen sent a card.

You didn't even have to fight for it.

She set the balloons next to the flowers that were starting to turn and hugged the monkey to her chest.

When she climbed back in bed, her head ached, her chest felt heavy, but her heart was full.

The ibuprofen and cough syrup Glen suggested wiped her out for a good two hours. She felt a little better when she climbed out of bed the second time that day but still knew she wasn't right.

Still, like anyone not on their deathbed, she tried to get a few things done. When she heard her doorbell for the second time that day, she thought of the monkey on her bed upstairs and wondered what Glen was sending her now.

A man holding an invoice greeted her with a smile. "You Miss Kildare?"

"I am."

"You asked for delivery in the afternoon." He looked down at her bathrobe and smirked.

Mary glanced beyond him to see the truck from the place she'd purchased her living room set.

"Right. Yeah . . . c'mon in." She opened the door wide and pointed to the room behind her. "It goes in here."

The man waved his hand behind him, signaling his help.

Then he bent down and picked up a box. "This was here."

She turned away and left the door open while the deliverymen did their job.

In the kitchen, she opened the box to find a case of chicken noodle soup. The card with it said *get well soon.*

Smiling as she pulled a can from the box, she sent a quick text to Glen. `Thank you!`

There wasn't a reply, but then again, it was close to midnight in London.

The time difference was becoming desperately old.

Between the soup, the new living room, and the feeling of being cared for, even from thousands of miles away, Mary fell into bed at close to eight, hugging her monkey and dreaming of Glen.

—

The day Glen was supposed to be flying back to the States, she got a text saying he was delayed a full day. He ended his text with `I'll make it up to you.`

Between all the hours she'd spent in bed and the time change, they hadn't spoken on the phone in two days. Mary used to think people who spent all their time texting polluted good communication. Now she realized that waking up to a text was her and Glen's way of saying they were there, and that they cared.

Mary forced herself into the shower early. Her cough was worse, but her headache and fever felt better.

Much as she hated spreading, or possibly spreading, germs, she had two clients who'd already rescheduled once on her calendar for the morning.

With a cough suppressant onboard and antibacterial hand wipes at the ready, Mary drove to work.

The parking lot was full, leaving her to use the spaces behind the building. In the most recent past she'd moved her car at lunchtime when several employees in the building left for lunch. She felt bad, but in light of everything crazy in her life, she felt justified in claiming a closer spot to the door.

Another message from Officer Taylor was on her phone when she turned it back on after her second client left.

"We brought Mr. Golf in."

Mary could tell from Officer Taylor's voice he didn't have good news.

"And?"

"He consented to the prints. He said, and I'm quoting here, 'I was never in that bitch's home, so go for it.'"

She closed her eyes. "He didn't match."

"Nope. There was a partial on the door to your office, but nothing matched what we found at your house."

"So where does that leave us?"

"Someone who has been at your office has prints on your mirror. My first suspect would be a boyfriend . . ."

"Glen and I were in New York when this happened."

"Right. The prints could have belonged to a friend who has been at the office and in your home."

Mary thought of Dakota, even Walt. But neither of them had been by her office in months . . . not since several weeks before Leo was born. "That isn't possible."

"Which brings us back to your client list as suspects. Just not Jacob Golf. Do you have cleaning people come to your house?"

"No. I can't afford that."

Officer Taylor sighed. "Then I suggest you pull out your calendar and take another look. How often is your office cleaned?"

"Once a week. There's a service that comes on Fridays."

"Find out how good they are about cleaning door handles. If we can narrow down a timeline on when that print was left, we might be able to narrow down suspects."

"There's no way this was random," she said.

"Not unless you bring people from your office into your home and have them in your upstairs bathroom."

Mary went ahead and drove to the deli instead of taking the short walk. Her head was already starting to pound, and she had no desire to cook when she got home.

The counter wasn't that busy. Mary flagged down Carla before she placed her order.

"What kind of soup do you have?" Mary asked.

Carla did a double take. "You sick?"

Mary puffed out her lip like a three-year-old. "I've felt better."

"I've got you covered." Carla scribbled something on her ticket and tossed it up for the cooks behind the counter to fill.

Mary caught the eyes of one of the cooks she didn't know by name. *"Enferma?"*

She understood the question and nodded.

The cook smiled with a short nod before placing a massive bowl up under the hot lights.

"This will do it." Carla placed the soup along with a basket of crackers next to her.

Mary didn't try to identify the type of soup before putting a spoonful in her mouth. It had a little kick of spice and a soothing feel as it filled her belly. "Perfect."

Carla leaned against the counter. "Hector makes a special batch every time the flu goes around. It's not even on the menu."

She waved to the cook. "Thanks, Hector."

Carla watched her take a few bites. "So where is your sidekick today?"

"My who?"

"You know, that guy who's always here with you."

Mary's first thought was Glen, but he'd only been here once. "You mean Kent?"

"Right. The man is going to turn into corned beef."

"He's in here a lot, I take it."

"Constantly. He always seems to be looking for someone when he walks in the door. My guess is that's you."

Mary felt her forehead getting hot with the soup. "I think you're right."

"He likes you."

Mary set her spoon down. "I know. I've told him no, but I don't think that's stopping him from hoping I'll change my mind."

Carla leaned forward on her forearms. "So how is it going with the *exclusive* boyfriend?"

Mary found her happy place. "He's fabulous."

—

Mary decided she spent her life on the phone. She'd just put a tea pod into her Keurig coffeemaker and pressed the button when her cell phone rang.

"Mary Kildare."

"You're a bitch!" Female voice, hostile.

Mary stopped looking through her mail. "Who is this?"

"I cannot believe you had Jacob hauled into the police station. First you tell him about my affair, then you do this . . . to what? Cover your ass?"

"Nina."

"You know, I was told that therapists were just as screwed up as their clients. But you take it to a whole new level."

It took every ounce of energy to avoid engaging in an argument. It was becoming increasingly obvious that the Golfs could both benefit from seeing a psychiatrist. "I'm sorry you feel that way. Please understand that after my last conversation with your husband, I had to go to the authorities."

"Do you have any idea how hard it was to walk away from that man, and now you're giving him all kinds of ammunition to blame me for everything. You're such a bitch. How do you even know a man was responsible for breaking in? Look in the mirror, women can be just as vengeful." The woman was hysterical.

"It's clear we're not going to have a productive conversation. I'm truly sorry you feel the way you do—"

"You're not sorry for anything. You will be. I'll make sure of it."

Nina hung up.

Mary tossed her phone on the counter. "I do not have the energy for this today."

She took her lukewarm tea outside on her back patio and tried to call Glen.

It went to instant voice mail.

"Hey, Glen . . ." She sighed into her message. "It seems like we're always missing each other. Let me start with the good news. I'm feeling a little better. Between the flowers, the monkey, and the soup, you're making me quite spoiled. Thank you for all of it. The bad news . . . Jacob wasn't a match on the fingerprints. Which puts us back at square one. Another one of my clients? Someone in the building . . . I don't even know where to start looking. I'm frustrated, but at least everything has been quiet. No peeping Toms or anything like that." She laughed at her words. "Now I have Jacob's wife on a rampage. Nothing I can't handle, but again . . . it's frustrating. Doesn't help that I don't feel a hundred percent. And I miss you. I really hope you miss me as much as I miss you. I know that sounds selfish and completely high school, but I would hate to be the only one this pent up with longing. Boy, that sounded terribly sappy. I should probably delete this message. I won't, but I probably should. Anyway . . . I'm home for the night. If you get this before ten my time, call me. I'll be in bed working toward that hundred percent mark for tomorrow. Talk soon."

She looked at the phone in her hand and opened a picture that was taken of the two of them when they went to Catalina. If it wasn't for the swimsuit, she'd make the image stick on her lock screen so that every time she glanced at the time, she'd see Glen's face.

—

Mary's phone started ringing every thirty minutes after nine o'clock. No one spoke, just called, breathed, and listened.

Her first thought was Nina. The woman wanted to upset her. What better way than to interrupt her sleep? By eleven, Mary turned off her cell phone altogether.

Eleven thirty her home phone rang.

The line was silent.

"This is the definition of harassment," she said into the quiet line. "Something I'll need to report to the police."

The line went dead . . . and at midnight, it rang again.

Mary unplugged the second line in her room and turned the volume off on the phone downstairs. She'd unhook the thing altogether but her alarm system connected through the landline.

By two o'clock she finally fell asleep. When she woke, her throat was sore again and her headache was back.

Chapter Twenty-Eight

Glen had to listen to Mary's message three times to hear the whole thing. Reception over the Atlantic wasn't always the best.

"I miss you, too," he whispered to himself. "You're not alone in that."

"Now you're talking to yourself." Jason smiled from the captain's seat of the cockpit.

"It was Mary."

"So I guessed."

"The only suspect they had just came back clean. His prints don't match the house."

"Maybe he wore gloves."

"Yeah, but someone left fingerprints in her house that matched the door of her office. Now she has irate clients and she's been sick all week. I just want to take her to the Bahamas until all this is past."

"She might like that."

"At least nothing new has happened. No dead cars or broken-in doors."

"Sad that you have to set the barometer so low."

"It makes me wonder if this is a onetime thing. Which I want, but then we may never know who did it . . . double-edged sword."

"Did she get the monkey?"

Glen laughed . . . "Wait, how did you know about the monkey?"

"Our secretaries talk."

"Yes . . . she got the monkey." What a brilliant idea that had been.

The words she'd used in her message replayed in his head and his smile slowly fell.

Glen opened his message center again and listened for the forth time. *Between the flowers, the monkey, and the soup, you're making me quite spoiled. Thank you for all of it.*

"What flowers?"

"Talking to yourself again."

Glen waved his phone in the air. "Mary said thanks for the flowers, the monkey, and the soup."

Jason shrugged. "And?"

"I didn't send her flowers or soup." The hair on the nape of his neck stood up.

"Maybe Dakota did. She's been sick. People send flowers when people are sick."

Logical. "Wouldn't Dakota leave a card?"

"I would think."

"Mary thought I'd sent them."

"You're the man in her life. It's safe to assume if she got anything from an admirer or even a friend without a card, she'd probably believe it was from you. Call her."

Glen glanced at his watch. "It's two in the morning there."

"Then call her in the morning."

He did . . . and the phone went to voice mail. "I'm home. Your message came through last night. No, you're not the only one. I miss you too much. I'm not happy to hear about your client, or his wife. I'm sure we'll have a lot to talk about this weekend. I thought the monkey was a stroke of brilliance. As for the flowers and soup, I'd love to take credit, but I didn't send flowers. I hope the soup was in a sealed can. Damn, saying that out loud makes me worry that it wasn't. Call when you get this message. Don't worry about waking me. I miss you, Mary."

—

There were squad cars outside her office building when Mary arrived.

"What now?"

She walked into the building to find three men and one woman in uniform standing outside her office door.

The door to the financial firm across the hall was open. The secretary pointed at Mary as she walked up.

"What happened now?"

"Miss Kildare?"

"That's me." Mary glanced around the policemen and noticed a mess of glass on the floor of her office.

"It appears that someone threw a rock through your office window last night."

She pushed past him to look at the damage. Luckily the treated glass kept the entire window from shattering, but whoever had done this had made sure they had a couple of handfuls of rocks. A half a dozen holes the size of her fist had taken out the floor-to-ceiling windows.

"We attempted to reach you before you arrived."

Mary covered a cough with her forearm. "Anything other than rocks inside?" She glanced around the small space, wondered if the property owner was responsible for the glass. Her pocketbook couldn't take much more.

"One of the rocks had the word *bitch* on it."

The Golfs. Could be Nina, maybe Jacob . . . Mary would bet money the phone calls the night before and the rocks in the window were the work of the same people.

"Is Officer Taylor on today?"

"Dennis?"

"I didn't catch his first name. He's been working on my case."

Mary dropped her purse on her desk as the glass beneath her feet embedded further in the carpet.

The officer used her office phone and handed it to her once Officer Taylor was on the line.

"You can't catch a break," he said.

"Broken glass, a rock with that special word on it." Mary saw the audience outside her office door. "The wife of the man you had in this week gave me an unpleasant call yesterday. Said a few things that make me think this is her."

"Mrs. Golf?"

"Yes. Then my phones rang all night until I finally turned them off."

"She called all night?"

"I'm not sure it was her. The caller breathed into the phone. Reminded me of my prom date working up the nerve to ask me out."

"Put Officer Murray on the phone," Officer Taylor told her.

Mary handed the phone back over, looked again at her feet. "Can I clean this up?"

The cop nodded and stepped out of the office.

She found a utility closet down the hall and brought back a broom and dustpan. She was bent over one of the chairs when her first client showed up. "Looks like we should reschedule."

Mary glanced up to find the female half of a new couple she'd been seeing. This would be the second time she had to put them off.

"I'm sorry. I'm having a bit of a domestic issue right now."

Her client looked at the mess. "You can say that again."

Officer Murray walked around her client, handed the phone over. "We have a few questions."

Her client backed out of the office. "I'll call."

Mary knew she'd never see the woman again.

Reports were taken, names and times from the previous night's phone calls were written down. The rocks inside the office were put in evidence bags, and Mary was left with a mess and unexpected ventilation in her space.

The police filed out of the office, leaving silence in their wake.

The secretary from next door poked her head inside. "You okay?"

Mary moaned. "I'm having a really shitty week."

"Looks like it."

They both turned to the sound of feet running up the hall.

Kent stopped short, out of breath. "I saw the cops outside."

Mary spread her hand as if she were on a game show showing the prizes. "Someone doesn't like me."

Kent hardly glanced at the damage before staring at her. "Are you hurt?"

"No. It happened last night. I just need to clean the mess, talk to the property manager about patching this up." Somehow she needed to do all this and see every client she'd pushed off until that night. All on a few hours sleep.

"I'm just across the hall," the secretary said.

"Thanks." Mary pulled her hair back and continued to clean up the glass.

"What time are you off tonight?" Kent asked.

"Late, but I'm okay. I'm pretty sure I know who did this, and other than being a pain, they're all bark."

"This doesn't look like bark to me."

She was pissed but didn't feel threatened. And it was time Kent understood she didn't need him running to her rescue every day.

"I'm all right. Please, don't feel obligated to watch over me. Glen will be here tomorrow. I'm sure we'll come up with a solution to all this."

The mention of Glen's name placed a strangled smile on his face. She didn't want to hurt the man, but he needed to get a hint.

"I see. I'm working late myself. I'll keep an eye out until Glen gets here."

"That isn't necessary."

He looked beyond her to the broken window. "Looks like it to me." He didn't give her more room to talk before twisting and walking away.

Glen woke to his phone ringing. "Hello?"

"I woke you up."

"Mary?"

Even mostly asleep, hearing her voice was nirvana.

"I wanted to call before I left the office in hopes you'd still be awake. I'll call in the morning."

"Don't you dare hang up." He pushed himself upright and turned on the lamp in his bedroom. "I haven't talked to you in forever."

"Message tag isn't the same," she said. "My phone keeps cutting you off."

"Your last message was sucked into cyberspace, too."

"I've tried calling all day. Was your phone off the hook?"

"About that . . ."

For the next twenty minutes Glen listened, steamed, listened some more. Ten minutes into the full twenty he pulled himself out of bed and started to shove clothes into a bag.

"And you're still at the office?" He'd caught that before she told him about Crazy Man, Psycho Lady, and the rock pitcher.

"I am . . . I've lost at least four clients from all of this. I needed to make up the hours."

No, she didn't . . . but he wasn't going to say that.

"Are you on your way home?"

"I'll leave when I hang up. I feel like I could sleep for a week. Don't plan any surprises. I'd just as well watch movies and eat ice cream in my pajamas all weekend."

He was pleased she didn't suggest he not come.

"Do me a favor. Call Walt and tell him you're on your way so he can keep an eye out."

"You of all people should know they left today. They put off the family as long as they could."

Mary kept talking, but Glen tuned out. He'd forgotten about Walt and Dakota's trip.

They were gone, and he was four thousand miles away. And Mary had some psycho . . . maybe more than one crazy . . . fucking with her.

"Call me when you walk in your door and set your alarm. I'll call you when I'm at the door so you can let me in."

"You don't have to rush here, Glen. I'm going home and burying my head in a pillow for twelve hours."

"And when you wake up, I'll be there making you breakfast."

"You don't cook."

"I can pour cereal."

"Glen, don't be ridiculous. Fly in tomorrow. I'll be fine tonight."

He flipped on lights in his bathroom and grabbed the overnight bag he had yet to unpack from London. "You probably will be fine, but I won't sleep knowing there is a possibility that you're not. Do you have the gun yet?"

"I pick it up on Monday."

He would much rather know she had it now, but at least the gun would give him some peace of mind after Monday. "I'm on my way. No use arguing about it."

"Fine! I don't have the energy to argue anyway. Me and my monkey are going to sleep like a rock. So knock hard when you get here."

He liked the thought of her curled up to *his* stuffed toy. "By the way . . . on your message you said something about flowers and soup."

"I did. They were thoughtful, thank you."

"Mary, I didn't send you flowers and I don't know of anyone who delivers soup."

She hesitated. "What about the flowers last week?"

The hair on his nape went to full attention. "The only flowers I've given you were on our first date. Did the card say they came from me?"

"There wasn't a card. There wasn't a card from the soup either."

He didn't like this . . . didn't like any of it. Who was sending Mary gifts? "Who knew you were sick?"

"About every client I have. I either rescheduled their appointment, telling them I was ill, or they came in and noticed themselves. None of them know where I live. It isn't like I give out my personal address."

"That didn't stop someone from breaking in the first time. Could Dakota have sent you—"

"No. I talk to Dakota almost every day. Told her about the flowers, sang your praises about the soup. If she was the one who put them on my doorstep, she would have said something."

He heard her sneeze.

"This is freaking me out, Glen. If you didn't send them . . . who did?"

"Someone who wanted to remain anonymous."

"Oh, no."

"What?"

"Nothing . . . I . . . he doesn't know where I live either." She was talking to herself.

"Who doesn't know where you live?"

"No one. I'm tired. I'm going home," she said.

"Call me when you walk in the door. I should be at the airport by then."

"I will."

"Promise me. In forty-five minutes if I haven't heard from you, I'm calling Officer Taylor."

"I promise. Please fly safe."

"I always do, sweetheart."

Glen hung up the phone long enough to reset a dial tone.

Trent answered on the second ring.

"I need a copilot."

"Hello to you, too."

"Now. I need you *now*. I don't have time to see who else is available."

"Is everything okay?"

"No, I don't think so. I have a bad feeling that won't go away. I wouldn't ask if it wasn't—"

"Glen, say no more. I'll meet you at the airport."

Chapter Twenty-Nine

Mary's car was parked all the way around the back of the building. She'd been so overwhelmed with the entire day she'd forgotten to move it after the other staff had left. She chastised herself for inviting problems and took a good look around the empty lot as she approached her car.

A shadow on the driver's door made her stop . . . but after a couple more steps, she realized it wasn't a shadow at all.

The word *slut* was written in what looked like a black marker on the driver's-side door.

"Damn it, damn it, damn it!" Mary was on the fast train to her breaking point. She walked around her car, found the same sentiment on the passenger door.

She swung the door open and threw her purse into the passenger seat.

"Mary?"

She swiveled to find Kent walking toward her.

"Hey."

"I heard you yelling."

She stood back and showed him her car.

"Oh, that's not good." He did a three-sixty turn. "Do you think whoever did this is still out here?"

"No. I think whoever did this is a *coward*!" She yelled the last word in case Mr. or Mrs. Golf was within earshot.

"Did you want to call the police?"

"No. I just want to crawl into bed and forget this day."

"I don't like this. You should call the police."

"I think I should go home. But thank you for your concern."

He stepped back when she slid between her door and the car.

"If you won't call the police, at least let me follow you home. Make sure you get there without anyone following you."

"You don't have to."

"I know. And your boyfriend will probably be upset, but if you were my girlfriend, I'd want someone looking out after you if I couldn't be there."

The mention of Glen reminded her that she was due to call him in less than thirty minutes. It also gave her some faith in knowing that Kent understood she wasn't available.

"Fine."

She waited until Kent brought his car behind hers before leaving the parking lot. Mary only lived twenty minutes away, and at nine at night, there wasn't much traffic to deal with.

All the way home she thought about the words on her car and what it would cost to have them removed. The insurance company hadn't yet settled the last bill for damage. She wouldn't be surprised if they canceled her plan. At the very least, her rates were bound to go up.

Mary signaled for her garage door to open as she pulled in her driveway.

Kent pulled in behind her and turned off his car.

She didn't want to be rude but had no desire to be social either.

"Nice neighborhood," he said when he shut the door to his dark sedan.

"It's quiet most of the time." Not at her place lately, but overall . . .

Kent stepped into her garage as she moved closer to the door leading into the house.

"I'm okay from here."

"You sure you don't want me to make sure everything is good inside?"

"I'm fine."

"Okay, then." He stepped closer, opened his arms with an invitation for a hug.

She thought about refusing, then figured hugging him and sending him on his way would be the quickest way to get rid of him. On Monday, she'd have a conversation with the man about boundaries.

She tried for the catch and release hug, only Kent held on. "I worry about you."

"I'm fine." She patted him on the back and tried to back away.

"I want to check out inside."

She pushed a little, to see if he was going to let her go without making things awkward. Apparently a boundary conversation wasn't going to wait. "I'm fine. Thanks again." Mary pushed this time.

Kent was bigger.

She felt one hand lose its grip but he held tight and slapped it against the button that closed the garage door.

Mary froze.

"I insist."

"Kent, you're scaring me. Let go."

"No. I don't want that." He twisted her toward the door, kept a grip around her waist. "Let's check it out."

Her heart started to kick and her eyes lost sight of everything that wasn't directly in front of her. She felt the entire length of Kent's frame along her backside, tried to put some distance between them. "Stop it. You need to leave."

He gripped the handle to open the door and gave it a massive shove, pushing her inside with the force.

The second the door opened, her alarm started to beep. The warning to disengage would give way to screaming for the police in less than a minute.

Kent grabbed her shoulders.

Her purse fell to the floor.

"Turn it off."

She shook her head and opened her mouth to scream.

Kent's firm hand closed over her mouth before one syllable left her lips.

Panic started to give way to common sense when she found it difficult to breathe through her nose.

Kent dragged her through the house to the control panel of the alarm. With his lips close to her ear, he said, "Turn it off!"

Mary looked at the keypad with vertigo setting in.

Think.

Think!

"Now, Mary."

She lifted a shaky hand to the device and turned off the beep.

Kent pushed her body against the wall and let loose his grip on her mouth long enough for her to suck in a breath.

"Don't scream."

"Why are you doing this?" Her words came out chipped and on the edge of breaking.

"You need someone to watch over you. You can't do that on your own."

"Kent, please." She felt tears in her eyes.

"That's more like it."

—

Glen sat in the captain's seat of the Challenger waiting on Trent.

The time on his phone inched closer to the deadline he'd given Mary to call him and panic started to set in.

"Thank you, gentlemen. We have it from here." Trent's voice came from the interior of the aircraft.

The sound of the door being shut and sealed, along with a light on his board telling him they were clear to move, had Glen in motion.

"Hey, big brother. We ready to fly?"

Glen tapped a nervous finger on the controls and looked out at the nearly empty tarmac while Trent slid into the copilot's seat. "She was supposed to call by now." It was exactly forty-eight minutes from the time he'd hung up with her.

"We're talking about Mary."

He started shaking his head. "It's bad, Trent. I'm telling you . . ."

"Then call her."

Glen looked at his phone as if it only had one direction of communication.

Then it rang, and he nearly dropped the thing on the floor. "Mary?"

"Is this Mr. Fairchild?"

Male voice that wasn't Mary. Glen wanted to scream. "I don't know who you are, but I'm in the middle of an emergency and need to leave this line free."

"Don't hang up. This is Essential Securitas calling. Your name is first on our list of people to call if a distress signal comes from the residence of Mary Kildare."

The blood from Glen's head threatened to drop to his feet and render him unconscious.

"Distress signal? What do you mean?"

"You are Mr. Fairchild?"

"I am."

"Good. We just received the distress code from Miss Kildare's home. The one she would put in during a possible hostage situation."

This is bad. This is bad!

"Mr. Fairchild, listen to me carefully. We need to respond quickly. There is a chance Miss Kildare mistakenly put in the wrong code. She's only had the equipment for a few weeks. We need you to remain calm and follow my instructions to ensure Miss Kildare's safety."

Glen was vaguely aware that Trent sat watching him. The lights on the control board were blinking. The air that would take him to Mary was just feet above him.

He sucked in a breath and unbuckled his belt. He signaled to Trent to switch places, which his brother didn't question and simply did.

"What do you need me to do?"

"You need to call Miss Kildare's home. I'll be on the line the entire time. If she answers the phone, I need you to talk to her. Do not, under any circumstances, say that I'm on the line or that I've contacted you. Do you understand?"

Glen knew he looked like a deer in the headlights when he rolled his free hand toward Trent to encourage him to move.

As the motion of the plane began, Glen concentrated on the man on the phone. "I understand."

"If in fact there is a hostage situation in progress, we need to do everything in our power to keep the hostage in place until the authorities can arrive. Do you understand?"

He sucked in a breath, felt his heart beating too fast for his chest to contain. "I do."

"This is often a false alarm, Mr. Fairchild. But even if you believe it is, do not say a word about our current conversation. Do you understand?"

"I get it. Are the authorities on their way?"

"Yes."

There was some comfort in that.

"When you're talking to her, I might talk to you. Understand she and whoever might be listening will not hear me. Do you understand?"

"I under-fucking-stand. Let's get on with it."

"Hold the line while I connect with the house with your phone calling."

Glen put his hand over the receiver and looked at his brother. "LA. Hurry." Yet even he knew the word hurry meant nothing in an airplane. There was only so much power they could use, with only so few hours in the air to make their destination.

Glen closed his eyes while he heard the phone tick off each ring as if it were a death bell toward a cemetery.

On the fourth one, she picked up with a tired voice. "Hello?"

He tried to stay calm. "Hey, Mary. I thought I asked you to call me when you got home."

"I, ah . . . just walked in the door." She hesitated. "There was traffic. LA, ya know?"

"I'm on the plane, just about ready to take off."

The sound of sniffles made him cringe. "I wish you'd reconsider. It . . . it's late."

They'd already discussed this.

"I told you I was coming."

"Uhm . . . I know. I'm just really tired."

She did sound exhausted.

"Are you crying?"

She sniffled over the phone. "Bad day with the rock thrower. I'm still sick." He heard her choke back another tear and Glen bit his lip to keep from mentioning it a second time. Mary didn't cry . . . he hadn't seen her shed one tear since he met her.

"I'll be there in a few hours. I have my key, I'll let myself in." Glen waited for her response, knowing what she said next would tell him if she was in trouble.

"Okay. Thanks again for the stuffed giraffe."

Glen squeezed his eyes shut and forced his hand to relax on his phone to avoid breaking it.

"You're welcome, baby. You'll feel better by morning. I promise."

"Okay. Good-bye, Glen." *Oh, fuck!*

He heard the click on the phone and waited until the security guy said something.

"Mr. Fairchild?"

"She's in trouble! Get the police there. Now!"

"Are you positive?"

"I'll bet my life on it."

Glen dropped the phone in his lap and stared down the runway. "Get this fucking bird in the air."

—

"That wasn't so hard, was it?" Kent's lips were close enough to her ear she felt his breath on her cheek.

Pull yourself together, Mary!

Think!

She blinked her eyes several times, pushing away tears she never let fall. Without Glen's voice making her soft, she tried to pull up the walls to deal with the man who was crushing her against the kitchen counter. She'd learned to live without emotions pulling her down at a young age; she didn't need tears clouding her actions now.

He could overpower her unless she could get him off guard.

"Why are you doing this, Kent?"

"Because you need me. You've needed me all along."

His grip around her waist, and his fingers digging into her chin, kept her from moving anything but her eyes.

Calm him down . . . let him believe he has the power.

The classes she'd taken in college to recognize psychosis started coming back. Identifying what she couldn't treat had been a big portion of her job.

"You've been very helpful."

"I have. You liked my attention. Even my flowers." He twisted her chin toward the flowers still in the vase on her counter.

"They're beautiful."

"Like you." He pushed his nose into her hair and took a deep breath.

She shivered. "Don't."

He snapped his head back.

"Please don't hurt me."

The grip on her waist loosened enough for her to breathe and not feel like she was going to break a rib in the process.

"I don't want to hurt you, Mary. I want to take care you. Didn't I show you how much you can depend on me? Haven't I been there every day since we met?"

"You have."

His lips moved close to her ear again. "Then you started pulling away. I don't like it when people want to leave."

"I didn't leave."

His voice started to clip and the grip on her waist tightened again. "You left all the time. You would think after the mess this house was in the first time, you'd want to stay and keep it from happening again. But no . . . you left again, Mary. Why did you do that if you weren't pulling away?"

"I have a boyfriend. I told you that."

He shoved the side of his hip against hers, pinning her against the counter with enough force to pull a cry from her lips. "Your *boyfriend* doesn't do anything for you. I'm the one who helped you with your car. I'm the one who makes sure you're safe at night. I'm the one looking over you. But he gets to fuck you. Where is that fair, Mary?"

She winced with the vulgarity of his words, his actions. "You're hurting me. Please stop."

"You need time to see how good I am for you. Then you'll understand. I'll make you forget him."

Borderline. The man had a borderline personality disorder, she'd bet her master's degree on it. Borderline with enough psychosis to force his way into her life.

"Did you break into my house?"

He took several breaths before he answered. "I came to see you. You were with him. I was angry."

She closed her eyes to keep from seeing him out of her peripheral vision. "And the rocks through my windows?"

"I'm a grown man, I don't throw rocks."

His twisted logic somehow made sense inside his head.

"Don't you see, you need me to keep away those nasty people who did that."

She nodded as if she agreed.

"Now . . . we're going to leave so I can help you."

She shuddered. "We don't need to go. I know you'll help now."

Kent started to laugh, slowly at first and then to the point where she felt his crazy coming on. "You will run the second my hands aren't holding you back."

"I won't."

"Don't lie." He jolted her from the counter and pulled her back against his chest. "We're going upstairs."

"Why?"

He didn't answer as he pushed her out of the kitchen.

She struggled against him and was rewarded by him slamming her shoulder against the wall.

Pain vibrated through her arm and down her spine.

"Don't make me hurt you."

She clenched her teeth together. "You're going to hurt me anyway."

"I don't want to. But sometimes when you're training someone, they have to learn through pain. The quicker you learn, the less it will hurt. I promise."

"Did someone train you, Kent?"

Emotion filled his face. "I learned quickly. You will, too."

Mary felt herself slipping into the role of a victim. The need to cry and beg sat close to the surface. She sniffled, from her cold or from fear, she didn't know.

Kent rushed her up the stairs, past her bedroom, and into her office.

Once again he used the force of his body to pin her against the wall and used his free hand to rip cords from the back of her computer.

"Put your hands behind your back."

"Don't do this. I won't run."

"Put your hands *behind your back*!" He grunted the last three words.

She wanted to scream.

Where were the police? Didn't Glen get the hint?

Didn't the giraffe comment make him understand she wasn't okay?

Kent got tired of waiting for her to move and grabbed the back of her head and smashed it hard against the wall.

Mary's knees buckled and she saw stars.

Kent followed her to the ground and bound her wrists together exactly where he wanted them.

He flipped her over and straddled her body. Kent looked down as if she were a puppy in need of a handout. "Look what you made me do."

Mary turned her head when he reached out to run his thumb on her forehead. It hardly registered that he drew it away with a splattering of blood.

The screeching of her phone pulled them both from the moment.

"I should get that."

They stood in a state of frozen time while it rang.

On number five, her answering machine in the kitchen picked it up.

Kent's shoulders slumped when the ringing stopped.

He lifted his weight and dropped it back down when it started again.

This time when it stopped, Kent lifted them both from the floor, out of the room, and down the stairs.

Mary tripped on her own feet trying to keep up and felt her ankle twist. They hadn't reached the bottom step when a voice on what sounded like a bullhorn blasted from outside. "Kent Duvall. This is the Orange County Sheriff's Department. We'd like to talk to you."

Thank God!

"Help!" Mary didn't rejoice long before Kent slammed her against the wall again, hitting her head in the exact same place. The stars she saw before were a distant memory as blackness faded in.

Chapter Thirty

Glen and Trent pushed the Challenger as much as they could but they were still hours away from California when a call from Officer Taylor came in.

"Mr. Fairchild?"

"Tell me she's okay."

"We *believe* she's okay."

"What the fuck does that mean?"

"What's going on?" Trent asked from the pilot seat.

Glen shook his head.

"They are still in the house and we're outside keeping him from taking her anywhere."

"Someone has her?"

"Yes. Holding her hostage at this point."

"Damn it . . . no, no, no."

"We have things under control. A hostage negotiator is en route. I need to know if you have any information about a man by the name of Kent Duvall?"

Something clicked, switched to a different circuit in his brain, and clicked again. "Yes . . . not much. He asked Mary out. I met him at the deli she goes to for lunch."

"Can you tell me anything more?"

Glen pushed his palm into his forehead as if that would knead free the information he knew was there. "Uhm . . . damn . . . her car. She told me he helped her jump her car when it didn't start."

"Did they date?"

"No." For a nanosecond he wondered if that was true or not.

Then Mary's words drifted into his head in her sweet voice. *I don't lie.*

"No. He wanted to. She told him no."

"Does he work in the same complex?"

"I think so. I'm not sure. Is he the one holding her hostage?"

"His car is in the driveway and we see a man and a woman inside the house."

"Get her out."

"We will, Mr. Fairchild. We're in the process of evacuating the surrounding houses. We have no idea if he has a weapon and we will not jeopardize the hostage."

The hostage.

The hostage.

"Her name is Mary."

"I know that, Fairchild. But I need to distance myself from that right now in order to keep everyone safe."

"You should have thought about that when you didn't take this case seriously."

He heard Officer Taylor muffle the phone and bark an order.

"When you arrive I'll let you past the police line only if you agree to remain calm and follow instructions. If you fuck that up, I'll make you leave. Do you understand?"

Why was everyone treating him like an idiot?

"I got it. Keep her alive."

"I plan on it."

Glen stared out at the black, moonless sky as Trent placed a hand on his shoulder.

—

Mary woke on the floor in her small dining room with her feet and arms bound and a pillow from the couch under her head. The irony of that would hit her later, but for now she thought of the pain in her shoulder, her ankle, and the side of her head.

She could see the flashing of red and blue lights from outside and hear the radios and the continual request that Kent pick up the phone.

Kent sat on the opposite wall, watching her and not moving. He'd taken a knife from her kitchen and sat scraping it against the new hardwood floors of her home.

For what felt like a decade, the phone would ring, be ignored, and stop.

After what had to be the twentieth time, the phone stopped ringing and Mary finally spoke.

"Kent?"

He glared up at her.

"They're going to want to know I'm okay."

"Shut up!"

Mary heeded the harshness of his voice.

When the phone rang again, Kent jumped to his feet, pulled the phone from the wall, and threw it through the kitchen window.

Mary cringed in the corner and ducked her head to avoid the spray of glass.

There was one brief breath before they both heard the phone ringing from the extension in her bedroom.

The voice on the loudspeaker blasted through the house a second time. "Mr. Duvall. We just want to talk to you."

Mary watched Kent's reaction wordlessly.

His jaw clenched and his hands fisted around the knife as he moved back into the corner where he'd been sitting.

"Kent?" She said his name as softly as she could and still be heard. "I know you need to think."

"Shut up!"

She sucked in a breath. "They're going to keep calling until they know I'm okay. If they know I'm okay, they'll give you time to think."

He glared. "What do you know?"

She tried to smile, knew it probably looked forced. And then Mary lied through her teeth. "I worked with a hostage negotiator for over a year." Actually, she'd read a few novels where women were held hostage and the theme had been the same. She prayed now the authors had done their homework.

"You're not a hostage."

She wasn't about to disagree with him. "They just want to talk to you."

The phone in Mary's purse, which was still lying beside the door leading to the garage, started to ring. It was well after midnight and not likely anyone but the people outside.

"They want to know you're okay?"

She nodded.

Kent scrambled to her purse, never truly standing up, and then over to her corner of the room.

He dumped everything out, took her phone, hovered a finger over the answer button. "Tell them you're fine." He put the phone on speaker.

"Hello?" The voice on the line was female and not familiar.

"Hello," Mary said.

"Miss Kildare, are you okay?"

When Mary hesitated, Kent placed a hand on her thigh and squeezed.

"I'm fine." She heard her voice waver.

"Can I speak to Mr. Duvall?"

Mary looked at Kent, who shook his head.

"He's not ready to talk yet."

"Okay. That's all right. I'm getting everyone calm out here. My name is Fiona. Tell him I'll call again in fifteen minutes. I want to hear what he has to say."

Kent blinked several times.

"I'll tell him," Mary said as if Kent couldn't hear the conversation.

The negotiator hung up.

It was pitch black and nearly three in the morning, and Glen waved hundred-dollar bills in front of the driver to move faster.

When he and Trent turned onto Mary's street, there were police barricades set up and no one was being let through. As much as he hated the scene, he knew that it meant Mary was still alive.

Glen turned to Trent inside the car.

"I'll call you from in there and let you know what's going on."

"I'll keep everyone up to date."

Glen felt the adrenaline rush from the rapid flight across the country dump into his system and tried to keep the emotion from taking over.

He shoved the door open and approached the officer keeping everyone out. "Glen Fairchild. Officer Taylor is expecting me."

A quick conversation on the radio and Glen was being led through.

The closer he came to the outside of Mary's condo, the harder it was to keep from running to the door and forcing his way in.

Police stood beside their squad cars. Several had guns pointed at the house.

Officer Taylor stood beside a tiny brunette wearing jeans and a sweater.

"Fairchild!" Officer Taylor extended his hand for a brief shake.

"I take it they're still in there."

The older cop nodded. "This is Fiona Ratcliff, the hostage negotiator."

Fiona Ratcliff didn't talk in pleasantries. "You're Mary's current significant other."

The word *current* took him aback. "Yes."

"Tell us everything you know about her home. Does she have weapons? Where are the phones? What can you tell us about her relationship with Kent Duvall?"

Glen stood staring at the home. "No weapons. She was picking up a shotgun on Monday. She might have a stun gun, she said she was going to get one, but I don't know if she did." He pictured her home. "There's a phone in her kitchen. One in the living room . . . no, wait. That one was destroyed during her break-in and I don't think she's replaced it. Another in her bedroom and a handset in her office." He leveled his eyes at Fiona. "And the only relationship she has with Mr. Duvall is in *his* head."

"Two minutes, Ms. Ratcliff," an officer standing one squad car away called out.

"You're a guest, Mr. Fairchild. I don't care what happens, you stay right there and wait like the rest of us. Got that?"

"I got it, I got it . . . I got it!" He was going to lose it was what he was going to do.

Ms. Ratcliff took a cell phone from her pocket and put it to her ear.

Glen heard her side of the conversation.

"How is everything in there?"

Glen placed his hands on the squad car to keep from running in.

"I just want to talk to you, Kent."

Fiona listened for the next thirty seconds, then removed the phone from her ear in obvious frustration.

"What's happening?" Glen yelled his question.

"The calls are aggravating him, and unless I can keep him on the line for more than two minutes, I'm unsure of how we're going to talk him out."

"We wait him out," Officer Taylor said.

Fiona's lips became a thin line with the scowl on her face. "I don't think so. He's taking his aggression out on the hostage."

The hostage. "Mary, her fucking name is Mary." Glen was getting tired of people talking about his lady as if she were an object.

Fiona lifted a hand in the air. "Mary," she said for his comfort. "We need SWAT. If I can't talk to him, I can't get him to come out on his own," she said to Taylor.

Taylor turned away and called the SWAT team in.

"How did she sound?" Glen asked Fiona.

"Tired . . . stressed. What she didn't sound was scared or hysterical. Which is good. If she can keep herself together, all the better."

"Mary's a therapist. She won't fall apart easily."

After close to six hours of sitting in the same position, with her hands bound behind her back, her ankles shoved together with the same cord, Mary couldn't feel her tailbone. The numbness was a relief compared to the pain throughout the rest of her body. There were times the silence actually had her closing her eyes, but then the phone would ring and the world came into grim focus.

"I took good care of you . . ." Kent stared at the wall above Mary's head as he spoke.

"You did, Kent."

"Just wanted to keep doing it."

"I know. I'm not sure if this was the best way."

He blinked repeatedly, as if his eyelid movement fueled his brain. "I do that."

This was the calm Kent she met at the deli . . . Mary just hoped that she could keep him talking.

"You do what?"

"People say I hold on too tight and don't let go."

All borderlines do, she wanted to say but didn't.

"But no matter how bad things got, you just kept pulling away. Why did you do that, Mary?" His eyes fluttered to hers briefly and then darted aside.

"I think it's because I'm an orphan. I had to take care of myself for as long as I can remember. I'm not used to depending on someone else."

Kent looked at her again, kept blinking. "I didn't know that."

She tried to smile. "Are your parents alive, Kent?" *Keep him talking, keep him calm.*

For a minute she wasn't sure he was going to answer her. "My mom was sick. Smoked. I was a kid when she left me."

"She died?"

He answered with one nod. "My stepdad trained me."

Trained . . . what was he? A dog? "He hit you."

Kent shrugged. "I didn't listen. He trained me to listen."

His troubled stare told her he was remembering dark times. "Do you have brothers or sisters?"

"Not anymore. My brother left after Mom . . ." He swallowed hard. "After. Ran away."

"Your brother was older."

Kent nodded.

"He abandoned you to your stepfather, who abused you." And for a borderline personality, the effect had to be devastating.

"He trained me."

"Your stepfather hurt you, Kent. You're a smart man, you know what he did was wrong. You know trying to train me is wrong."

His eyes traveled to hers, revealing physical pain. And in that moment, she felt sorry for the boy inside the man.

"How do you want this to end, Kent?"

"I want you to go away with me."

She tried to look as empathetic as possible. "They will never let that happen. And I'm in love with someone else." The confession, the realization of how deep her emotions for Glen were at that moment had tears in her eyes. "You need someone to love you and take away some of the pain inside."

He ran a hand through his hair. "I fucked this up."

"You can unfuck it up."

"How? How can I? You'll never want to see me again. They're going to throw me in jail."

"They will and then you'll have an evaluation."

"I'm not crazy."

She hesitated to say more. "I didn't say you were. Maybe they can help you so you don't mess up like you said you did this time. But you need to end this first without anyone getting hurt. You survived your stepfather, have learned to live your life with a respectable job. You can survive this. You work with lawyers, Kent. You know I'm right."

Kent didn't respond with words. He started tapping the back of his head to the wall behind him.

The fifteen minutes were up and the phone started to ring.

Kent ignored it.

Mary didn't know police procedure, but she could guess that no communication would make the police think the worst. "Please, Kent. Answer the phone."

He kept hitting his head, ignoring her and the ring.

"I don't want them to hurt you."

The ringing stopped for less than a minute and started again.

Kent slid the phone across the floor until it hit her legs. He followed with the knife in his hand.

Mary tried not to flinch as he twisted her around and sliced away the cord binding her hands. Blood rushed into her fingertips with such a force they were difficult to move.

"Answer it," he told her before scrambling back to where he'd put the impression of his head into her wall.

Her fingers shook. "Hello?"

"How are you doing, Mary?"

"Good. Better."

"We got a little worried when you didn't answer the phone."

"Kent was removing my restraints."

"Wonderful. Perfect. Can I talk to him?"

Mary moved the phone toward him. "She wants to talk to you."

He shook his head.

"He doesn't want to. I'll call you back when he has something to say."

"I'm calling back in ten minutes."

"Okay."

Mary disconnected the call and rubbed her wrists. The red welts would eventually give in to purple bruises, much like the rest of her body . . . but she could deal with that.

"I can't feel my toes," she told him. "Can I take this off?"

He glanced at her, then returned his stare to the wall.

She took that as a yes and the hope that she'd actually walk out of the house without the need for gunfire looked more like a reality. Removing the knot he'd placed in the cords on her feet took five minutes and three broken fingernails. The swelling and pain in her right ankle made her wonder if she could walk on it.

The blank stare on Kent's face told her he wasn't really listening, but Mary spoke anyway. "I'm going to call her back, tell them I'm walking out."

He turned his head and stared.

If she were being honest with herself, she would say she felt sorry for the man. Then the mental inventory of the pain shooting from all over her body reminded her that he'd done this to her. His twisted logic of training her.

Not his fault, not completely.

He pushed away from the wall. "I'll walk you out."

"No!"

He looked hurt.

"They have guns."

The knife he'd held sat at his fingertips. They both looked at it.

Kent pushed the knife across the floor, out of reach, and rested his hands on his knees.

Mary picked up the phone.

"Mary?"

She hesitated.

Waited.

"I'm sorry."

Chapter Thirty-One

When the sun started to rise, the magnitude of law enforcement standing by came into full view, and Glen started to panic.

The last phone call put everyone on edge.

SWAT surrounded the house from all angles. Their angry guns and full gear brought back every action movie he'd ever seen. Only this wasn't something he was watching while eating popcorn and trying to move to second base with a woman.

No, the woman he wanted to run every base with for the rest of her life depended on these people to do their job and get her out safely. The inability to do anything but watch gutted him.

The phone in Fiona's hand rang and they all stared.

Relief washed over the negotiator's face. She placed a hand over the receiver and yelled to everyone listening, "The hostage is coming out."

Every sense in Glen's body stood at attention.

Fiona turned back to the phone. "Slowly and with your hands up."

Glen inched his way to the front of the squad car.

Officer Taylor pulled him back. "Don't panic now, Fairchild. Let us do our job."

A hush went over the posse as everyone watched the front door as if their lives depended on it to open.

The door squeaked as Mary's frame filled the doorway.

She had her hands up, like she was the criminal, and she walked as if every step was an effort. Once she walked out of the shadow of the house, Glen felt a knife in his chest.

Her face was swollen, bruised, with a big section of her hair matted to the side of her face with blood. She limped like a zombie from one of those apocalyptic movies. And she was crying.

He started to push his way past Taylor.

"No, you don't."

Glen resisted at the same time that one of the SWAT team members rushed to Mary's side, grabbed her by the waist, and all but picked her up off her feet to bring her behind the police line.

Only then did Taylor let him go.

Glen reached her in six strides, pushed his shoulder under hers, and relieved the SWAT officer of her weight.

"Baby, I'm here." He was in motion; his free arm came up behind her knees and lifted her off the ground as he ran her to the waiting ambulance.

Mary buried her head in his shoulder as she wept and repeated his name.

The paramedic guided him toward the gurney. He gently laid her down, but she wouldn't let go. "I'm not going anywhere."

Her vise grip broke his heart.

"Let them look at you, baby. I'm right here."

He pried her hands free of his neck and held on to one of them while the medics pushed the gurney into the ambulance.

Chaos erupted behind him. A male voice barked orders over the loudspeaker, telling Duvall to walk out on his own.

The media, who had set up cameras before Glen had arrived, were in a state of animation as they scrambled to capture shots of Mary, of the house . . . of the officers in motion.

Glen climbed into the back of the ambulance along with the gurney and continued to tell Mary she was safe and he was there.

The noise from behind them disappeared when the doors of the ambulance slammed shut. The sirens proceeded to drown everything else out.

He glanced down at their clasped hands and noticed the welts on her wrists.

A little part of him died inside.

—

Everything moved around her as if she were in a tunnel.

All Mary saw was Glen.

It was as if her body and mind stopped functioning on their own the moment she was out of crisis. She knew she was safe and allowed everything to shut down.

Glen kept asking her if she was all right.

She told him she was.

They both knew she was lying and neither one of them acknowledged it.

The staff in the emergency room handled her as if she were a frightened child.

She took five stitches to her temple, had a nasty ankle sprain that required an Aircast and crutches, and a stupid broken clavicle, which made the crutches nearly impossible to use. Mary couldn't remember the shove, the blow, or the training that had managed that injury.

The police questioned her in the hospital. A psychiatric crisis counselor insisted that Glen leave the room long enough for them to talk.

No one told her what had happened to Kent and she didn't ask.

It surprised her. The desire to not ask and not want to know the outcome of the man who'd put her through hell for nearly twelve hours.

Someone would eventually tell her what happened, but for now . . . she only thought of herself.

She held Glen's hand in silence, their communication nothing more than a look and a smile.

Later, Mary overheard Trent talking with Glen outside her temporary room at the hospital. "Dakota and Walt are on their way and Mary Frances and Burke have already landed."

Glen spoke in a hushed whisper before returning to her bedside.

"The doctor isn't going to admit you."

She attempted a half smile. "Too many germs here anyway."

He smiled and rubbed his thumb over her knuckles. "Exactly."

"I'll sleep better at . . ." The word *home* twisted in her gut. She placed a hand over her lips to keep from vocalizing her distress. Tears welled. The very tears she'd finally gotten control over once she'd reached the hospital and the doctor stitched her up. "I can't go back there."

"Of course not. I have everything arranged."

Mary nodded and didn't even ask.

Between the medications she'd been given and sheer exhaustion, she fell asleep in the back of a town car as Glen took them to a hotel.

It registered that she'd made it to a room; a suite . . . and Glen tucked her into bed.

"Don't leave," she told him as the lights dimmed.

"I'm right here, sweetheart. You'll never be alone again."

Mary woke with a start. The dream was part memory, part horror.

A gun had gone off . . . there was blood.

"Shh! It's okay."

Glen held her in her sleep. She attempted to move closer and whimpered in pain.

She rolled back to where her body didn't protest. "God, it hurts."

Glen scrambled out of bed. "I have medicine for you."

Mary pushed herself up, noticed it was full dark outside.

When Glen stepped back from a small service bar with water and a pill, she accepted both.

"Thank you." She swallowed them down and smiled. "Even smiling hurts."

Glen kissed her temple as softly as he could to still register a kiss. "I wanna lie and say you look better."

She managed a breath through her nose and counted it a blessing. "I do feel a little better. I think there might be a spot on my left thigh that doesn't hurt . . ." She was joking . . . but now that she took stock of her pain . . . maybe not.

"You hungry?"

"What time is it?"

"Doesn't matter. I have a half a dozen people waiting to run for you."

"That's sweet. Nobody has to jump."

"You've slept for eight hours and I can't imagine you ate since dinner two nights ago. Besides, the pills I just gave you say you need food with them."

"Fine . . . something simple. Soup."

Glen sprang from the bed, poked his head out the door, and said something to someone on the other side.

He told her it was after three in the morning.

Dakota and Walt had rushed home to find they couldn't get back in the neighborhood, and the three of them were in a room down the hall.

Mary Frances and Burke had been diverted to the hotel when the hospital had discharged her and had finally retired in another room. Trent and Monica were in a conjoined room to the suite Mary and Glen were now in, and Monica was working on getting her some hot soup.

Mary's only comment was "Mary Frances and Burke had better have separate rooms."

Glen started to laugh. "You sound better . . . you look like shit, though."

"So we're being honest now?"

He leaned close to her on the bed. "I've never been more scared in my life, Mary."

"This ranks up there for me, too."

He kissed her hand.

"I didn't see this coming, Glen. I probably should have, but I had no idea he was a hot mess inside."

"I know . . . it's over now. He'll never be given the option to hurt you again."

A part of her wanted him to clarify his prediction, but she didn't want to know. Not yet.

Glen told her anyway. "They took him into custody."

"He's certifiably crazy," she told him.

"I'm sure they will figure that out."

She thought of her home . . . the dining room. "I can't go back to that house."

Glen gave a tiny shake to his head. "Done. You never have to go back."

"But I—"

"But you nothing. I'll take care of it. I'll pack your stuff, hire a real estate agent . . . we'll get it on the market."

"And where will I live?"

"I'm taking you home with me."

She stared at him.

"You already have a drawer there . . . why not half the closet?"

"Glen . . ."

"No. I thought I was losing you tonight. I thought your good-bye meant that was it. I'm being given a second chance here and I'm taking it. So unless you're appalled at the idea of moving in with me, then this discussion is over."

Maybe it was the medicine kicking in or her head still spinning from the day, but his plan sounded really good.

"And my clients?"

"There are people in need of counseling in Connecticut, too."

"What about Dakota? Leo and Walt?"

"What about them? Jump on a plane."

She started to shake her head.

"No." He took both her hands in his and ducked until their eyes met. "I've fallen in love with you. So unless I'm completely alone in this feeling, I need to push this idea into your head."

Adrenaline rushed through her veins with his words.

Then her inner counselor kicked in.

"It's not uncommon for people to label affection as love in times of crisis. What you're feeling might be fleeting."

Glen shook his head. "That is not what this is. I thought of you every day I was in London. I leave you and can't wait to get back. I look at my phone ten times more a day just hoping I missed the buzz in my pocket to find a text from you. I can't think of tomorrow without you. I love you. It's that simple."

Mary felt a tear on her cheek.

She sat forward, ignored the pain in her shoulder, and kissed him. "You're not alone," she told him. "I kept thinking you were the wrong guy for me, and then you had to go and prove me wrong."

Glen smiled and pushed into her kiss.

Her body whined and he instantly released his hold.

"Sorry."

"It's okay. We have all kinds of time for that later."

Epilogue

"I can't believe you're getting married." Mary stood beside Mary Frances wearing a mauve dress suitable for a maid of honor, while Mary Frances wore cream.

"Well, I can't live in sin, now can I?"

Mary was positive the comment was meant for her. Mary Frances kept her opinions about Mary's living arrangement with Glen to herself. After the crisis in California, true to his word, Glen had a moving company pack up everything she owned and ship it to Connecticut. Within a month, Dakota and Walt listed their condo and moved to a crazy big house in San Diego. A month into the move, Mary was well enough to miss her BFF and ask Glen to send a plane.

Adjusting to life on the other side of the States was made easier with an airport close by and a man who loved her at her side.

The network of marriage and family counselors Mary belonged to happily took her referrals of clients.

Here she stood, three months after relocating her life, putting the finishing touches of makeup on Mary Frances before she accepted a husband into her life. "You could live in sin . . . but my guess is that wouldn't fly with the people on your Christmas card list."

"Could you imagine the gossip?"

They both chuckled at the thought.

Mary sat back. "There. Perfect."

Mary Frances looked at her reflection in the mirror and smiled.

She really was a beautiful woman, made more so by the light inside her soul.

"Now, as much as I might not like your questions . . . I feel the need to ask if you have anything you need to know about your wedding night."

Mary Frances started to chuckle, and then started to belly laugh. "Oh, dear . . . that is funny."

"I'm serious."

Mary Frances laughed harder.

"What's so funny?"

"Oh, boy." Mary Frances got ahold of her laughter. "Sweetheart. I'm old enough to understand the mechanics of sex, and I'm fairly certain Burke will be careful with my delicate frame."

It hurt to keep smiling when Mary wanted to cringe at the thought of Mary Frances doing the naked tango with Burke. But she endured the pain and listened.

A knock on the door of the church was followed by a voice. "Five minutes, ladies."

Mary Frances actually appeared nervous.

Mary took Mary Frances's hands in hers and met her eyes. "I know today is about your becoming a wife. A proper wife with all the things that come with it . . . but . . ." Mary had been contemplating this question for years, and today seemed the best time to ask.

"But what, dear?"

Mary felt her eyes swell with tears. "I want permission to call you Mom."

Mary Frances pulled in a sharp breath, brought their joined hands to her lips, and choked back tears. Without words, she pulled Mary into her arms and hugged her hard.

"Is that a yes?"

Mary Frances nodded and pulled back to look at her. "I have waited so long for you to ask. I knew in my heart the day would come. I love you so much."

Mary blotted tissues under Mary Frances's eyes. "You're making your makeup smear."

"I don't care. I'll be crying all day anyway."

Mary fanned her face with her hands to dry her eyes. "Well, *Mom* . . ." she tested the new name on her lips and enjoyed the taste. "There's a handsome man out there who will be squirming in his shoes if we don't get moving."

"Okay." She twisted toward the full-length mirror and ran a hand down her belly. "I should not be this nervous."

Mary leaned her chin on her mom's shoulder and smiled at her through the mirror. "Sex is going to be awesome."

The older woman instantly flushed.

"Oh, that's a much better color for your cheeks," Mary said. "Now let's go."

The church had done a wonderful job decorating for the ceremony. Something Mary hadn't seen coming. As hard as it was for her mom . . . and it did take some thought to think of her in that way . . . as hard as it was for her to leave the convent, it appeared as if the church hadn't left her.

Some weddings are simply a formality in the lives of those taking their vows. But for an ex-nun and a widower, there wasn't a dry eye in the church. The Mass took nearly an hour and every minute was precious in Mary's heart.

When the priest asked Burke to kiss his bride, instead of feeling uneasy, Mary cheered on the inside.

The reception took place in the hall of the church.

Mary watched her mom and Burke greet their guests and smile for pictures once the meal was over. All the traditional fanfare that went with a wedding didn't go undone. During the planning, Mary Frances attempted to downplay the party, but Mary refused. So did Burke's children. Whether the couple wanted it or not, there was cake, and the first dance . . . the removal of a garter, which Mary Frances practically had on her ankle. And the tossing of the bouquet.

Mary didn't stand up when the emcee behind the microphone asked for all the single ladies to gather around.

Dakota bounced seven-month-old Leo on her knee and nodded toward the group of women. "Get up there."

Mary grasped Glen's hand on the table and leaned into his shoulder. "I don't feel very single these days."

"I love you, too, sweetheart." Glen kissed her briefly.

"Yeah, well." Dakota reached across the table and picked up Mary's left hand. "Looks like you're still eligible for free flowers."

Walt shook his head in laughter.

Glen nudged her shoulder. "Go ahead."

Jason, Trent, and Monica had happily accepted the invitation to the wedding, so the entire table encouraged her to go.

"Fine, fine." Mary stood and joined a dozen women huddled in a corner.

There were heckles and a couple of women in their thirties started kicking off their shoes to dive for the bouquet.

She watched the wedding director position her mom in front of the women. A fake throw and a picture came first, then she turned around for the real thing.

Mary caught everyone at her table staring and holding their breath. Poor Glen wouldn't be given a moment's peace if she caught the darn thing.

The crowd started to count down for the toss.

Mary Frances played along.

"Three . . ."

"Two . . ."

On the word *one* Mary Frances turned around and met Mary's eyes.

Then, before the women in the crowd could protest, she walked directly up to Mary, grabbed the hands that Mary had glued to her sides, and shoved the flowers into them.

Laughter erupted from the crowd. It grew louder when Mary Frances turned on her heel and pointed a finger directly at Glen.

Mary felt the need to crawl under the table.

Instead of waiting for her to return to the table, Glen pushed his chair back, stood, and straightened his jacket.

The crowed parted as he approached.

He leaned down and kissed her mom's cheek and winked.

Then he smiled at Mary and slowly bent down on his knee.

The blood drained from her face when the reality of the moment hit her.

Cameras were flashing left and right. Someone with a video camera stepped in front of the line.

"I love you, Mary. The past seven months have been the happiest of my life. I want the next seventy years with you by my side." He reached into his coat pocket and removed a small velvet box and opened it. The round solitaire was the size of her thumb but didn't sparkle as much as Glen's eyes did with his smile.

Mary felt happy tears drop from her eyes. She placed a hand alongside Glen's cheek. "I love you so much."

"Is that a y—"

"Yes, yes . . . a thousand times yes."

Glen took the ring from the box and slid it on her finger before swinging her into his arms and taking her lips as his own.

Dakota was cheering the loudest while everyone else clapped.

When Glen finally set her down, he leaned his forehead against hers. "I'm going to make you happy."

"You already do."

Glen shook his head. "You haven't seen anything yet."

Mary kissed him again.

Glen kept his lips molded to hers as he took the bridal bouquet from her hand and threw it into the crowd.

It landed directly at Jason's feet.

# Acknowledgments

Phew . . . another book finished and ready to share with the world! It's always such a bittersweet moment when I sit down to write the acknowledgments for an individual book. Bitter because the ride is over . . . and sweet because the ride is over. Writing is a bipolar experience . . . just roll with it.

As always, thank you to my agent Jane Dystel and her entire team at Dystel and Goderich Literary Management. You help keep me sane in this crazy business.

My editor Kelli Martin for pushing me to reach new levels with every book.

My publisher, Montlake, and the team it takes to turn every manuscript into a novel.

Now on to a few people who opened up their areas of expertise and answered my questions.

To Julianne Gentry and her husband, John, for taking me up in a single engine four seater and not killing me. Taking the controls of an aircraft was never something I thought I'd see myself doing, but boy am I glad I did. John's stories of his years as a pilot had us all laughing and added depth to *Not Quite Perfect* in ways I couldn't do alone. P.S. I still think we need to fly to Vegas . . . fuel is on me! Hint, hint!

Thank you Robert, the Jet Guy, for answering my questions about the private jet business. One of these days I'll have to book a private charter. I might need to write a few more books first.

To the former nuns out there who have the courage to leave the church when they find their calling somewhere else. While Mary Frances's story was completely fictional, I have at least one point of reference who shared with me her struggle.

Stay strong, ladies.

Now back to Marina Adair.

Fellow author, newest bestie . . . and overall amazing woman who I admire more than you will ever know. We jump on planes to see each other, and spend more quality time together than I do with my own family members who live an hour away. Friends are people you choose, and family are people you're stuck with . . . I've adopted you, my friend . . . so you're stuck with me. Love and Kappa Sigma Hottie Sisters Forever!

—Catherine

About the Author

New York Times, *Wall Street Journal*, and *USA Today* bestselling author Catherine Bybee has written twenty-four books that have collectively sold more than two million copies and have been translated into twelve languages. Raised in Washington State, Bybee moved to Southern California in hopes of becoming a movie star. After growing bored with waiting tables, she returned to school and became a registered nurse, spending most of her career in urban emergency rooms. She now writes full-time and has penned the Not Quite series, the Weekday Brides series, and, most recently, the Most Likely To series.